After reading five pages of *Bone Broth*, I thought, *I know these women*--Justine, Bev, and Myrtle. They could have been a dozen of former classmates at my 50th Vashon High School reunion who were still playfully fussing, fighting, and fawning over the good old days in the Pruitt-Igoe housing project. They were "among a different breed of naysayers: those who prided themselves on being part of the first batch of blacks to move from the chaos and crime that mostly defined the inner city and settled in one of the safer districts of North St. Louis County." One of those districts being Ferguson, Missouri, known for the protests after the tragic death of teenager Michael Brown.

This novel's relationships reflect a kaleidoscope of colors and patterns that change a close-knit family and an almost-family over time. Husbands, wives, children, best friends, and lovers struggle to reevaluate long-held beliefs and life decisions.

Ellis ably reveals painful family secrets and generational trauma that unfolds during and between two racially charged periods in St. Louis history. She draws parallels between a mother's foray into activism in the early 1970s and a daughter's immersion into grassroots organizing in the Bay Area in the 2000s. After the daughter Raynah's 20-year absence from her hometown, "She was left fighting to reconcile two pasts, two regions, two worlds."

—Vivian Gibson, *The Last Children of Mill Creek*

Lyndsey Ellis's beautiful debut novel, Bone Broth, is a heartfelt and moving portrait of a family riven by secrets and lies and the weight of history and legacy. Set in a volatile Louisiana, this emotionally rich novel skillfully dives into class and race and desolation and redemption through the siblings Raynah, Theo and Lois, their mother Justine, and their various homes and what and who they see as home. Ellis has a keen eye for the ties that break, and bind, be they family or friendships. Bone Broth is a complicated novel about complicated times and one readers will find unputdownable."
—Soniah Kamal, author of *Unmarriageable*

Set in the aftermath of the Michael Brown protests in Ferguson, *Bone Broth* follows the lives of Justine, a newly widowed woman, who despite seeing an end to a marriage that was rather complicated (they lived apart), is still struggling with the next stage in her life. She has three kids who have distanced themselves in various ways and are struggling with their own losses. When her eldest daughter Raynah starts a social justice museum, she uncovers a secret about her mother that calls into question everything she's believed about her family. Ellis has written an absorbing and nuanced family drama, packed with St. Louis details and unforgettable characters. *Bone Broth* highlights the burdens of racism over generations and the resulting trauma that can ensue, and how activism, while vital, can lead to burnout with its own lasting scars.

—Daniel Goldin, Boswell Book Company, Milwaukee, WI

BONE BROTH

A Novel

Lyndsey Ellis

HIDDEN TIMBER BOOKS, MILWAUKEE, WI

Hidden Timber Books
6650 West State Street, #D98 Milwaukee, WI 53213
hiddentimberbooks.com

Publisher's Note: This is a work of fiction. Names, characters, places, and incidents are a product of the author's imagination. Locales and public names are sometimes used as historical reference. Any resemblance to actual people, living or dead, or to businesses, companies, events, institutions, or locales is completely coincidental.

Cover Design by Jade Burel @ jadethedesigner.com
Book Layout: Morrison © 2017 BookDesignTemplates.com

BONE BROTH/ Lyndsey Ellis. — 1st ed.
ISBN 978-0-9906530-3-5

For Us.

The struggle is eternal. The tribe increase.
Somebody else carries on.

—ELLA BAKER

CONTENTS

Part I

Justine

Frank looked pretty in his casket. Suit creased. Hair conked. Rings shining.

In the church, the organ's throaty hum clashed with the sound of a helicopter chopping through the air outside. Justine pushed down her disgust at the idea of another protest headed for disaster on the streets. She followed the long line of people chirping their approval for Frank as they viewed his body. She ran a gloved hand over the front of her childhood friend's obituary, a photo of a much leaner, younger, and mustached—but equally handsome and fashionable—Frank.

Justine reread the words underneath the picture:

Franklin Obadiah Crawford
Sunrise: April 8th, 1949—Sunset: September 1st, 2014
Light & Abundance Missionary Baptist Church
St. Louis, Missouri

"Sharp, ain't he?" Bev smiled and rubbed the casket's shiny wooden edge.

Justine grimaced. "Looks a little pale to me."

"Quit lying. You would've never known anything was wrong with him."

Justine ignored her best friend. She fanned herself with the obituary and dabbed her flaming face with a handkerchief. In the hour they'd been at Frank's funeral, the sanctuary had turned into an oven.

A blanket of heat rushed over Justine—through her pantyhose, up her girdle, and forcing itself into all her pores.

Forget hot flashes, she thought. Maybe it was actually happening. Maybe she was being burned alive, from the inside out, in front of everyone, for her own good. A grim but deserving price to pay for the death of her husband last month.

Justine knew she wasn't completely responsible for what happened with Wesley. He wanted it, and made her want it too. But how could she prove that? What could she say for herself? *My husband ordered me to help kill him, so I did?* Her defense sounded weak and bizarre. Even Wesley wouldn't have believed her, if he hadn't done what he did.

The truth was absurd. Justine hadn't told a soul. Definitely not her kids. Not even Bev.

It made more sense to create a new truth. A few weeks after Wesley's funeral, Justine started stealing from the funerals of dead folks—some she knew, but mostly those she didn't—not to be sordid or cruel, but because she wanted to recreate her past with truths that came from other people's past.

The helicopter outside sounded like it was about to land on the church's roof, its angry blades were thrashing so loud. Chaos ruled these days. People getting shot. Do-gooder protests. Reality TV. Fake meat. Not that things were perfect years ago, but Justine wasn't getting any younger. It wore on her to keep up now. Caring too much and trying to understand everything exhausted her. She'd done enough caring and understanding, only to end up here: at this funeral, her own husband dead, with memories strong enough to set her on fire if she didn't take control.

"Scratch my back," Justine told Bev. She wiggled, trying to get the itch out of her shapewear.

"No," Bev said. "Hurry up and get what you need so we can go. It's hot as hell in here."

Behind them, a man loudly cleared his throat as if in agreement. Justine faked a sniffle and wiped the corners of her eyes to buy his sympathy and more time.

There was a thrill to it, being a funeral thief. Dead folks couldn't fight back. The real damage would come from the families of the deceased if they found out, which was why Justine had remained careful and choosy until now. She'd foolishly asked Bev to bring her to see Frank in exchange for her promise to visit an elders' support group for grieving spouses. Now, they were both admiring the good looks of a corpse Justine was preparing to steal from; the body of a man whose past had once been tied to her past. The same man who had been claimed by a stroke just weeks after offering his condolences for Wesley's passing.

She scanned Frank again. He looked like he was sweating. On his temples sat tiny beads of fluid, shiny and bold as fruit flies on a freshly baked cherry pie.

Justine never saw a corpse sweat before. She wondered if her nerves had her imagining things. Maybe the moisture on Frank was a bad reaction to the embalming chemicals. But then, why would dead bodies be allergic to anything?

The idea got Justine remembering them all as kids living in the Pruitt-Igoe housing project, something she did more often now that Wesley was dead. Frank was a spirited boy who came to St. Louis with his mother and grandmother from some town in Alabama. He always had a smile on his face, with dimples that cut into his cheeks, and he was fiercely energetic. But he was also a runt—a twelve-year-old stuck in a seven-year-old's frame, with bones not quite strong enough to handle the body slams and choke holds from Wesley, his best friend Beans, and their crew when they had wrestling matches. But the boys took Frank into the fold, mostly because they could weasel him out of his lunch money, and teased him for his smallness and his pretty-boy appeal.

Once after getting roughed up, Frank started playing with Justine, Bev, and some of their girlfriends when they were still allowed to hang out in the back of the building after school. And that's when he tried to kiss Justine, before she pushed him into a bush full of poison ivy. His arms immediately got so swollen, red, and welted, and they all spent the rest of the afternoon dousing him with water from a nearby hose.

Justine fanned Frank with his obituary, real tears coming to her eyes. This was why she preferred the funerals of strangers: they required less feeling, which kept her from getting sloppy.

Wesley would've said it was a dumb move—even for a woman—to drop in on Frank's service, but how could she not attend? Besides Bev, Frank had been the only person from their childhood who Justine cared to keep up with after life had scattered them in different directions.

Everyone else she knew from those days was either dead, crazy, relocated, or worse: they were showing up at annual "family resident" reunions where, as Wesley put it, some folks were fool enough to celebrate the time they spent being miserable together in Pruitt-Igoe.

Bev cleared her throat, echoing the man behind them. Justine decided on one of Frank's cufflinks—the one thing that would hold together the fabric of that day with Frank and the water hose in her mind. Seeing them all together again as carefree kids, still sheltered from the world's woes.

Justine leaned into the casket to whisper her last goodbye. She touched Frank's hand, which was surprisingly cool, and with one quick tug, pulled off the gold piece.

*

The next day brought clear skies and no traffic, but the outskirts of downtown St. Louis looked like a bad thrift store. Broken shopping carts, vagrants' clothes, and abandoned flyers from another protest littered the sidewalks.

This was a bad idea. Bev's bribe. The elders' bereavement group. Wesley, if he was still living, didn't need to assure Justine this whole plan was a mess, although she knew he would.

She checked to make sure Bev's car doors were locked. What terrified Justine most was that there was no way out.

She was here now. Trapped, looking at used condoms and different colored hair extensions and scribblings of NO JUSTICE, NO PEACE! on cardboard signs scattered across the pavement.

As they drove around another pothole, Justine fantasized about jumping out of Bev's station wagon. Bev took the backstreets and rode the brakes, so Justine figured, even at her age, she wouldn't suffer much past a skinned knee, maybe a dislocated hip. She'd seen enough action films to know she just needed to roll and protect her head.

"Don't try anything stupid," warned Bev.

"Too late," Justine said, "I'm already with you."

They approached Tender Mercies Center for Elders' Independence. The midmorning breeze, already plagued with humidity, tickled Justine's forehead under her newly styled bangs. Letting Bev give her a haircut was the only highlight of this whole deal. The bangs brought life to Justine's face, as Bev claimed they would, especially since Justine still refused to wear makeup.

Once they parked, Bev turned off the engine and fiddled with the ends of her neck-length burgundy wig, twisting it this way and that. "Do me a favor, Justine. Lighten up. Stop being so damn critical for once in your life."

Justine grunted. "Critical? Do you see where we are? You brought us to this war zone and you expect me to relax."

"Stop exaggerating. We've lived through worse." Bev opened a tube of Vaseline lotion and glazed her hands with the moisturizer. "You promised, remember? I got you to Frank's funeral yesterday so you could do your little stealing—"

"It's not stealing," said Justine. "The man's dead."

"I don't give a shit what you say. It's stealing, and you know it, and it's a wonder no one's caught you yet. This'll help. Trust me."

Justine sighed, resisting the urge to argue. Every day, it became more clear why she'd made the right decision by not confiding in Bev about what happened to Wesley. Justine could almost hear her husband in her ear, insisting the only way a word of anything ever got out was because Bev couldn't keep her mouth shut. As much as she hated the way Wesley grumbled about everything Bev did when he was alive, Justine knew he was always right about that point.

"You better not steal from my funeral," Bev told Justine. "I'll come back to haunt your ass."

They walked toward a large building that was shabby on the outside with rusty wind chimes and an unraveling welcome mat at the door. Once inside, Bev linked her arm through Justine's and tightened her grip until Justine could feel their bones rubbing together. They took the elevator to the twelfth floor and stepped into a lobby that was too bright and colorful, like a daycare, but with cheap and ratty carpet. Supermarket music played in the background.

In the hallway, the walls were lined with staged photos of smiling senior citizens in cardigans. Again, Justine thought of Wesley and knew he'd say she was plain stupid for letting Bev drag her to this place.

"Good Lord," she muttered, "these people are old."

"It's an elders' center," said Bev. "We're old, too."

Justine recalled when Ms. Jenkins, the widow who lived next door to Bev in Pruitt-Igoe, got stuck in her hallway's pile of burning trash. Someone on their floor, Justine couldn't remember who, called the fire department, but the neighborhood hoodlums drove them away by hurling bricks and bottles at them from the building's roof. The closest fire extinguishers were gone or broken, so Bev and her aunt beat out the fire with blankets and drove poor Ms. Jenkins to the hospital, where she later died from her burns.

Thinking back, Justine wondered about Ms. Jenkins's age when she made her transition. Her guess was the woman was old, but not really that old. Justine and Bev were just teenagers at the time, not realizing there were levels of old. To them, everyone with gray hair in Pruitt-Igoe was feeble, luckless, or just plain invisible. Justine never imagined that one day, she'd fall into the same category.

In the elders' center, they neared a conference room with its blinds drawn. Justine grimaced at a poster that read HANDS UP DON'T SHOOT on the closed door. Underneath it, a white board read KNOCKING IS FOR STRANGERS. YOU'RE AMONG FRIENDS. COME IN.

As soon as Bev opened the door, they were hit with a chorus of hellos from people standing in a buffet line. A large conference table swallowed the center of the room, surrounded by chipped oak chairs and paintings of fruit bowls and flower gardens. Water marks looked like a dried-up river on the ceiling, and dusty windows overlooked Laclede's Landing. From where Justine stood, the Gateway Arch was nothing more than a tiny slab of metal bent over a pool of mud, broccoli-head treetops, and toylike buildings.

She studied the group of participants—both men and women, different ethnicities, all looking over seventy—hovering over the open pots. Her stomach curled around the smell of hash browns and strong coffee as steam rose from their plates piled high with food.

"Why aren't you eating, darling?" A potbellied white man nodded at Justine and took a seat across from her at the conference table. His cheeks were big and red, like tomato stains on his face.

"Leave her alone, Phil." The dark-skinned woman sitting next to him took a swig of her coffee. She wore glitter eyeshadow. Bright pink lipstick spread over her teeth when she smiled. "I'm Ingrid," she told Justine. "Folks call me Grit."

A short Hispanic woman in flower-print culottes with bleach stains waved at Justine from the far end of the table. "And my name's Rachel Beth. Folks call me Rachel Beth."

Her face was as much golden as it was wrinkled, like the skin of fried chicken. She rushed over to Justine and extended her hand with childlike excitement.

"This is Coconut, the sock monkey." Rachel Beth shoved her faded striped toy at Justine. It was missing an eye and wearing pants that matched its owner's, minus the bleach spots. Justine pushed the toy away and shut down Wesley's voice in her head telling her to spit on it.

"You better grab a plate before we start," Grit said. "Ain't no food like free food."

"I don't eat everybody's cooking," Justine told her. She crossed her legs, meaning for it to be the period in her sentence.

"Nice seeing you two again," Bev said to Grit and Rachel Beth as she sat next Justine. "This right here's my best friend, Justine Holmes."

"And who are you?" Phil asked Bev.

Justine snorted into Bev's ear. Bev ignored her, but Justine knew she felt silly, learning she wasn't as remembered as she thought she was.

"Beverly Thompson," she said. "I know it's been some time, but I'm glad to be back. I'm one of those with the runaway spouses. Guess you could assume he's dead now; nobody's heard from Beans in over three decades. My heart still aches, though, and nobody knows that kind of hell better than the folks in this bereavement group."

"Honey, I know what you mean," Grit chimed in. "It's hard losing a husband. I lost four and each took a piece of my heart with them."

Justine mumbled her apologies, hoping Grit would go away, but she kept yapping about how the Lord was her man now. Her savior this and her savior that.

The woman's talk and gaudy way she was put together struck Justine as what she must've looked like to some women she'd met in the spring of '71. She and Wesley had moved from Pruitt-Igoe to North St. Louis County with the money Wesley had been saving since '67 from his factory job. At the time, most of Justine's family and friends from her old neighborhood didn't have cars to drive into the secluded suburb to come see her. With the exception of Myrtle across the street, all of Justine's new neighbors were white, and there were no Black churches, or clubs, or any gathering places in the area. She took to Myrtle more quickly than she expected, but the woman was a bit of a wild card whose time was mostly spent caring for her gardens and the sassafras tree behind her house, or tending to her pregnant, unruly teenage daughter, Dani.

Justine grew lonely and bored with Wesley working all the time, and when she discovered she too was pregnant, her isolation swelled to a dangerous level. She searched the classified ads section in Wesley's newspapers after he left each morning. What Justine was looking for, she hadn't really known. Wesley had been insistent that no wife of his would step foot in any workplace as long as he was breathing and able-bodied, so finding a job was out of the question.

Justine soon stumbled on an ad about a Black women's tea and bridge club that met twice weekly just one street over from hers. The next day, she found herself in a living room among three other women in their early twenties, all clad in silk pleated dresses and matching designer jewelry.

Sonya, the hostess, was fair-skinned with a fashion model's long neck. She had straight teeth and thick black eyebrows. The hair on her head was dyed blonde and so wavy, it looked like packs of dried ramen noodles floating above her shoulders. Within ten minutes of being in Sonya's house, Justine learned the woman's husband was one of the first African American circuit judges in St. Louis, and they were both college-educated North Carolina natives with no children.

Sonya had just opened a new dry cleaners with money from her husband's savings. This was just a starter home, the woman kept insisting. Their goal was to eventually move to a dream residence in the South County suburbs, a two-and-a-half story house her husband planned on building from the ground up one day.

When it wasn't Justine's turn to play cards from her hand, she'd sat on her palms, ashamed of her fourth ringless finger as she listened to Sonya and the other women exchange stories of their spouses' elaborate proposals. With Wesley, there had only been enough money to sign marriage papers at city hall and the promise of a down payment on a ring for Justine once they were fully settled into the new house, a feat she wouldn't see come into play until all of her kids were in grade school.

As Justine's fingers numbed under the seat of her skirt, she felt more and more out of place, consumed by the dishes in display cases, family heirlooms, designer furnishings, and degree certificates hanging on Sonya's walls. She remembered getting misty-eyed until the paint from the Cadillacs sparkling in the woman's driveway gave her a splitting headache. In the end, she made up some lie to the bridge women and left with no intention of returning.

"I'll be back," Justine said to a rambling Grit, and anyone else who was listening.

She rose from the table in the senior's center and went to the restroom, where she called her youngest daughter, Lois, on her cell phone. No answer. Reluctantly, she called the only other person she knew could be reached.

"What."

"Don't 'what' me," Justine told Raynah, her eldest daughter. "Come get me."

"I thought you and Ms. Bev had a deal."

"Forget Bev. I'm ready to go now."

Justine heard heavy breathing over the phone. It sounded like Raynah was smoking again.

"Have you seen or talked to your sister today?" Justine asked.

"No, why would I do that?"

"I'm not kidding, Raynah."

"I'm not kidding, either. Try calling her."

"I just did," Justine told her. "She's not answering. Can you not be an ingrate right now and bring your behind down here?"

"Just tell Ms. Bev to take you home. You two shouldn't be out there anyway."

"Oh, hush," Justine said to her daughter. "You think I care about a few protests right now? What, will I be mistaken for one of these professional rioters? This is your type of crowd, not mine. News flash: that boy wasn't the only person who died last month. Not that it matters to someone who missed her own father's funeral."

There was a click on the other end of the line. Justine speed wiped the sweat accumulating under her armpits with damp paper towels and called Raynah back.

"Mama, I'm not doing this with you today."

"I'm in a bind, Raynah. You think I enjoy asking you for anything? I agreed to check the place out. I did and I don't like it."

"You mean you've already found fault with everything and everybody."

"No, it's just not a good fit," Justine said.

"Then do what I said and tell Ms. Bev to get you out of there."

"She's not leaving early."

"Call A Ride comes that way," Raynah said.

"Are you crazy? I'm not doing that. Might as well take the bus."

"Well, then, I guess you're stuck."

The word 'stuck' came at Justine hard through the phone. It sat with her, a sixty-five-year-old woman who never learned to drive and filled her days by sitting in an empty house, sifting through coupons and watching soap operas.

"Mama, you hear me?"

Justine hung up and returned to the elders' group, where everyone was now listening to Grit talk about insomnia and fear of a dislodged stent. The man sitting at the head of the table politely cut her off after Justine took her seat. He was tall, with a fair complexion and a thin but firm build. The man's hair was multicolored, like a calico cat's, and cropped close to his scalp. He was handsome. Maybe too handsome.

"Hi," the man greeted Justine. His blue eyes immediately threw her off guard. They were a lullaby, soothing and warm, like Justine always imagined the ocean would be. She looked away, afraid she'd get lost in them and forget to look mean.

"What's your name?"

"Justine," she said in a small, dumb voice.

"Justine what?" the man asked in an equally small, dumb voice but baritone and laced with a Southern drawl. It reminded Justine of her favorite Ghirardelli dark chocolate candies that Raynah had always shipped to her when she was living in the Bay Area. They both knew Justine could've bought the brand from a local store, but it was something deeply special and intimate about the kind Raynah sent from the factory based in San Francisco.

Now, Justine found herself savoring each of this man's words like she did each bite of those candy bars. Still, the mirroring in his tone cut her like a shard of glass wrapped in silk.

"Justine Holmes," Bev answered for Justine. "She's my best friend and she's happy to be here."

"I see," the man said. "Well, I'm Richard McKline, the facilitator of this group. Great to have you, Justine. We were just checking in. Would you like to share how you're feeling today?"

The man held Justine's gaze. She looked down at his fingers, which were long and slender with bristly black knuckle hairs. He leaned forward, elbows against the table, and placed his hands inside his crossed forearms.

"You can say anything, really," he assured. "Doesn't have to be about how you're feeling. Just tell us what's on your mind."

Despite feeling drawn to the man, Justine decided he was too calm and observant for her liking. She found it intrusive, suffocating. What right did he have to poke at folks' lives? Examine their pain, their feelings? Wesley would say the man was jiving.

"Tell me something, Mr. McKline," she said.

"Just Rich, please."

"Okay, Rich. Why do you have all these pictures of smiling senior citizens out in the hallway? Is this group some kind of joke to you? Can you even relate? Or, is this—what do the kids call it these days—a side hustle?"

Rich looked confused, then embarrassed. "Of course I can relate," he said. "Would you like to hear my story?"

"No, I don't want to hear your story," Justine told him. "I want you to answer my question. What's the deal with all the goofy photos in the hallway?"

"I don't think they're goofy at all," he said. "They reflect the environment that we're trying to set. One that's vibrant and harmonious and inclusive."

Justine glanced at Bev, who looked evil enough to slap her. Still, she was liking the way Rich wore his nerves. The way he shifted in his chair as forks stopped clinking and mouths quit chewing. Everyone seemed to be holding their breath, eager for what would come next.

"But why do they all smile if they're representing us?" Justine asked. "We're all supposed to be these older, frail folks who are grieving, right? The pictures aren't realistic."

"She's got a point, man," Phil said, the toothpick in his mouth nodding in agreement.

Rich flashed Phil a tight smile. He loosened the silk tie around his neck and rubbed a hand through the small spikes in his hair. Justine could almost see him arranging words in his head.

"It's very real, Justine," he told her.

"Mrs. Holmes."

"Okay, Mrs. Holmes. Grief comes in many forms, so I think the smiles in the photos represent hope in the midst of circumstances. I'm afraid I can't speak for the photographer, but you should bring your concerns to management if you feel strongly about it. Anything else you'd like to share?"

Justine folded her hands in her lap and looked past Rich at the clock on the wall. It was almost half past eleven. Another hour of this charade, and she could be done with it. Home free, where she belonged. Never to see or hear from these pitiful strangers again. Until then, she would keep her mouth shut and let the others babble about themselves. A bunch of nonsense, Wesley would say.

"Rich, can I check in now?" asked Rachel Beth. She raised Coconut, her sock monkey, in the air.

"Yes, go ahead, Rachel Beth," he said. "But try to keep it under two minutes."

"Okay," she agreed. But the woman blabbed on about her dream of using Miracle Whip as an aphrodisiac on a blind date and how Coconut, her sock monkey, was allergic to new people who didn't smile.

*

Myrtle's kitchen was stuffy with the smell of maple syrup and dirty hair. Two mobile fans, hoisted in opposite corners of the room, blew lint and hot air everywhere. On the countertop closest to Bev's makeshift styling chair, a small television displayed the stern talking heads of news anchors between flashes of protesters gathering in the streets the night before. Some, women and children holding picket signs over their heads. Others, shirtless young men with bandanas over their mouths and their arms lifted in the air.

"Turn off this mess," Justine told Bev. She waved a large spoon in the direction of the TV. She was tired of seeing the hysteria that was gripping St. Louis, all in the name of social justice. Wesley would say it was all a sham to lure misguided youth. "These rioters always think they're doing something uplifting."

"Don't think you're fooling anybody, heifer," said Bev. She turned the television channel to a rerun of the Bobby Jones Gospel show and dabbed at the gunk of hair grease on the back of her hand before rubbing it into Myrtle's scalp. "You put up a good fight yesterday, but I saw the way Rich had you melting."

Justine ignored her and stirred a bubbling pot of grits on the stove. She dumped bacon from a skillet onto a plate and gave Myrtle a piece of the meat. She considered propping open the back door for fresh air but didn't want to deal with the alley rats that liked to eat through the screen. Right now, the last thing Justine had the patience or energy for was digging up more sassafras root in Myrtle's backyard and extracting its oil to kill off the little critters.

The idea nearly made Justine laugh. To think alley rats were one of the things she and Wesley had tried to leave behind when they moved away from the inner city. Back then, everything about the life they'd chosen in the North St. Louis County suburbs after moving from their old neighborhood had been new and different and clean. Most of her then-neighbors weren't open to Black residents, so they socialized in the privacy of their backyards, kept their grass cut, and regularly took out their trash. Now, here she was, worrying about poisoning rodents from the same neighborhood's overfilled dumpsters and clogged sewers.

"Anyway," Bev said. "I hope you have a better check-in speech prepared next time."

"There won't be a next time," Justine told her. "I'm not going back. I told you that and I mean it."

"Give it another try." Bev rotated her curlers in the ceramic iron stove. "At least get to know Grit. She's sappy as hell and uglier than a prune, but she's a good talker. I know you don't want to hear it, but you could learn a whole lot from Rich, too. They're a good bunch once you get used to them."

"I don't want to get used to them."

"Right, because stealing from folks' funerals is so much better," said Bev, rolling her eyes. "Leave the dead alone. What do you do with the shit you take from them anyway? Sell it? Put it on an altar? You better not be reusing it."

"I bury it in the backyard," Justine said flatly.

"That's not funny."

Justine raised her eyebrows. "Am I laughing?"

"Well, shit, you're burying something," Bev said. "Wesley's gone, okay? And, he's not coming back, thank God. Whatever you've got bottled up in you, it's got to come out, one way or another. Or else you're going to end up like Beans. I wouldn't trade a day I spent with my husband, but I knew something in him stopped clicking right." Bev covered Myrtle's ears with her hands. "Same for this one right here," she whispered.

Justine looked at Myrtle and remembered the woman she saw from her bedroom window almost thirty years ago. The way Myrtle clawed at the stretcher's bloodied sheet the night they brought home the dead body of Pete, her oldest grandson. Pissing down her overalls, she was so mad. Breaking a police car's window with one of her high heels before several officers tackled her to the ground. That mouth of hers, working and twisting like some demon doll.

"Quit talking about me like I not here!" Myrtle bucked her eyes and knocked Bev's hands off her head. Her faded dungarees hung off her sickly thin body. The ruby pumps she still insisted on wearing look busted and small on her flat feet. Justine gulped back the emotion forming in her throat.

"Hush and put this in your stomach," she said, and gave Myrtle more bacon.

"I hear Ahmad's coming back from California, too," said Bev.

"Where'd you hear that?" Justine wiped her fingers on the apron around her waist. She hadn't meant to sound so curious, but the thought of Myrtle's youngest grandson returning to town was more than she was prepared to take in.

"I overheard some of the ladies down at the shop talking about it while they were waiting to get their hair fixed. One of them is good friends with Ahmad's aunt in Oakland. Lois didn't tell you?"

"No, she doesn't have anything to do with that fool," Justine said, her anger rising.

"How do you know?" Bev asked.

"Because I know."

Justine threw Bev a look that signaled she wanted to end the conversation. Thoughts raced through her mind quicker than she could grasp and process them. Was Ahmad returning to St. Louis for good? Did Lois know about this? If so, why hadn't she said anything? Was she part of the plan that led him back?

Justine hated letting herself wonder about Lois getting caught up in another heated fling with the same man that left her stranded years ago. Lois was good and grown enough to make her own decisions now, but in the past two years, she had been through hell after losing her and Ahmad's only child, Quentin, to a stray bullet fired in his apartment complex. If anyone needed a bereavement group, it was her—but Lois insisted on hiding behind her career.

Ahmad returning would only create the worst kind of storm. He had been senseless and wrong for running away in the first place. Abandoning a then-pregnant teenage Lois, along with his own grandmother who had fallen apart after his brother, Pete's, murder. Justine knew Ahmad hadn't been given the best circumstances, dealing with the absence of his mother, Dani, who'd become addicted to drugs and left him and Pete in Myrtle's care when Ahmad was barely in middle school. Leaving home was the best way Ahmad probably thought he could survive something else so tragic. But, why so far away, and for so long? Wesley used to say a man like that was as good as dead to everyone.

"Lois would be crazy to get involved," said Justine.

"Why?" asked Bev. "They have a history. Plus, I hear Ahmad's done pretty good on the West Coast. Made a little name for himself as a journalist."

"Tuh." Justine rolled her eyes.

"Well, that's what I was told."

"Like I said, Lois is not getting caught up with that. Now, Raynah on the other hand ..."

"Just stop. Not everything"—Bev made a circle in the air with her curlers—"is Raynah's fault."

Justine pursed her lips. She didn't feel up to explaining. While in California, Raynah claimed to have fallen out of touch with Ahmad, but Justine never believed her. The two of them had grown up together in the same neighborhood, same church, same schools. They were close in age, Raynah being older than Ahmad by a couple of years, and both had lived in Oakland since the late eighties. They both clung to that childish ambition of changing the world.

"When's the last time you seen Theo?" Bev asked, changing the subject.

"I haven't," Justine told her.

"Since when?"

"Wesley's funeral."

"Hot damn," Bev said. "And, before that, it was when? Election season?"

Justine tested the grits from the tip of her spoon. They were too salty and scalded her tongue.

Earlier that year, Justine had returned home with Wesley from his dialysis treatment to find Theo at her door with a camera crew at his heels. One of the newspapers was doing a story on him ahead of his run for alderman. They said they wanted to learn more about his upbringing so people could get a sense of his human side.

"What human side?" Justine remembered Wesley asking as he eyed his son suspiciously. "He's the alien in this family."

Justine laughed off the remark with Theo and his entourage, but she knew it was the bitter truth. Theo was always tragically different. She'd wanted to protect him from his differentness since the moment he left her body. Unlike Raynah, he didn't roar radically with balled fists like he was angry for being born. He didn't fall out of Justine in a hurry, eager to meet the world like Lois, either. He barely whimpered when the doctor cut his umbilical cord. His purple, mashed face already looked like a worried old man. When Justine held him for the first time, she watched him blink slowly and tiredly, as if he was coming to a sad realization that no one else knew yet.

That day at the house, she saw those tired, slow lids flutter quickly to mask the hurt as Theo blushed and chuckled in front of his reporters. He made up some corny joke to downplay his father's cruelty. Then, he apologized to Justine and Wesley for the last-minute meeting and for not dropping by more often.

It was enough to get Justine talking about what it had been like raising her youngest and only son, but Wesley wouldn't budge. At the end of the interview, instead of joining her and Theo for a family snapshot, he spat on the lighting equipment and hobbled back to his own house next door.

"Theo calls a lot," Justine told Bev.

It wasn't really a lie. He did call, but it was usually at the worst times, like near midnight when Justine was already in bed. Or on a Sunday afternoon while she was at church. And he never left messages or answered when she tried to call him back.

"These damn kids," Bev said. "Just be glad he's making something of himself while he's busy forgetting about you. Hell, I only see Pinch when she needs money or a babysitter. The others only come around for the holidays. Why? Because they need money or a babysitter. I might as well have 'bank' or 'daycare' tattooed on my damn face."

She frowned at the hot comb's hiss on Myrtle's hair.

"Look, whenever you're upset about having to make an appointment to see Lois and Theo, think about how often you get to see Raynah, now that she lives next door to you. Nervy heifer, ain't she? Hasn't changed one bit. Couldn't make it back from California for her own father's funeral, but she was there to take his house off your hands."

"Why didn't you wash her hair before you started styling it?" Justine asked Bev, changing the subject. She didn't feel like being angry at Raynah right now. She nodded towards Myrtle dozing in her chair, bacon bits clinging to her chin.

"It's not happening," Bev told her. "Hard enough getting her to take a bath these days."

She pointed her hot comb in the direction of the personal care assistant cleaning the front room. "This new girl has another thing coming when she tries to hose Myrtle down. Third damn PCA this month. Talk about a handful, honey."

"I didn't sell my kids to no Jesus!" Myrtle blurted, her eyes bucking again. "They took them. They took them all!"

"I know, honey," Justine said. She tore up another piece of bacon and, this time, hand-fed her neighbor.

*

Lois was late as usual. She didn't call or come inside. She just blew the horn.

"What's wrong with your mouth and hands that you can't phone me when you're running behind?" Justine asked, getting inside her daughter's silver Mercedes. The car reeked of iced coffee and designer perfume. It was almost too much for Justine's stomach, with the lingering smell of bacon grease and Myrtle's sour hair from earlier that morning. She sucked her teeth and lowered the window.

"How are you, Mama?" Lois asked in that I'm-more-civilized-than-you way of hers. She ran a manicured hand through the thick curls that shaped her plump face. "I was stuck on a conference call on my way over."

Justine switched the radio station from jazz to gospel as they backed out of the driveway. She wanted to ask Lois if she knew about Ahmad returning, but something told her not to. Lois's response could go one of two ways, and Justine wasn't ready to handle the betrayal of her daughter's admission to knowing and not telling, or worse, being lied to.

"You're keeping the air conditioning on with the windows down?" Justine asked her daughter. "Must be nice to have money to blow."

Lois turned the fan off. Her obedience annoyed Justine. Ever since she was little, Lois prided herself on being the angel in the family. Back then, it was a comfort Justine realized she needed against Raynah's smart mouth, Theo's coldness, and everything Wesley. But, as she got older, Lois's squeaky clean ways became her weapon. Justine rarely let it disarm her anymore, but she regretted how it tempted her to pick on Lois.

"How was the elders' group yesterday?" Lois asked.

"I don't want to talk about it." Justine opened her coupon book. They hit a speed bump and a bunch of the tickets fell on the floor. Justine reached down to grab what she could.

"What happened?"

"Nothing," she told Lois.

She spread the coupons out on the dashboard and was reminded of the deck of cards she used to lay out for spades games with Wesley during their long rides in the '68 cinnamon Oldsmobile. He bought the car after they moved to North St. Louis County, and it was fierce with white leather seats and a new engine that roared to life. Every time Wesley turned the key in the ignition, Justine felt like she was part of the car, her bones purring against its cool, stiff seat cushions.

Before the kids came, playing cards and eating pork rinds in the car was just as sacred to them as Saturdays full of sex, whiskey, and Johnnie Taylor songs. Everything sounded clearer, tasted fresher, and felt better. They craved their time together with the naïve intensity of two lovers who didn't know how to break each other yet.

There were things Justine knew she'd had no instruction on—growing up poor, being married, raising three kids—but it was life; like anyone else, she got by. She wished she could've said the same for getting widowed. Wesley hadn't been that great of a human, much less a husband. He was a workaholic who rarely spent time with Justine or the kids and he'd had enough women to start his own tribe. Still, no one taught Justine how to survive without him.

It was the loneliness that got her. When Wesley was alive, Justine thought she'd known the feeling well. She knew now that the isolation is what caused her to drift. To wander into places she had no business going, with people she had no business meeting (the "justice junkies," as Wesley once called them) and ultimately, do things she had no business doing.

Fortunately, Justine came to her senses and rededicated herself to the quiet suburban life. A life that Wesley always insisted made Justine the envy of every woman she'd grown up with, whether they admitted it or not. Even as Justine immersed herself into being the perfect homemaker, mother, and wife, she'd never been totally convinced by her husband's view. She became less convinced as the years passed and the two of them grew apart.

By the time Wesley died, it was beyond pointless for Justine to reconsider the life she'd chosen. She got so mad with Wesley for being dead. She hated him for leaving her alone with his shadow and a pain she couldn't see around, under, or through.

"Nothing happened," Justine told Lois again. She avoided her daughter's eyes and pushed her coupons back into one neat stack.

*

The grocery store was a mess of people and shopping carts. Lois grabbed a small basket and headed toward the vegetables. Justine got a cart and wound up in the dairy section where it was less congested.

She never liked crowds, but the open space was too quiet and terrifying. Suddenly, she wanted the warmth of other bodies around her. Chatter in the background and feet scraping the ground. Whatever it took to distract her from feeling like her chest was caving in.

Justine realized she'd been staring at milk containers in the dairy aisle for too long and walked to the yogurts and cottage cheese. Everything looked so sterile and deserted and mean. The words on packages were all fuzzy and spiteful. The tile floor's blinding whiteness sneered at her.

The snack aisle seemed even more troubling. Every woman Justine passed had a man on her arm, or a grocery cart piled high with food that she was probably excited to take home and share with her partner.

In the canned goods section, there were women with more baskets filled with more groceries. They walked by Justine, stealing glances at her empty cart. She thought she saw the corners of their mouths curl upward into smug grins or downward into sympathetic frowns. She noticed her own hands shaking when she yanked cans off the shelf.

Everyone pretended to shop in the frozen foods aisle, but their eyes pricked Justine like a bed of pushpins. She knew they thought she was too stupid and lonely to know she was being stared at. To them, she was just some helpless old woman with a basket full of space. Them, with their overloaded carts, and their family-sized entrées, and their loving spouses.

The glass doors of freezers opened and smacked shut. Justine felt sealed into place in the biting cold air.

"Excuse me, miss. Can I get by, please?"

The male voice behind Justine was young, high-pitched, and tinged with scorn.

"Hey ma'am," a female voice, openly angry, chimed in. "You mind moving your cart?"

Justine shivered. Her heartbeat with an explosive pound that vibrated through her torso down her back. Her hands fell from the cart to her sides. The heaviness in her legs worsened as she tried to keep walking. With each step, it felt like she was lugging sandbags across the floor. People were attacking her with their stares, their whispers, their finger-pointing.

"You left your cart here in the middle of the aisle, ma'am."

"Miss, aren't you coming back for your groceries?"

"She won't move her things out of the way!"

"Wrong cart," Justine heard herself say. Her voice was soft and quivery. She got mad at herself for not being strong enough, for bending into the ugliness around her.

"It's the wrong cart!" she screamed at the ceiling. "It's the wrong cart!"

Justine closed her eyes and let her purse dangle against her leg. She couldn't stop, even as her shrill screams turned into hoarse yells and hot water trickled down her face. Around her, feet scraped the floor, and hands clutched her arms.

"I know her. Let me through, please."

A familiar baritone voice, silky and Southern, tugged at Justine. Suddenly, she was at the elders' group again, sitting with Bev and watching Rachel Beth wave her sock monkey. The images around her were so real. The discussion, so clear.

"It's okay."

Justine looked at Rich, her mouth still twisting and spurting. His arms around her, his body warmed her like a heated blanket before she went limp. She felt his eyelashes stroke her forehead, calming her back into the light.

*

Outside, the sky held a brash sun surrounded by clouds. Rich sat with Justine on a bench near the store's entryway.

The silence between them was wide and brutal.

"You don't need to be here with me," she said.

It hurt to talk, so she drained the Styrofoam cup of water given to her by store personnel. The stale tears on her jaws stretched like dried glue. She felt wobbly and exhausted, wanting to just disappear and sleep.

Justine couldn't help imagining the disgust on Wesley's face if he were here. Seeing, through his eyes, how desperate and pathetic she must've looked, sitting there being pitied by a man she barely knew.

"It's fine," said Rich. He leaned forward against his knees. Justine let her eyes travel over his calico buzz cut and Mr. Rogers sweater. The tufts of hair on his knuckles and those eyes the color robins' eggs when he turned back to her.

"So, who are you," she asked, "and what else do you do besides lead elders' support groups and pick up distressed widows in your spare time?"

Rich sat up and squeezed his creased slacks at his knees. He didn't smile, but he spread his lips to expose his teeth.

"Not much these days. I'm a retired school superintendent and widower. I decided to become a certified peer specialist about six years ago. My parents came here from Louisiana before I entered middle school because they got tired of pretending they were white sharecropper and Black servant, rather than husband and wife." He raised a finger in the air. "Oh, and I don't eat dairy or drink alcohol."

"You're some piece of work," Justine said, shaking her head.

"My wife, Agnes, used to tell me that all the time."

"What happened to her?"

"Car accident. Her inhaler ran out, and I was drunk again. She couldn't wake me up and tried to drive herself to the hospital."

Neither of them said anything for a while but Justine felt something inside of her loosen. It was hard to look at Rich, so she stared at the pieces of Styrofoam she'd torn apart and laid on her skirt.

"I was probably more of an asshole to her after she died," Rich continued. "Blaming her for looking the other way. She knew about my relapse. I could barely find our bed most nights, much less hide the bottles. She wouldn't say anything to me about it, though. Guess she thought her silence would shame me into rehab again."

"Did you have kids?" Justine blurted. Immediately, she regretted engaging him.

"One son, Blake. He's in prison. Murder and armed robbery."

She envied Rich's careless honesty. He listed personal tragedies like bullet points on his life's catalogue. Each word struck Justine like a punch in the neck. He exposed his teeth again, this time smiling, when he noticed her stunned expression.

"We're pen pals," Rich said. "I go up to visit him a lot."

"At least you know where your kid is. Check-ins always matter," said Justine, hating herself more as she said it. She realized she shouldn't be concerned with painting Rich a brighter picture. She shouldn't be concerned at all.

"Took some time," Rich told her. "But right now, he doesn't have much choice."

Justine pursed her lips and sat on her hands to keep quiet and still. There was a chance he'd leave her alone if she just stopped everything.

"Do you have kids?" Rich asked.

Exhaling, Justine began gathering the torn bits of Styrofoam on her lap.

"One I only see when he's campaigning for alderman. Another I see when she's forced into mother-sitting me between her real estate property showings. The other one, my oldest, just relocated back here from the West Coast. I see her all the time, whether I want to or not." Rich looked muddled.

"She inherited my husband's house after he died," she told him. "He lived next door to me."

Justine almost laughed at the way Rich tried to contain his curiosity. Instead of asking more questions, he sat back on the bench, folded his arms, and crossed his legs at the ankles.

"Years ago," she continued, "Wesley decided we should sleep in separate beds. Then, a few years after that, he decided on separate houses. He died before we could get a divorce."

"Interesting," Rich said.

"Yeah, especially over the holidays."

They both chuckled. Justine kept pouring the Styrofoam pieces from one hand into the other.

"How'd he go?" asked Rich.

Justine paused and sucked the inside of her cheeks.

"Slowly," she finally said.

"I'm sorry," Rich told her.

"I'm not." Surprised at her own casual response, Justine squished the cup's contents between her palms. "It was his time. I just hate accepting it."

"Yeah," is all Rich said. He poked his lips out like he was going to start whistling, but he didn't. They both just sat there, listening to the crows cawing over their heads.

Justine thought about mentioning the random funerals she attended, but then reconsidered. Why bring up more than she had to? As it was, Wesley would hate her for opening up to someone—a stranger—about her family. His death.

"There you are!"

Lois scurried over to Justine. Even in the wind, her curls fell effortlessly back into place like some model in a hair shampoo commercial. A lanky, teenaged boy in a store uniform trudged behind her with grocery bags.

"What happened?" Lois opened her arms out to Justine. "Crying over spilled milk?"

"Actually, it was more like spilled frozen lasagna," Rich joked.

Lois looked at Rich, a speck of hostility in her eyes. She forced a quick, polite smile. Justine introduced them, repulsed and tickled at the idea of them hitting it off.

"Great to meet you," Rich said. He offered his hand to Lois. "Your mother and I were just getting some fresh air. She had a little scare, but she's alright. The more she engages, the better off she seems. Maybe you can help persuade her to come back to our elders' group."

Justine sucked her teeth. The damn elders' group. Right now, she didn't want to be reminded that it was how she'd met Rich. In the group, he was still his sweet self but not as reachable. Out here, he was both. A person who just showed up when he was supposed to.

"If I can get her to tell me what happened during the last group first," Lois said. She raised an eyebrow at Justine.

"I told you, nothing."

Lois adjusted the purse on her arm and put on her shades which meant she was ready to leave.

"Let's go." Justine looked around for a trash can. "Rich, I didn't think we'd meet again like this. If I never see you again—"

"You're welcome, and you will."

He removed the Styrofoam pieces from Justine's hands, piece by piece.

"Don't count on it," she told him.

From the side mirror of Lois's car, Rich looked small and fictional to Justine, like a tan Ken doll with a buzz cut. He stood there next to the bench, watching the Mercedes as they turned out of the parking lot. His shoulders were slightly hunched and his hands still holding pieces of the Styrofoam cup. Justine felt herself smiling and stared out the passenger window so Lois wouldn't see.

Raynah

Nearly every time Raynah looked at her mother, she saw someone who was deeply opposed to living. A nesting doll, afraid to shed her outer shells.

From the living room, she watched Justine sit barefoot at the dining room table and flip through a Schnucks coupon book. As if it was normal to leave the heat turned off in mid-November just to preserve the latest batch of roses from another funeral.

"These flowers stink," Raynah said to her mother. "They make my head hurt."

Justine didn't respond.

"Whose funeral did you crash this time?" Raynah asked. She pulled a small sympathy card out of the bouquet sitting on the coffee table and eyed the message written in sloppy cursive letters. "Another random person? One of Sir's old friends?"

Raynah rammed her tongue against the back of her front teeth. It felt more ridiculous using the word *Sir* now, after her father's passing, than it did when he was alive. Raynah couldn't remember what she had called him before the name stuck. She knew it was never anything as normal or endearing as *dad*. Sir wasn't the warm type and, strange as it was, Raynah admired him more for his stubbornness. She remembered her father telling Justine to give her and her siblings a choice between Sir and his first name. To Raynah, he didn't look like a Wesley. Lois and Theo felt the same way and from that day forward, he was Sir to them all.

"I know you hear me over there," Raynah said to her mother. Her nose ring twinkled in the living room window's reflection. She ran a hand over her shaved head, which also glistened and overrode the faint shadow of stubble on her scalp. She was ready to leave, but Lois was late again and Justine still couldn't be trusted alone.

"If all you came over here to do is complain, you can go home." Justine kept her eyes on the coupon book. The bouquets of dried flowers and mounds of papers and photos that surrounded the dining room table made her look even smaller. The navy housecoat she wore was clean but outdated. Several rollers poked out of her matching hairnet.

The more Raynah criticized her mother's exploits, the sooner she hoped Justine would give up her obsession of attending and stealing from the funerals of strangers and acquaintances. At first, it was just the typical funeral program, but eventually she started bringing back sacred belongings left inside the open caskets of dead folks—handwritten letters, broaches, bandanas of slain gang members—and tucking them in a corner on the living room console.

Raynah recently noticed her mother returning with only bouquets of flowers that were gifts to the grieving families. Sir's passing, Raynah believed, had become too big in Justine's mind. The elders' bereavement group had been a letdown. No one could make Justine go back, especially not after her breakdown in the supermarket a few months ago.

"I just don't get the whole switch to roses when it's freezing outside," Raynah told her mother. She adjusted the blanket she'd taken from Sir's old recliner next door and hugged it tighter over her shoulders, the cotton still thick with the scent of aftershave, cigarettes, and sweat.

"Because they make me feel good," said Justine. "You got that ugly spread on. Now, hush.

"I ran into Pinch the other day in the Loop," Raynah said. "I never noticed the resemblance when we were kids, but she looks just like Ms. Bev."

"Mm-hmm, the girl cusses like her, too." Justine licked her thumb and turned a page in her coupon book.

"Every woman can't be a respectable woman like you, Mama."

"Why do you still go down there?" Justine asked. "That area's almost as bad as the city and downtown combined. Don't you watch the news?"

"No it's not," Raynah argued. "And where else am I going to go? Not like I have many choices here."

"Don't go anywhere. Be like normal folks and stay in the house."

"Right," said Raynah, "And on occasion, I can step out to crash a funeral."

"Well, if it makes you feel any better about missing your own father's, be my guest."

"I'm joking."

"I'm not," Justine said. She put down the coupon book and rummaged through papers on the table, folding some down the middle and tossing others in the wastebasket. "California's made you crazier than a fool. Keep going to these dangerous places if you want. I guess you'll really be a free spirit if a bullet hits you."

"There's things worse than bullets," Raynah muttered.

Justine's obsession with safety was stifling. Don't go there, watch out for this, keep away from whoever. Raynah never thought her mother's paranoia could be worse than it had been when she was growing up, but she was wrong. Every day, Justine proved she could go a little more back-ward. Midwest suburban life had sedated her. Made her as dead and blind and unfeeling as the funerals of the folks she stole from. If it wasn't for the flavor Ms. Bev added to Justine's life—the kinds of so-called ghetto behavior from citified people that her mother liked to turn her nose up at—Raynah knew Justine would be nothing more than a grumpy woman choking on her own fears and boredom.

"Where's your sister?" Justine asked.

"On her way."

"When are you going to tell her about Ahmad?"

"What is there to tell?" Raynah asked. "If you're implying I knew he was coming back home, you're wrong. If you're implying something else, after all these years, you're dead wrong. So just stop."

"I'm not implying anything," said Justine. She cut the soiled edges from a battered flyer. "I just think Lois should know that Ahmad's back in town. And who better to tell her than the person who's lived closer to him than the rest of us?"

"No," Raynah told her mother. Sir's smell, along with the tired chug of a train nearing on the tracks at the street's end, pulled at her. "It's not my responsibility."

"Nothing is, apparently."

The two of them sat in a stiff, resentful silence until Lois's Benz finally crawled into the driveway. From the window, Raynah locked eyes with her younger sister prancing toward the house, a grocery bag at her hip.

"You're late again." Raynah stood back on her legs and held the door ajar. She marveled at how the years had changed Lois without really changing her. Her sister was still a wannabe diva with oversized Chanel sunglasses sitting above her sharp nose. A two-toned bob, just the right kind of kinky. Brown lip liner around her bronze lipstick. Hardly fat, but fleshy in her fitted pantsuit. If Raynah had to guess, she'd say the weight gain was from antidepressants; Lois had a lot to be sad about—living under Justine's thumb, her demanding career, a slain son—but here she was, trying to hide behind the image of success.

"There's more stuff in the trunk," Lois said, pushing her way inside.

"You should've called," Raynah told her.

"No, you should've switched shifts with me when I asked you to. Traffic's always a mess right now."

"If you'd time yourself better, there wouldn't be an issue."

"Where do you need to be at this hour?" Lois asked, "You have a real job now?"

"That's not the point, Lo." Raynah trailed her sister into the kitchen. "Learn to respect other people's time. Pretend I'm one of your fucking class-act clients if you have to—"

"Watch your mouth in this house," snapped Justine. She hobbled into the kitchen and clapped her hands at them the way Raynah remembered her doing when she and Lois quibbled as kids. A silver ringlet shook against her temple.

"You should be proud, Mama," Lois said, placing her grocery bag on the counter. She recurled the rogue strand of hair around Justine's roller. "This is the most she's said to me since she moved back. I guess it's better than her being holed up all the time next door."

"Jealous?" Raynah pulled a gallon of milk from the bag, opened it and drank from the container.

"Don't be silly," said Lois. "No one's mad you got Sir's house. This neighborhood's not exactly a prize anymore."

"What, it's too Black for you now?"

The milk carton was slippery with moisture in Raynah's hands. She placed it on the counter and glared at Lois. She was tired of the way people talked around being surrounded by Blackness. In Lois, she heard the same abrupt coldness as in newscasters' tones when they announced another shooting or robbery in what—they said—was once a "quiet" area, a "nice" neighborhood. People at the stores, the library, the post office, the bank, all referred in passing to parts of North St. Louis County that had really "gone down" over the years.

The worst critics, Raynah noticed, were usually white, which was to be expected. But Lois, like Justine, was among a different breed of naysayers: those who prided themselves on being part of the first batch of Blacks to move from the chaos and crime that mostly defined the inner city and settle in one of the safer districts of North St. Louis County. They were the original minorities to flood the white spaces of Florissant, Black Jack, and Ferguson. And, in their minds, they were the real Black middle class—openly nostalgic for that window of time that existed before everyone else caught up with their social and financial aspirations. They resented the uncouth behavior being brought into the suburbs which, they believed, stirred the new wave of *white flight*: a mass migration of white people returning and rebuilding parts of the inner city that they'd once abandoned. The land was incredibly cheap, and the all-brick homes more spacious and durable.

"Don't put words in my mouth," Lois told Raynah. "What I mean is this area's no longer the same neighborhood it was when you left."

Raynah cocked her head to the side. "In other words, it's too Black for you. Why don't you do something about it, like move out of here, instead of complaining so much?"

"Trust me, I'm on it," said Lois. "I've been trying to talk Mama into getting out of here, too. You'd both sell these houses if you knew what was good for you."

"Hell no," Justine told her. "You be a realtor outside these walls, but talk like you have some sense in here."

"Fine," said Lois. "You two keep being stubborn. Don't say I didn't warn you."

"I'm not selling Sir's house," Raynah asserted.

*

Once outside, Raynah lit a cigarette. It felt good to get away from Lois's pearl-clutching act inside Justine's house. Raynah traipsed across the lawn, returning next door to the house she inherited from Sir. She slumped into a folding chair on the porch and stared at Ms. Myrtle's sassafras tree looming over the roof from her backyard—the one she used to see Justine picking from to make bone broth when she or one of her siblings was sick. Its bright green bushiness, dotted with purplish fruit; the sweet-smelling leaves that reminded Raynah of her favorite Fruit Loops cereal as a kid. She eyed Ms. Myrtle's bed of mums and overgrown hedges across the street. The blue painter's tape crisscrossing over the woman's doorbell. A cobwebbed shutter dangling from the house's hinges.

Raynah would never admit it to Lois, but her sister had a point. The neighborhood she remembered and loved during her childhood was no longer the same. All around her, property seemed to be in a state of decomposition, changing into something that didn't feel homey or recognizable. The walls weren't splattered with human shit like some parts of Oakland or downtown San Francisco, but what had once been a space that residents—both Black and white—took pride in was now becoming a debacle.

Raynah swallowed the knot in her throat and took a drag of her cigarette. Since the return from Oakland in September, she had been in a dance between crippling nostalgia and extreme bitterness. She missed the California she once knew. The people there, but also the landscape. She craved San Francisco's dreamy fog. The taco trucks and hills of colorful homes in Oakland. The Pacific Ocean gleaming from the docks of the Berkeley Marina, and the vast beauty of Stinson Beach.

The Bay Area expanded Raynah's world in ways she never imagined. She enjoyed books and friendships during her stint at UC Berkeley in the late 1980s before moving on to dabble in film and nonprofit life. When that ran its course, she immersed herself in grassroots organizing. There was no sense of permanency in the years that flew by—just new opportunities constantly forming.

Now, back in St. Louis, the only places where Raynah came close to feeling that alive was in pockets like the Delmar Loop or Maplewood. Sometimes she explored South City's Tower Grove area, but resented what was once dismissed as a seedy section morph into a new urban renewal project for hipsters.

Raynah would've loved to wrap the recent experiences in her hometown into a neat, pretty box and label it "transition." But the reality was clear: in a three-month span, the last twenty years of the life she'd created for herself in the Bay Area came crashing down. She was left fighting to reconcile two pasts, two regions, two worlds.

Next door, Lois emerged from Justine's house. She retrieved a jumbo nail kit wrapped in a gold ribbon from the trunk of her car and bounced across the street to Ms. Myrtle's house, where she placed the box between the main entry way and the gated screen door.

"What's she going to do with that?" Raynah asked.

"Keep her feet clean," said Lois, returning to Justine's driveway.

Raynah imagined Ms. Myrtle, once a short, stocky woman in high heels and men's overalls, crouching over her bed of chrysanthemums. A six-pack of Stag beer leaning against the porch's handrail to jump-start an afternoon of gossiping and people watching with Justine.

"The Ms. Myrtle you once knew is no longer there." Raynah pointed to the weeds on their neighbor's lawn. "Her brain died with Pete. You remember Pete, right?"

Lois's face twisted in disgust. Raynah watched her sister dissolve under the weight of a lost memory they shared, both of them standing among the crowd in Ms. Myrtle's yard, viewing a bloodied stretcher be pushed into an ambulance.

"So, what do you suggest, Ms. Fight The Power?" Lois asked. "A beret? Brass knuckles? Do tell."

"You would've been better off getting her beer, is all I'm saying."

"Whatever." Lois opened her car's back door. "Come help me with the rest of these bags."

"Nah, looks like you have it all together," Raynah told her.

"What's that supposed to mean?"

"Whatever you take it to mean."

Lois sighed and closed the door, careful not to let it slam. "Why's everything always a struggle with you?" she asked Raynah. "This isn't California. You don't get points here for being the rebel."

"I guess it's more fitting to be the puppet."

Lois stared at the patch of grass between their parents' houses. "I don't know what else to say to you anymore," she said. "Would it be too much for you to just be cordial sometimes? Have a little class. You'd get along much better in the world."

"Says the woman who's never left St. Louis."

Lois put the grocery bags on the ground and marched closer to Sir's house. Raynah could see the large vein that protruded from the middle of her little sister's forehead whenever she was angry.

"That's right," said Lois. "Forgive me for being too concerned with priorities while you and Ahmad were away, doing God knows what."

Raynah sat up, her temper rising. She knew it was only a matter of time before Lois started hurling Ahmad into the conversation and letting her suspicions get the best of her.

"You're on that again?" Raynah flicked the ash accumulating from her cigarette in her sister's direction. "For the hundredth time, why the fuck would I sleep with Ahmad?"

"Say what you want," Lois told her. "All I know is while you two were busy trying to reinvent yourselves, I was building a career. Helping our parents. Raising my son."

A darkness spread over Lois's face at the mention of Quentin. Raynah knew the conversation had gone too far. Still, as much as her nephew's death hurt Raynah, she wasn't about to let today be centered on Lois's trials. She wasn't going to give her sister the satisfaction of being a victim by consoling her. If that's what Lois needed, which she almost always did, she could run back to Justine and they could lose themselves in each other's misery.

Raynah frowned, her nostrils flaring. She took one last drag of her cigarette, smashed it on the bottom of her shoe, and went inside Sir's house.

*

"Bitch, I'm tempted to add vodka."

Pinch placed the glass of cranberry juice on the bar's countertop in front of Raynah. She rolled the top ball of her tongue ring back and forth across her lips. Her makeup shimmered under the kaleidoscopic lights reflecting off the dance floor behind them.

Raynah shrugged and sipped from her glass. She welcomed the warm feeling that came with seeing her closest childhood friend again after running into her the other day.

The third oldest of Ms. Bev's six children, Yolanda, who everyone called Pinch, was now a far cry from the scraggly tomboy with scraped knees and missing hair barrettes that Raynah remembered. She'd blossomed into a tall, voluptuous woman who sashayed, rather than walked, behind the counter where she greeted customers and made their cocktails.

"Not if you don't want an ambulance outside here soon," Raynah joked.

"Seen it all." Pinch wiped the countertop with a towel. "We get sloppy drunk folks all the time."

"I'm not talking sloppy. I'm talking sick."

"Whatever, bitch. We get those kinds, too."

"I'm sure."

Pinch laughed and flung the damp towel over her shoulder.

"Still can't believe you went off to college in Cali and never learned how to hold your liquor," she said to Raynah. "Bitch, what was y'all doing on the weekend? Bacardi ain't but twenty bucks and was probably ten back then."

"Don't start," Raynah told her. "Those days are exactly why I slowed down."

Someone called Pinch's name down at the other end of the bar. She waved and stuck out her tongue.

"Be right back." Pinch winked at Raynah. "You be good."

Raynah rolled her eyes at Pinch. She squinted at the clock on her cell phone. It was only going on five o'clock in the evening and already, the dive bar was becoming packed with patrons. Raynah glanced around the small place again. She watched the growing number of customers around her flocking to the bar to order drinks. A group of twentysomethings, clearly tipsy, bounced on the tiny dance floor in the center of the bar to an old Missy Elliott song. An explosion of orange velvet cushion booths lined the walls. Above the seats were photos of St. Louis favorites over the years—the world's largest Amoco sign on Skinker Boulevard, Imo's Pizza off I-64, the old Woolworths in Midtown, Velvet Freeze Ice Cream, Northland Shopping Center, London & Sons Wing House, the marquee for River Roads Mall, Crown Candy, the Checkerdome before it was demolished, and an unfinished Gateway Arch as it was being built.

From the outside, Raynah would've never guessed the ounce of magic this bar held. It was situated in one of the worst neighborhoods in St. Louis, a run-down, crime-infested area that many people knew to avoid stopping in. Raynah sometimes felt guilty for avoiding some sections of her hometown, only going if an errand called for it, or to visit relatives and rekindle old friendships. But, there was something criminally demeaning about seeing crater-sized potholes in the streets, boarded and abandoned storefronts, and the skeletons of badly burned houses next to residents living only a few feet away. All of it was a sore on the eyes, memory, and spirit. The ghastly message that poor people deserved constant reminders of their powerlessness.

With this in the back of her mind, Raynah forced herself to accept Pinch's offer to hang out at the bar when they'd exchanged numbers the other day. She hadn't confirmed when she would visit, in case she changed her mind. But the exhaustion of unpacking and sorting through Sir's old things after the confrontation with Lois, coupled with her disappointing job search, had put Raynah in a sour mood that afternoon. She knew she had to go somewhere before her feelings suffocated her.

"You hear about Genie?" Pinch approached Raynah again on the other side of the counter. Instead of scratching her scalp, she firmly patted the side of her head. Even now, she was the only person Raynah knew who could bring back the freeze hairstyle from the 1990s and wear it well like the trend had never faded. It must've been a talent she'd inherited from Bev after all those years of watching her mother create and remix styles for clients.

"Who's Genie?" Raynah asked.

"You know, Lance's cousin who used to drive Solomon's bum pop truck. Hurt my heart when they moved to the South Side. I used to have big feelings for him."

"Who, Lance or Solomon?"

"No, bitch. Genie."

"Girl, who are these people and what happened to Genie?"

Pinch held up her finger and made a Long Island for one of her new customers. When she returned to Raynah, her hand was upside her head again.

"You'd know Genie if you saw him," she said to Raynah. "Yesterday, he got into a scrap in here with another dude over some girl. Got his shit broke and everything. I hear he's in ICU with one collapsed lung."

Raynah whistled in disgust. The news was tragic but she couldn't help wondering where Pinch was going with her random story. As if Pinch could read her thoughts, she raised one of her perfectly arched eyebrows at Raynah.

"Bitch, didn't you say you was looking for a job? Genie's not getting out of the hospital anytime soon so his gig at the History Museum is open. You better apply now before they fill it."

Raynah smiled in spite of herself. She hated the thought of benefitting from another person's tragedy. Still, joy swelled in her chest. Finding work hadn't been easy. Since moving back home, Raynah had applied for jobs all over the city—ones she knew she was more than qualified for—and went on countless first-round interviews that never led to a callback or follow-up meeting. Meanwhile, food, utilities, occasional entertainment, and the gas in Raynah's jalopy wasn't taking care of itself. Sir's house desperately needed repairs, too, so Raynah had resorted to pinching off the safety net she'd built during her six years as a program assistant for a design firm in Oakland to get by.

"Don't get too happy," Pinch told her. "It's only part-time."

"That's a start."

"Yeah. I'm sure your mama will be proud."

By that, Raynah knew Pinch meant Justine would get off her back about being unemployed and venting to Ms. Bev about her firstborn being such a disappointment.

"You know it." Raynah laughed and shook her head. "Things would be so much easier if the two of them didn't go looking for trouble."

Pinch snorted. She got a straw and drained the rest of Raynah's fake cocktail. "Ms. Bev and Ms. Justine."

"AKA, the Black Thelma and Louise," added Raynah.

"Nah, the Black Lucy and Ethel."

"Wait, I got one." Raynah held up her hand. "The Black Laverne & Shirley."

"What about Ms. Myrtle?" Pinch asked. "We can't leave her out."

Raynah drummed her knuckles on the counter, her eyes wide with excitement. "The original Salt-N-Pepa featuring Spinderella."

"Bitch, Spinderella?"

"You heard me!" Raynah said. "There'd be no group if she wasn't spinning shit behind the scenes. She was cold back in the day, don't get it twisted."

Pinch popped her tongue. They both burst into laughter at the memory of their mothers hanging out with Ms. Myrtle back in the day.

"So, why you really here?" Pinch finally asked Raynah. "I know it's not to sip on some stale-ass cranberry juice and compare our mamas to old-school legends."

"I don't know." Raynah shrugged.

"You miss your daddy."

Pinch's truth stabbed Raynah so hard, she bit her nails to keep from crying out. Sir had only been dead for a few months and for some reason, Raynah couldn't conjure up a single physical image of her father. No smiling face in a family photo. No cutting glare when someone said the wrong thing. Not the playfulness in his eyes when he flicked shaving cream at her on the mornings Raynah snuck into her parents' private bathroom before school. All that was left of him in her memory was a growing black dot where her father's handsome face had once been.

"Yeah. So?" was all Raynah could think to say. She kept her eyes on the counter and sucked air through the straw in her empty glass.

Lois

Lois called her son right after it was announced that the cop who fatally shot Michael Brown wouldn't be indicted. Quentin was dead, but she called anyway and held the phone to her ear like he would answer. After the fifth ring, she hung up, sorry for what she'd just done. Again. Hungry for peace, she unplugged her alarm clock and, with the help of sleep aids and wine, slept for three days through sirens, chants, fires, and glass breaking outside her home.

At some point, Lois dreamed of a bear being attacked by shadowy figures. It screamed in a man's voice and was beheaded. With a squishy thud, the bloody matted fur fell on the ground and rolled onto Lois's bare feet. She woke up rattled and dry-mouthed in the wee hours of Thanksgiving morning, listening to her stomach growl in the dark until she dozed again, and rose to the sun's midmorning assertiveness that swallowed the house.

Lois showered and stared at her puffy face in the bath-room mirror. Her whole body hurt. An invisible stone crushed her throat.

After getting dressed, she read and answered emails in her office on her desktop computer. She brewed coffee, cooked eggs, and ate in silence. She washed dishes, changed her bed linen, and charged her phones. Then, she sat in the living room and listened to voicemail messages left by missed callers.

There was a message from Jillian, Lois's accountant and best friend. Her nasally voice screeched into the phone.

"Lo, you there? Listen to me. Go straight home, okay? I'm headed out of the office now. Things are getting out of hand. The boards on these windows are already being tagged. Eggs, dirt, rocks, sticks ..."

Something shattered in the background. Lois heard Jillian yelp into the phone.

"... the church is having a peace and healing service to-night. We should go. Call me later, okay?"

Lois downed the last of her coffee, remembering that she had mentioned to Jillian that she might go to church with her once the verdict came. They were supposed to mourn together. The thing was, even as they were having the con-versation, Lois knew she wasn't going. Something about attending service felt hollow and wrong.

Over the years, Lois had grown to despise their church, an elaborate building with 3D ceiling murals, heated pew cushions, and an underground theater—everything that attracted many of St. Louis's professionals. The congrega-tion was sizeable but bland, like food that was never properly seasoned. Lois missed the storefront church of her childhood. The bold, milky warmth of anointing oil trapped in the worn carpet. Its crowbars on stained glass windows and the uneven wall paint weren't the most pleasant things to look at, but after some time, seeing them made her feel secure and special enough to hold the building's flaws. At her old church, Lois felt seen and inspired. People were expressive, defying the veil of sophistication that was now her world.

The next message was from Justine.

"This is your mama, girl. Don't tell me you're at work while these fools are tearing up the place. Ring me. Bye."

Lois deleted the message. Sometimes she could live with Justine's sass, but too often, her mother sounded ignorant and heartless—incapable of sympathizing. After Sir's death, it seemed she cared more about the dead than the living; the proof was in her silly addiction to hijacking funerals.

Part of Lois also believed Justine enjoyed the way St. Louis was being nationally demonized. With every day that passed, her mother's complaining became more pointed and self-righteous, as if she found twisted pleasure in seeing the mistreatment of residents groveling for justice in the streets.

Lois wanted the Justine that raised her to come back. She missed the mother who jumped on the bed alongside her and her siblings to Kool & the Gang's "Jungle Boogie" on Saturdays while Sir was away at work. The mother who slipped Lois Tootsie Rolls when she cried at the sight of the large conveyor brushes in the gas station's tunnel car wash.

The woman who replaced the Justine she knew was becoming impossible, and Lois envied her siblings for being better at handling her. Theo always knew how to make himself unavailable and Raynah, for all her faults, was admirably brutal, always challenging Justine, even when a confrontation wasn't called for.

But as much as Lois hated enabling her mother's foolishness, there was something about Justine's criticism, as piercing and awful as it was, that consoled her. At forty-one, being single and now childless, was no glamourous journey. The fussing reminded Lois that she mattered to someone enough to be mothered; that she was reliably loved.

The voicemail system's automated voice belted out another number, timestamped from that morning. A familiar dread pricked at Lois as she waited for the message to play.

"Happy Turkey Day, lady! Let's catch up over brunch and Black Friday sales tomorrow. Maybe we can go to that new soul food joint in Pine Lawn and I can finally try some grits, or what is it? Chicken and waffles! My treat, yeah? Hit me back!"

Dawn calling at a time like this was weird. Experience had taught Lois that when things weren't all sweet potato pie and Tyler Perry movies, Dawn was the white acquaintance who disappeared. When things calmed down, she eventually returned, careful to avoid topics that triggered debate and quick to hurl distractions in discussions that were out of her comfort zone.

The last time Lois remembered Dawn reaching out was Fourth of July weekend, when she invited Lois to a soirée for real estate professionals. Lois lied and said she'd made other plans, when really, she didn't want to risk being the only person of color, besides service workers, in the building.

Ever since Lois met Dawn in real estate school back in the late '90s, Dawn was that girl who insisted on being friends. They both were the youngest in their class, so it was a natural gravitation. The two of them studied together in late night cram sessions and knocked back cocktails during post-test celebrations, but they were never as close as Dawn would've liked because right away, Lois understood something: Dawn was obsessed with Black when it was on her own terms.

It was almost as if she expected Lois to be her personal tour guide through contemporary Black experience. She was in Lois's face, gushing with curiosity and grabbing for details about everything she assumed was connected to Lois: where to go for the best soul food, how to twerk, who to contact for weed.

Lois knew their relationship was toxic, but she was determined to keep Dawn around, even if it was at a distance. She enjoyed having access to the right people, with the right benefits, and figured she could cut ties as soon as things became as draining as they were insulting.

There was still one unread message. A 510 area code. From Oakland. Like Raynah's.

On impulse, Lois deleted the message. She slumped into the sofa and pushed down thoughts of Ahmad. She couldn't go there. Not today. And even if she could—which she wouldn't—there was little chance of receiving a call from Ahmad. He hadn't returned home since Quentin's funeral two years earlier, not even to visit his grandmother, Ms. Myrtle. Few things, besides the current and highly publicized hell in Missouri, could bring Ahmad back and not even that was enough to stir the pot of his cluttered history with Lois.

To keep her mind from wandering, Lois dusted furniture, mopped floors, vacuumed curtains, reorganized cabinets, and folded clothes. By noon, she was washing and hand-drying all of her dishes in the kitchen.

While working, Lois saw a black cat bathing itself in the window of a house across the street. Its glossy fur shimmered like ink melting under the sun's blinding white rays. The cat's golden eyes, feverish and slanted in their sockets, were like a hushed flame afraid of its own power. Wary of getting lost in them, Lois closed the blinds and retreated back into her bedroom.

*

"Your mama's looking for you."

"Hi, Ms. Bev."

"Don't 'hi' me," Bev grunted into the phone. "I said your mama's looking for you. Why you sound like that?"

"Like what?"

"Like somebody ripped your damn throat out and put it in backwards."

Bev's voice fell into her beauty salon's symphony of women's chatter, dryers buzzing, and the clinking of equipment in the background. To hear better, Lois muted the television in her bedroom where she'd returned after last night's deep cleaning and quiet weeping. Unable to sleep for more than a few hours, she rose before sunrise and watched Lifetime movies. She glanced at the clock on her night stand. 10:03 a.m.

"How was your holiday?" she asked Bev.

"Girl, what holiday? I got stuck cooking greens and cakes for badass kids who act like they don't know my address any other damn day of the year. Your mama wasn't any help either. Shit, all she did was sit and read me the latest eulogies of folks whose funerals she stole from."

"Sounds fun," Lois said. A pang of regret hit her when she thought of Justine eating dinner at her best friend's house, alone with none of her own children to keep her company during the first major holiday without Sir. She shook off the feeling, wondering why Bev hadn't called Raynah or Theo. And why wasn't her mother looking for them? Justine, of all people, knew how hard any holiday was on Lois. This time, she'd have to look elsewhere for her emotional punching bag.

"Yeah," Bev continued. "And now, I've got all these heads I have to do today. Why don't you come down here and grab a plate?"

"No, but thank you," said Lois. The thought of leftovers from a traditional Thanksgiving meal made her queasy. She didn't have the energy or the appetite.

"You don't have to eat it right away," Bev told her. "Just something to hold you over for the weekend. Maybe take it with you to the office on Monday."

"That's okay. I'm fine, Ms. Bev. Really."

On the other end, the background noise in Bev's shop stilled. Lois heard the faint hiss of a running faucet and paper towels crumpling. She imagined Bev drying her hands, a flip phone nestled between her meaty shoulder and the wig she'd decided to wear today.

"Lois, between me and you, I don't think you're fine. When's the last time you went anywhere, besides work and your mama's house? The protests outside aren't worse than anything that's going on inside your head. You need to do something. Get some fresh air. Quentin would want that. You know he would."

Hearing Quentin's name said aloud prickled Lois's skin. She wanted to scream at Bev and demand answers. Why did she think it was okay to be so thoughtless? How could she fix her lips to prescribe such an easy solution? What right did she have to make assumptions about who wanted what?

"Sorry," Bev said, as if reading Lois's thoughts. "I know it's not my place to—"

"I have to go now, Ms. Bev. Thank you for calling."

Lois hung up and gathered the crumpled mounds of used tissue on her satin comforter. She stretched and took in the room's moist, briny smell—the aftermath of her tears—as she stood in front of her vanity table. Her skin, usually bright and honey-colored, looked aged and gray. She poked at the dark circles under her eyes and massaged her cheeks to stop the muscles in her face from twitching.

Bev's advice hung in Lois's thoughts and the sting of her words lingered. Even if she wanted to get some fresh air and do something—which she didn't—what would she do? It exhausted her to think of options, so she returned to her bed and her movies.

At half past noon, Dawn called back with an invitation to brunch. It still struck Lois as odd of her to reach out during a time of so much panic and terror in the city. She probably needed a favor, or worse, wanted to vent about her own problems. Lois wasn't excited about hanging out, but she was bored and needed something to numb the dark spell trying to consume her thoughts again. Desperate and antsy, something inside her screamed yes.

The soul food joint that Dawn mentioned was closed. They ended up meeting at her favorite place in Clayton, a posh tea bar with antique furniture and indoor fountains. The restaurant's location was a far cry from the city's raging ghosts that were just miles away. On Lois's drive over, she was hit with the sobering smell of smoke and the charred remains of buildings. She could almost taste the bitterness of tear gas and spray paint fumes.

"I knew you wouldn't let me down." Dawn squealed. Her brown moppy hair, streaked with dirty blonde highlights, bounced as she embraced Lois in the restaurant. She gave one of her hugs with the extra squeeze at the end.

"Do I ever?" Lois asked her.

"Only when you're not answering your phone."

"Yeah, sorry. I haven't been myself lately."

"Hate to hear that, hon." Dawn made a sad face and picked up her menu. "Anything I can do?"

"Not really," Lois said. "I'm fine. Just more tired than usual. You know, with all that's going on and—"

"Looks like they have apple cider mimosas again." Dawn beamed and pointed to the fall specials. "Let's try it, yeah? I've been a little out of it myself. Maybe that'll give us a nice energy boost."

Lois forced a smile. "I'll try anything if it makes me feel less dead."

"Oh, you poor dear," said Dawn. "I wish you'd mentioned this earlier. I would've picked you up instead of having you drive to meet me here."

She reached across the table for Lois's hand. Eyes watering, Lois waved her off and studied her own menu. She knew Dawn was just being polite. Unless it was to show property for business purposes, the woman rarely went anywhere outside of her own glossy neighborhood. Several times, Dawn made it clear she didn't feel comfortable in some parts of St. Louis, even North County.

As much as Lois hated Dawn's dismissal of the area she'd called home all her life, she knew it was true. The same neighborhoods Lois once worshipped as a kid and teenager now had litter cluttering the sidewalks and the nearby wooded parks. On the main roads outside of the residential spots, pawnshops, check cashing centers, and liquor marts replaced the indoor malls, family-friendly landmarks, and prominent grocery chains. Shops that Lois frequented would be open to the public and then one day, without warning or explanation, they weren't there anymore. More and more, she noticed vagrants parading intersections in search of food, money, sometimes shelter. Witnessing her neighborhood being taken apart, in so little time, was like grieving over the death of someone close to her all over again. Each day, Lois felt more of herself slipping away, eroding with the suburban perks that once defined her childhood.

Being in real estate had become Lois's refuge. She believed this career was her calling. It wasn't just about selling houses. Lois was handing people—mostly her people—their dream. A tangible one. Or, what was left of it.

Many of her clients were first-time property owners, re-alizing a goal that went beyond their own vision and dated back to earlier generations who'd prayed and worked and sacrificed for someone in their family to eventually earn their way to the American pie. Through Lois, clients were able to see the best version of themselves and their ances-tors, and in return, they adored her for it.

To remind herself of the impact her work had, Lois kept all of her gratitude gifts from past clients. She still had the wedding invitation after her first sale from a twentysome-thing Rwandan couple who she helped close on their first house in the states. Another couple—middle-aged St. Louis natives with teen triplets—gave Lois a handmade vase, plated with twenty-four-karat gold, that she had framed for her home office. Not that she was looking for anything, but nearly twenty years in real estate had also earned her an-tique Persian rugs, invitations to baby showers, VIP concert tickets, designer jewelry, autographed books, luxury ball-point pens, and a host of thank-you cards, some of them stained with the tears of Lois's clients as they handed them to her in exchange for the keys to their new house.

All of this, Lois tried to keep in mind when she wanted to complain about the skeletons of her lost neighborhood. But, every year, with an economic downturn affecting areas that had once been well kept and easily sellable, it became hard-er for Lois to adapt. More people were renting instead of buying, because things like rotting trees and broken cars sitting in oil-stained driveways were bringing down the property value in her most targeted areas. The more Lois complained, the more it felt like she was turning into her mother. So, she mostly learned to keep quiet about her frustration, especially in front of people like Dawn who used any excuse to trash-talk her neighborhood.

A thirtyish Hispanic man with a unibrow promptly took Lois and Dawn's orders. He told them his name was "Riq," short for Enrique, and that he was a Wash U student pursuing his PhD in sociocultural anthropology.

"What do you plan on doing with that?" Dawn asked him.

Her question to Riq reminded Lois of the time she bought Quentin new shears on Amazon a month after he graduated from barbers' college. They were emerald green, her son's favorite color, and Lois remembered hovering her mouse over the confirmation button on the computer in her office, her belly knotting. The years of pride on Quentin's lengthy summer outings with kids from respectable families, enrollment in Missouri's best private schools, and a partial scholarship to study architecture at St. Louis University deflated.

Barbers were good, Lois knew, but it was a life for the mediocre. The average. There were worse things than dealing drugs or winding up in prison. To Lois, remaining just above the poverty line, never having a mortgage, and working through the standard retirement age were equally a death sentence. But Quentin was pigheaded and wanted to forge his own path however lowly and generic it seemed.

Lois tried hard to get a handle on her emotions as she watched her son ruin his adulthood. Like every mother, she was afraid the world would crush him under its biased, corruptible thumb. She couldn't shake her jealousy of Quentin's courage to be his own person, an opportunity Lois never had. And, as hard as it was to admit, she was angry with herself for feeling entitled to her due rewards as a selfless mother. For investing in programs that were "ethnically gratifying" and exposing him to St. Louis's upper-class pocket of somebodies. For ceaselessly instructing her son on things a young man like him needed to do in order to survive:

> *"Stay away from dark colors."*
> *"Hoods and caps cause trouble."*
> *"Don't stare at anyone too long."*
> *"Hold your chest in, son."*
> *"Try not to take up so much space."*
> *"Never run; walk fast, if you're in a hurry."*
> *"Keep your hands where everyone can see them."*

When Quentin moved out, it hurt Lois more than she let on. It was a wonder he'd never reached out to Ahmad and run away to California, a decision that would've killed her. Fearing it might one day come to that, Lois confirmed the Amazon order and had the emerald shears shipped to Justine's house where they'd planned a surprise graduation party in his honor.

When the package arrived, no one had heard from Quentin in a while. He was happiest when off to himself, but it wasn't like him not to check in with Lois for days. She panicked when she learned Justine hadn't talked to him either.

Lois left dozens of messages on Quentin's phone and circled his apartment complex, hoping to get a glimpse of him inside the lobby or on the steps that led to the building's entrance. She drove around town, paying close attention to young men with her son's build and complexion. She looked for the copper-brown cheekbones scarred from acne, the bushy eyebrows which won him the nickname "Grinch," and the gap in his teeth that he never wanted to correct.

Hours later, she learned her son was gone. Dead. A victim of crossfire in a drug bust between his neighbors and the police.

"I'm going to study people, I guess," Riq told Dawn. He chuckled shyly and tucked a chunk of his wavy black hair behind his ear. Lois noticed a spider tattooed on his neck. She concentrated on the design until the pressure around her torso relaxed.

"Good for you," said Dawn. "As long as there's money in it, go for it. You'll need it once those student loan bills start rolling in."

"I'm on scholarship."

"Gotcha." Dawn handed Riq one of her business cards. "I can help you find a nice place if you're looking to stick around after graduation. Bad credit's fine. We can fix you up to lease."

Riq stuffed the card in his pocket and went to put in their orders.

"Bad credit?" Lois raised her eyebrows at Dawn. She fiddled with her silverware, irritated by her colleague's assumption.

"What?" Dawn's reaction, laced with innocence, nearly made Lois bang her fists on the table and leave.

Dawn leaned in, a sly look on her face. "I bet you he's gay."

Lois chewed on Dawn's words, her anger thawing. "Really?"

"You didn't see that extra pep in his hips when he walked away? Nice, round ass, but I know gay when I see it."

Suddenly, Lois saw her brother, Theo, when he was a teenager, razor bumps bulging from the strong jawline he'd inherited from Sir. He was wearing his faded Mr. T shirt and flipping through X-Men comic books on his bed. One shoe off, the other on. Door more open than closed. Guarded but tender eyes.

"God, I wish my son had that problem," Dawn said. "If parents could actually choose which hardship they had to endure from their kids, I swear I'd take 'Hi Mom, I'm gay' any day over a son who doesn't talk to me at all."

Riq came by with mimosas. Lois had hers to her mouth before he could walk away. The drink was cold but lacked flavor. She swished it around in her cheek pockets, savoring the fizz before she swallowed.

"I told you he moved out, right?" Dawn said. "I mean, I knew he was trouble the moment he hit eighteen, but never like this. Drugs, fights, girls, you name it. He's like a different person.

My husband wants to get him counseling. He thinks he's depressed or something. Depressed from what? I mean, what the fuck. Really? He's got everything a young man his age could want. Always has. It'd be a different story if he'd been raised like, you know ... if he'd been in some way disadvantaged."

Before Lois realized it, she was nodding in agreement. She leaned forward and propped her head between her hands. It was going to be a long day, she realized, but there was no use in letting whatever Dawn said trigger her and make her act unreasonable. Lois knew she wasn't the only person in the world with problems. She wasn't going to let this woman see her sweat and fall into the dangerous thought pattern that all people who looked like Lois were insular and acted like the world revolved around their own misery. She would do better. She would be the exception.

"I told him, 'You want to be a thug?'" Dawn punched the air between her and Lois with her finger. "'Not under my roof, bud. Go somewhere else.' And he did. My only kid."

"I'm sure it's a phase," Lois told her. The tips of her ears warmed. She licked her lips and buried them between her teeth. It occurred to her that she could stay this way for the rest of their time in the café. It might actually be a relief to watch Dawn drown in her tears and her mimosa.

By the time Riq returned with their meals, the afternoon crowd had piled into the café. Lois avoided eye contact with Dawn as she drowned her waffles in syrup. She slowly picked at the soiled bread, aware that an empty plate was an invitation for Dawn to start talking again.

*

An hour and three mimosas later, they were outside Nordstrom, witnessing the aftermath of a Black Friday demonstration.

"We could hold off on shopping until next weekend," Dawn said. "I wasn't expecting it to be this lively."

Lois pretended not to hear her. She walked faster across the mall's parking lot, past the police cars and the crowd of protesters, trusting that Dawn would follow. Men and women, young and old, Black and white, filled the main entrance, thrusting their NO JUSTICE NO PEACE signs over their heads. Chanting and occasionally shouting obscenities at the officers that surrounded them in the distance.

Instinctively, Lois combed the crowd, searching for Raynah. Although it would've made for an interesting story to share with Justine later, she was relieved not to find her sister. When Raynah returned to St. Louis after their father's funeral, it was clear she wasn't the same person who'd left. She'd foolishly immersed herself into all things Black and radical. To Lois, it was both brave and stupid. Not that she didn't care about the plight in her community; she just couldn't accept that it was all she had to care about.

"God, nothing's off limits," Lois heard Dawn mutter behind her. "Can't we just shop in peace?"

They entered Nordstrom and beelined to the women's section. It was warm and roomy. Everything seemed slow and muffled against the disruptive show outside.

Fuzzy from drinking, Lois wandered between the aisles of designer clothing. She flicked through dresses on the clearance rack, carefully stroking the fabric of gowns that made an impression. An old Gloria Estefan song purred over the department store's speaker, and she sang along softly.

"Let's play a game, shall we?" Dawn draped one arm around Lois and held up a blue lace cocktail dress. Her face was checkered with red blotches and the smell of cigarettes hung on her breath.

"Pick one and get dressed," she said.

Suspicious but amused, Lois found a beige floor-length gown, sleek and fitted, with colossal sequins outlining its

leg slits. She tried it on in the women's dressing room ca-
tercorner to the racks of clothing. It felt snug and expensive
against her body. The dress's thick crisscross straps hid her
stubborn lower back folds and the ruffled bustle curved
nicely around her buttocks, accentuating her shapely hips.
She felt like her old self again—shining and elegant.

Dawn walked barefoot in a circle in front of the double
mirror outside the dressing room. Her thin, long legs poked
out of the leg slits on her gown as she exaggerated each
step. To Lois, she resembled a living porcelain doll. Smooth
and perfectly sculptured.

Like schoolgirls, the two of them sashayed across the
carpet in their gowns toward the other end of the department store. They stopped in the juniors section, where
three square stands were positioned across from one of the
double-door exits. Only one of the three glass platforms had
a mannequin, clad in a denim jacket and leather fitted mini
skirt. The stark white figure's faceless head jutted out at an
unnatural angle, while its arms, hips, and legs bent into an
evocative pose.

Dawn winked at Lois and climbed onto one of the bare
podiums.

"Let's see who can hold it the longest," she said, motioning for Lois to join her.

"Come on now, this is silly," Lois told her. "How old are
we?"

But, when Dawn didn't answer, Lois found herself
scrambling up the other platform. Instantly, she felt giddy
and uninhibited. She laughed with Dawn and exchanged
funny faces while they imitated the mannequins' voguelike

poses, stood frozen—doll-like and dignified—until she saw a familiar face through the exit's glass doors.

Ahmad.

He was burlier than Lois remembered, dressed in a snug V-neck sweater and wrinkled jeans, a Black Lives Matter cap covering his head. Third in a cop-escorted line of demonstrators plodding towards the opened rear of a paddy wagon. Hands behind his back, the cuffs around his wrists twinkling in the midafternoon sun.

"Hey, you're kind of good at this," Lois heard Dawn say beside her. Lois remained still, her insides twisting with shock and desire as Ahmad looked in her direction. Their eyes met, and she felt herself falling.

Theo

Theo found Alex's house just after sunrise and pissed on the porch. He watched steam rise from his splashes on the cobblestone steps, not stopping or looking up when he noticed the blinds shuffling from inside a room on the first floor.

"What the hell are you doing?!" Alex emerged from the house's custom-made entry doors, his gray robe stirring behind him in the wind. A cloud of horror and confusion thawed the anger on his face. Behind him, the voices of young children floated from the house's open entryway.

"It's okay, kids." Alex positioned his body directly in front of Theo's to block him from sight. "Daddy's just talking to a friend. Go help Mommy with breakfast." Theo shook himself and zipped his pants.

"You have ten seconds to get your ass off my property." Alex removed a cordless phone from his robe's pocket and held it up between them.

"Or what, man?" Theo said, unmoved. "You'll do more damage? Haven't you done enough? I'm just here to return the favor."

"Get the fuck out of here. I'm not going to say it again."

"Alex, I thought we were friends. Boys. Homies. You'd really call the cops on me? This thing you've got for smearing my name is getting out of hand."

"What are you talking about?" Alex asked.

Theo pulled a folded newspaper from a pocket inside his jacket. Just touching it made him nauseated. He threw the paper on the lawn beside them, hoping it would land on the right article. It did.

"Look, man." Alex shook his head. "I've been meaning to meet with you. That wasn't supposed to be out yet. The book's not even coming out for another few months." The book.

Something heavy landed in Theo's stomach. Up until then, he hadn't publicly acknowledged the claims about unpublished material that was out there somewhere, being printed and prepared to eventually be pushed out into the world. Rumors, he knew, came fast in this business. He'd had several mounting, especially after last summer's Ferguson crisis when he was accused of not doing enough to defend protesters and reporters like Alex in North County, who fought and documented the unfolding events. He was dismissed as a cop lover, a fraud, a traitor to his people, for choosing to not become involved as several of his incumbents did.

It wasn't so much that Theo didn't support the underdogs and essence of activism that represented the scene. As an alderman representing the Central West End in St. Louis

City where he'd lived for the last seven years, he just hadn't felt it was his place to step in and publicly ride for Ferguson residents. As it was, North St. Louis County still served as a bittersweet remnant of years in his life that he didn't want to face.

Still, the deeper Theo dove into politics, the more false fires he had to extinguish. And although the evidence in Alex's book was there, part of him desperately hung on to the idea that this was another falsity designed to test him. That part of him felt justified in redirecting conversations with his colleagues and ignoring his assistant when she tried to give him the newspaper. The part that, after leaving the office last night, caused him to drink heavily, in order to numb the dread of having to do what he was doing at Alex's house; to send the message that Alex's irresponsibility wouldn't be tolerated or impossible to outdo. Now, the admission stood between them on Alex's porch, invisible but present, waiting for Theo to make his next move.

"I didn't mean for you to find out this way, man," Alex said, tightening the belt on his robe. "Let's discuss this on Monday. What's your schedule look like?"

"You can't be serious. My ass is on the line and you're telling me to deal with it during normal business hours."

"Keep your voice down, okay?" Alex looked behind him at the open door that echoed toddlers' coos and dishes rattling in the kitchen.

"You know I'm suing you for character assault, right?" Theo told him. "You, your image, and your Goddamn gingerbread family won't have a dime when I'm done."

Alex came closer, his slippers inches from the puddle of piss on the ground. "You're making this bigger than it is.

This is my story, my memoir. I didn't name any names, and I didn't give any clues, so what's the issue?"

Theo flinched. He couldn't believe what he was hearing. "St. Louis alderman isn't a clue?"

"So I'll call my publisher and have them change some things."

Theo imagined the sweet pain of his fingers breaking as they dove into Alex's face. He clasped his hands behind him to curb the temptation. "How stupid do you think I am? No way would a publisher change things this late."

"So what if they don't," Alex said, his voice tinged with new anger. "Who do you think you are, man? You think anyone's gonna give a damn about connecting dots? This is St. Louis. We're not talking a bestseller here."

Theo rocked back on his heels, marveled at how his ex-lover could be as naïve as he was brilliant. He was once attracted to Alex's innocence and loved him almost as much as he'd loved Pete, his first partner and neighbor across the street from his childhood home. But since their introduction, their first drink, and their first tangle in bed together, Theo also recognized the danger. Knowing Alex meant Theo had to peel back the worst version of himself—the arrogance, the self-delusion, the exaggerated masculinity—to find, at the core, a person grappling with denial, dismissing his bisexuality as this thing that men like them just sometimes did.

"Who are men like us?" Theo once asked.

"You know," Alex said airily, "men who need a little variety."

Theo couldn't be mad. Sometimes, he needed to believe that too. And there was no room for judging since he and

Alex were different shades of the same cowardice. Regardless of how different their public lives were, they both worked hard to maintain the straightlaced prestige they'd scrupulously built.

So, instead of arguing with Alex that night, Theo did a line on one of the *Maxim* magazines sprawled on the table of a hotel room they shared for the weekend. Then, he watched Alex lather his face with shaving cream in front of the mirror, the wedding band on his left hand covered by a dirty Band-Aid.

Looking back, Theo figured his name must've been on Alex's chopping block for some time now, probably since their messy breakup over a year ago, if the book was already due for release in the spring. But he couldn't understand how anyone would be blind enough to believe it wouldn't leave the city, especially after last year's eruption in Ferguson.

St. Louis, Theo knew, was deceptive. Unassuming. It was small, until it wasn't anymore. People on the outside thought it was a Midwest relic, known for an arch and not much else, and people on the inside were too busy with their lives to care about things spilling outside of city limits. Still, hearsay was hearsay, and everyone was likely connected to relatives or associates who lived in a popular Sunbelt state or coastal area.

Theo could've moved after graduating from high school, like most of his classmates who were eager to leave their hometown and explore the world. It wasn't that he didn't consider it; he just never took seriously the idea of inserting himself into another region. He wasn't swept away by an urge to meet new people, try different things, taste exotic foods, or any of the stuff that was supposed to make life more interesting. None of it was real to him. St. Louis was far from perfect, but it was his. He decided early on that he'd stay and make a life for himself there.

In his teens, Theo had plans on working in the construction industry—he knew he wasn't the university type—but he also didn't want to be caught up in the mind-numbing routine of a factory worker like his father. Unlike politics, which later seemed to fall into Theo's lap, he was always drawn to construction's unglamourous nature. He liked the muscle and grit that was linked to the job. It seemed hands-on and masculine. The work seemed to fit his personality: heavy-duty and fixed. A constant, through any condition.

It was why Pete loved him, and why Theo hated loving Pete. Big dreamer that Pete was, he always claimed Theo's steadiness turned him on. Theo remembered laying on Pete's chest for hours with his Walkman headphones on, liking the way his head bobbed in time to the music while Pete flexed his pecs. He wanted to freeze-frame those moments. They were enough for him, but then Pete would blab about making it big in some place like New York or Paris, either in basketball or his real first love, photography. His talking almost always led to a heated semiargument before it led to one of the main things that brought them together—libido.

"I don't need this in my life right now, man," Theo told Alex. He took a few steps back from the mess he'd made, and from Alex and whatever it was that they were or weren't anymore. He wanted so badly to crawl into himself and reverse everything.

Alex rolled his eyes.

"You never need anything in your life right now." There it was. The heartbreak.

Alex spat on the ground between them. His saliva landed in Theo's urine. Theo examined its distorted shape and counted the number of bubbles glistening inside it, anything to avoid the torment in Alex's eyes.

To his advantage—and later, his detriment—a ruined adolescence had taught Theo caution. Certain rules needed to be followed to exist underneath people's interest. For this reason, Theo was proud he wasn't a good-looking man, not in a charming, robust way like his father. He had Sir's cleft chin and his stubbornness. That was it. He was never crushed on in grade school and never had to indulge in the silliness of puppy love. In junior high he was secretive, terrified of his own indifference to the pecs growing beneath the braless shirts of girls he'd grown up with, and the sweaty camel toes inside their leggings on hot summer days.

He once ate pussy in his high school locker room, mostly out of boredom, after ditching detention with a girl from his shop class. Like Theo, she was average-looking and hid her brilliance underneath her nasty girl reputation. She made herself horny bragging to Theo about her sex with Pete. Theo got a hard-on from listening, but wouldn't stick it in when she slid off her panties. He looked at the girl, lying there on the rickety bench, with a skirt around her waist and her legs open. She smelled tart, like old soap. The meat softened between his own legs as the wet pink of her middle stared back at him. He warned the girl they'd get caught if he humped her on the noisy bench and pulled her thighs close to his face.

In those moments, Sir always came to mind. Theo could feel his father scowling at his hesitation, pointing out what he failed to do, laughing at his clumsy manhood. It hurled him back into memories that he couldn't outgrow, like when his father made him wear one of his mother's wigs as punishment for not returning a girl's kiss in their church's basement one Easter Sunday. Or, when Theo got the air knocked out of him for trying to hold his father's hand as they crossed the street. He must've been five years old then, with eyes only for jawbreakers and action figures. He couldn't shake off the hostility clouding Sir's face and the power of his disappointment spreading in Theo like serum trapped in his little veins, even as the pain in his crushed chest wore off.

Theo felt Sir's poison resurrect itself in his body after his first kiss with Pete. The night they were caught, when the flashlights spilled through Pete's car windows, his father's toxins screamed inside of him, bounced out of his pores, and traced the disgusted smirks on the officers' lips as he struggled to get his clothes on in the backseat.

"How did you really think all this was going to play out?" Theo asked Alex. "You really think you can just write it off as a dumb phase that happened before you came to your senses and matured into a family man? All this, because I quit you?"

Alex laughed, his voice cracking. "Was I supposed to just go away? Pretend it never happened?"

"That was the idea," Theo said.

"You're a cold motherfucker, man."

Theo turned up his collar and mashed a patch of dewy grass near the folded newspaper with his shoe. He felt his lips hardening in the frigid air, licked them, and surveyed the neighborhood. The street was void and sleek, a frozen black stream separating the rows of brick luxury homes. Above them, the sun was still a youthful peach glow steadily climbing the sky.

Alex's mouth started moving again as he spewed words.

Ignoring him, Theo returned to his SUV and left.

*

Justine answered the door after the first knock. She was holding a creased coupon book to her chest.

"I know I taught you about coming to folks' houses un-announced," she said, stepping aside to let Theo in. "You must've been hoping I wasn't here again."

Theo stood there for a while, like he always did, tracing the iron swirls on the screen door with his eyes, waiting for the familiar dread clenching his stomach to loosen. He was relieved, and ashamed, when the weight dissolved from the comfort of remembering Sir was dead.

Times like this confirmed why he chose politics, or why politics had chosen him. Theo was tired of letting bits of the past—especially those containing Sir—dictate his thoughts and feelings. It made him feel like he was constantly being pulled back into a vacuum of chaos that he saw no way of escaping.

Aside from all of its challenges, politics, in its purest form, was all about moving forward and building better futures. It all sounded cliché, but from the moment he at-tended his first town hall meeting over three years ago, Theo felt compelled to be part of something that took him out of the depressive sphere of looking back. Since then, he'd let politics consume him, thankful and well aware of the time it took away from family and this house that soured his spirit.

Inside, it smelled like sweat, washing powder, and something sweet baking. Theo sat on an arm of his mother's living room sofa, one of the only areas not covered in house junk, or worse, the items she secretly collected from folks' funerals. He scanned Justine as she placed the coupon book in an uncluttered spot on the end table. She had on a plaid duster, but her silver ringlets were wound into a bun at the top of her head, and her honey-brown face seemed to pop out at him. He rose again, realizing she had on makeup.

"You look nice, Mama. Going out with Ms. Bev soon?"

"No," Justine told him. "She's the last person I'm in the mood for today."

Theo followed her into the kitchen and stood against the wall between the table and the door. From the small window over the sink, he could see inside Sir's old bedroom next door. It looked the opposite of Justine's house—stark and abandoned. With the exception of the opened curtain, everything was the way his father had left it, from the bed linen to the Old Spice bottles neatly lined against the mirror on the dresser.

"For all her freedom fighter antics, your sister can be the biggest wimp," Justine said when she caught Theo eyeing Sir's room. "She barely goes in there. I walked into an oven when we donated the last of his shoes the other day and convinced her to let the room breathe while there's still a nip in the air. Her broke behind can barely afford caulk for the bathroom, much less new wallpaper."

Theo chuckled, more out of disgust than amusement. How ironic, he thought, that Raynah, Sir's favorite—his golden child—was living out her days as a washed-up intellectual who couldn't pay her bills on time. Save for the property she'd inherited from their father, she had nothing going for her but her Black pride babble.

"It's not too late to sell the house," Theo said.

Justine wiped the table with a damp dishrag. "Now you sound like Lois."

"Is that supposed to be an insult?" asked Theo.

"It is, if you're okay with getting rid of something your father worked hard for."

Theo stuffed his hands in his pockets and let the back of his head bump against the wall. When it came to Sir's property, he knew his opinion didn't matter. And he didn't really care to have one, for as long as he'd stayed away. Still, it was pitiful and exhausting to see Justine side with a dead man who'd moved out of the house they'd shared for four decades just to get away from her. Even worse, his father had moved next door to keep tabs on her and have access to familiar booty whenever it occurred to him that he was still married.

The busy spell that overtook his mother after the funeral meant nothing. It was a cover-up, like the makeup Sir once banned, now defiantly smeared all over her face. Justine could throw out every stitch his father owned, go to all the strangers' funerals and elders' grief support groups in St. Louis—or wherever Ms. Bev was dragging her these days—but his mother was still a smudge under Sir's rotting thumb. Sir was very much alive, in Justine's head, and she seemed content with being strung along.

"You run into Beth lately?" She asked him, raising her eyebrows.

Theo shook his head, politely taking the punch. His mother was a fool, but she was no dummy. She was always good at seeing into him, and everyone else, and she wasted no time pulling off scabs when she felt she was being silently judged.

"That's too bad," said Justine. "She should hear about your father directly from you and not someone else. That girl put you through school. At least you could call her."

"Yeah, maybe I will," Theo lied. He looked at his mother again as she smiled at him sweetly, draped the dishrag over her shoulder, and sat down at the table.

Justine never liked Beth. Theo remembered how childish his mother had acted, covering her ears and whining to Sir about a migraine as he broke the news to them about his engagement to a lawyer that was thirteen years his senior. Surprisingly, Sir gave his blessing, and Theo thought he'd never be happier to finally be on the inside of his father's approval.

Justine, on the other hand, grew into a ball of hatred designed to destroy Beth. First with her indifference and then with her sharp tongue, which knew no boundaries. By the day of the wedding, she'd resorted to sabotage, showing up late to the ceremony and spilling punch down the back of Beth's dress at the reception.

Beth had her own peppery personality, but she handled Justine with sympathy and respect. To her credit, she put up with a lot of things because she loved Theo. He didn't love her back—not in the same way—and didn't know a man in his right mind who'd marry her in his early twenties, but he did it anyway, mostly to kill the rumors surrounding him after Pete's death.

By then, he'd been scared into only dating girls and liking it. Most of them were predictable and not as discreet as he would've preferred, but he was lonely with hormones that defied his caged heart. When Theo met Beth in passing at a construction site he was working on, he suspected she was more experienced, but never thought she'd turn into anything more than a bed buddy.

Despite the age difference, he quickly learned they shared a lot of commonalities. Like Theo, Beth was the youngest of her siblings and a loner, addicted to CNN and Pixy Stix. She was carefree but ambitious, and wasn't interested in playing the mind games he associated with females. She wasn't self-conscious about her midnight skin or her lisp, and she had a mole in the middle of her chin that he liked to trace with his tongue. Just her smell—Nivea moisturizer and cinnamon-flavored gum—kept his dick hard.

Theo knew he'd ask Beth to be his wife when he woke up one morning with her name on his mouth. What he didn't know was how impossible it was to live with someone he was waiting to love. Within three years of their marriage, Beth had enrolled Theo in business courses at night school and funded the launch of his construction business, but there was little else he enjoyed. He could never shake the disgust gripping him when she cuddled next to him on the sofa. Or, the fury of seeing tampon tubes laying in their bathroom's trash can every month. Or, the hopelessness when she showed him the positive pregnancy test.

Beth wasn't the clingy type; she had a flourishing career that kept her busy. But becoming a first-time expectant mother in her mid-thirties and being the youngest to make partner at her law firm, she faced some physical difficulties. She wasn't close to any of her rural Kentucky–based relatives, and Theo soon found himself alone in her web of panic and despair. Sir would've knocked his balls off if Theo expressed his regrets to him, and there was no use asking a spiteful Justine for support. Raynah was still out in California, and his darling Lois—his "little big sister," as he affectionately called her, the only one in his corner during their teenage years—was in her own struggle; a single mother abandoned by Pete's baby brother and Theo's ex-best friend, Ahmad, who'd also flocked to the West Coast in search of sanity after Pete's death.

Since everyone was unavailable at the time, Theo dealt with Beth for a torturous four and half months, hating her and his unborn child. He didn't want a boy or a girl. He feared what the world would expect of them, and the horror his child would face if they couldn't measure up to the standards that society felt compelled to set.

And what if the baby turned out like him? The real him.

The question ate at Theo as he found it harder to bury his secret cravings for men, his resentment of Beth, and his anger for letting himself get caught in the snare of her fairy-tale life. He began wishing her womb away every time he passed by the ultrasound photo on the fridge.

As his wife's baby bump grew bigger, so did her health complications, and Theo wished harder, praying to a God he'd given up after Pete's death. He encouraged Beth's determination to keep working, knowing it would add pressure. He imagined a random vitamin deficiency or bacterial infection. During the day, he fantasized about the possibilities; at night, he dreamed of Pete's crushed skull on the train tracks, white bone protruding from his first love's lustrous Jheri curl and a hollow heart where the kingly, broad nose should've been. When he woke, his only relief was fucking Beth in the ass. And, when that was over, he faced the wall away from his wife, too exhausted by guilt to sleep.

There really was a God because the news came one day, just like that. Theo rushed to the ER when he got the call about Beth's tumble in their garage. Sobbing, he kicked off his work boots and let his wife hold him in her tiny hospital bed. He kept one hand on her protruding stomach, not totally convinced it wasn't a trick until the doctor assured him that the bulge would eventually disappear.

"We'll try again," he whispered, but silently recounted where he'd hid the divorce papers.

"You should call her," Justine repeated with authority, her eyes blazing into Theo's. "The last thing you need is a reason to make her more bitter."

"Got it, Mama. Can we drop it already? That's not why I'm here."

"Right," said Justine, checking on the dish in her oven. "So, why are you here, son?"

Theo ground his teeth. He didn't know why he was there. Maybe it was a knee-jerk reaction after that morning's bullshit run-in with Alex. Maybe he needed the rare, twisted comfort that his mother and childhood home still gave him. Or, maybe he was just putting off the humiliation of realizing he'd left the damn newspaper article at Alex's house while on his way to the gym to burn off steam.

Thoughts about the article dragged his heart up his throat again. What would he do, or say, when the book came out? It was unlikely that Justine would read it—the only things in print that she cared about were the newspaper's obituary section and her coupon books—but public commentary would spread as people drew inferences. He'd relive his shame when chatter about Pete erupted. And, like then, his mother would make things worse by never asking him about it directly and instead stiffening her jaw in contempt when he came around. Only this time, she wouldn't be able to hide behind Sir.

"I just stopped by to say hi," he told her.

Justine hooted as she set the pound cake on top of the stove to cool. "To what do I owe this honor?"

Before Theo could respond, she stepped back and pointed to her face.

"The one time you don't show up with your camera crew, I wear makeup. Irony's something. Have a seat."

Theo sniggered and pulled a chair from under the table. He wanted to ask his mother about the makeup, and why today, but didn't. She really did look pretty.

Part II

Justine

"Say something."

"No."

Rich sat up in Justine's bed and turned on the lamp. She turned on her side away from him, hoping he'd finally give up and go back to sleep. Instead, he just sat there, listening to her breathe. She could feel him staring.

There she was, naked in bed with a man. She pulled the covers up to her neck so Rich couldn't see all of her flab in the light. "Stop," Justine said. She was irritated with Rich's eyes on her.

"Go," Rich told her.

"I mean it."

"I mean it, too." Rich held her gaze. "Go."

Justine closed her eyes and sighed. Wesley would kill her if he were alive. He was still her husband. On the other hand, it wasn't like she and Rich were in Wesley's bed. They did what they did in a house that had technically belonged to Justine for years since the day Wesley moved out and decided she made a better next-door neighbor than a wife.

When they were together, Wesley rarely touched her. After the kids came, their lovemaking—if one could call it that—was always sloppy and heartless. Justine preferred to sleep through it, or go over the day's to-do list in her head, practicing when to insert grunts and moans to make things go faster.

With Rich, it was different. Their energy, their personalities, their bodies fit together like scattered puzzle pieces reuniting over time. What began as reluctant conversation in the elders' support group at Tender Mercies and a messy day at the supermarket last September eventually led to a random follow-up phone call from Rich, asking Justine if she'd be back to the group soon. Somehow, that led to a one-on-one home-cooked meal he made for Justine in her kitchen, which led to them eventually learning other parts of their hidden selves.

There was a lot Justine had forgotten, like how to hold her lips for a kiss and the warmth of a man's hand on her skin. Rich was so careful and attentive, it made her both sad and aroused.

Justine leaned back against the headboard. When Rich rubbed his eyes, she stole the moment to take him in. The rise and fall of his stomach under the bedsheets. His shoulders and bare chest that were distinctively lighter than his muscular forearms. His thin lips and long nose. The salt-and-pepper hair cut close to his head.

He caught her staring. "What?"

"Just thinking," she told him.

"About what?"

"Stuff."

"What kind of stuff?"

"Just stuff." Justine tossed a pillow at Rich. "You keep asking me questions and I'm going to kick you out."

The concern in Rich's face turned to confusion and hurt. Justine thought his silence would be a relief, but all it did was make her feel cramped by his genuine curiosity. If Rich wanted Justine to give him her version of a Lifetime story, he was in for a letdown. If he hadn't figured out yet that she wasn't into sharing her innermost private thoughts and feelings, it was his own fault. Not hers.

It wasn't that Justine didn't get urges to talk deeply with a companion. She did, more often than she liked to admit, especially after Wesley's passing. But lately, the things that were going on, both inside of Justine and around her, just seemed too difficult and shameful to explain. Too big for her to call out and slap a name on, or give meaning to.

Talking, it seemed, would only make the issue morph into something hideous and overwhelming. Justine couldn't take that chance. She wasn't about to tell Rich about her thing with funerals. Why would she? Where would she start? How could she put into words that, since her breakdown at the supermarket last year, every funeral she attended was also attending her?

The reason Justine had started taking things from funerals in the first place was to fill, or at least blend, the unwanted parts in her past with pieces of other folks' past. But her dramatic episode in the store—something she never spoke of, or let anyone else speak of—opened a portal in her that had once been closed. Since then, with every deceased person she stole from to add to her collage of unfamiliar pasts, Justine was getting large doses of her own past hurled back at her. Bittersweet things, like her childhood, and the Wesley she knew—and liked—before they were married, tempered with her days living in Pruitt-Igoe.

Last week, Justine had attended the funeral of a woman she'd heard of but never met. LaVerne Mabrey had been a flourishing barbecue restauranteur in her heyday, but had lost her business and her fortune after getting shut down multiple times for not passing multiple health inspections. The procedures were supposed to be conducted once a year, but as LaVerne's name and operations grew in the city, it was rumored that she'd made many enemies, particularly white competitors who resented her success. Some said LaVerne had died alone and nearly penniless, but Justine had noticed that the woman had been draped in a designer mink boa, the same as she probably was accustomed to wearing back when she was still financially well-off. Then, under LaVerne's fur wrap, Justine saw the sleeves of her blazer was tattered with several loose threads.

She snatched the longest hanging piece of thread she could see on LaVerne's jacket and tucked it inside her purse. It reminded her of one of the most vivid moments she hadn't thought about in ages. A time when her mama slapped her for declaring that she didn't want to be Black anymore. At the time, Justine was nine years old and sick of their one-bedroom unit in Pruitt-Igoe. Along with everyone else, her family called it the "poor man's penthouse," a place they assumed would be a fresh start after her father's discharge from the Korean War. Ma put every dime from her wages at the local grocer into securing their new home through her boss's connections.

The units were welcoming at first, with brand-new carpet, sparkling kitchenettes, and clean white walls. The living room—also Justine's bedroom—was the size of their old shoebox apartment, with large windows that Ma cracked open at night to help cool the plastic on her sofas. Justine slept on the sleeper couch with an old foam mattress that was flipped and replaced several times. She was a bed-wetter—scared of everything from roaches and overfilled dumpsters to Ma losing her job and Pop not being able to live with them anymore because his presence threatened their welfare assistance.

The only time Justine wasn't scared was when her father stayed the night. He was a big mountain of a man with dimples that softened his face. And he had the voice of God when he sang. He usually joked about his injury in the war and how it made him into both a local disgrace and semi-legend. Ma hated Pop for starting his own band, using the money from his veteran's benefits to buy used instruments for friends to keep them off the streets. But Justine remembered the way Ma's tone softened once the sidewalk jam sessions turned into paid club gigs in the Gaslight Square district and on the East Side.

When Pop couldn't see Justine and her mother because of his travels on the road, or because of interference from Social Services, home as she knew it became hell, with the growing number of Pruitt-Igoe's scary vacant units, stairwell winos, break-ins, and knife fights.

That's when she got fed up and told Ma what she did. Justine was surprised when her mother hit her, but it really burned when she was called a thoughtless little girl. Truth was, Justine put a lot of thought into what she'd said. Beneath their music and Kool-Aid smiles, tragedy was scattered on the streets, in the stores, at the salons, everywhere. To Justine, it seemed that if they weren't Black, maybe they wouldn't have been hated and feared like they were. Maybe some of their neighbors wouldn't have turned sick inside and used that hate or fear to hurt each other, or those who tried to help them. Then, maybe old Ms. Jenkins, the widow killed in the trash fire, could've lived out her last days in peace, dying the way God wanted her to.

Justine took back the pillow she'd thrown at Rich. He let her, but gently held his hand over hers while she repositioned the cushion. That alone made Justine jumpy and reticent. She tried to figure out a way to peel his eyes off of her without snapping at him again. "My kids are taking me out later today."

"That's great," said Rich.

"It's not," Justine told him. "It's a surprise. I hate surprises."

"Do they know about us?"

"Of course they know," she lied. She remembered the last time Theo visited, two months ago in January. The way her son gaped at her for wearing makeup. How it was so tempting to cut short his company out of fear that he'd be there when Rich arrived for their weekly meetup.

"Good," said Rich. "I was starting to feel like your dirty secret."

"Secrets can be good."

"Yeah, when you're young and on the prowl. At our age, it's not sexy anymore."

"Speak for yourself." Justine stuck out her tongue and enjoyed Rich's laughter. When he turned over on his stomach, she traced the maze of small moles on his back.

"Frankly," she said, "the less I know about any of my kids, the happier I am. It hurts sometimes, but it's for my own good."

Justine's skin felt heavy from realizing her own carelessness. She remembered what Rich told her about his son, Blake, being sentenced to life behind bars that day in the store. The cruel reminders of his only child's crimes lessened by letters and monthly visits from a rehabilitated alcoholic father who indirectly killed his mother.

The crow's feet in the corners of Rich's eyes sealed into a smile meant to pad Justine's regret. This would've never happened if he hadn't needed to talk so much. Why couldn't he just leave things where they fell? Maybe he deserved to have his curiosity backfire.

"How'd we get on this subject?" Justine asked. "Can we change it?"

"To what?"

"Anything."

"Okay," said Rich. "Let's talk about the real reason you have me here wide awake with you at three o'clock in the morning. And I don't want to hear you're thinking about nothing."

Justine threw the heavy comforter over her head so he could no longer see her. Next thing she knew, he was leaning into her and kissing her face through the covers, like the patient fool that he was.

*

The sassafras tree in Myrtle's backyard looked puny against a day that was struggling to open its eyes. Not at all like the massive shadowy trunk with twisted mittens for leaves that Justine was used to seeing over the years. The way it was out-of-sight should've made her feel secure and relieved, but it didn't. With every glimpse of the delicate greenery folding in on itself, Justine felt like something was collapsing inside her. Becoming scabby, hardened, and gnarled like the tree's bark. Her skin started quivering, as if hundreds of tiny invisible bugs were crawling over her. To distract herself, she plucked the tree's smallest and closest leaves—next to the bright yellow flowers that firmly announced spring's arrival—and hoped it wouldn't be noticeable that so many of them were already gone.

"What the hell's that gonna do?" Bev disappeared into the morning's thick fog and returned holding dozens of larger leaves. She split them between both their baskets.

"I don't need that much," Justine told her.

"It's not all for you, heifer. What about the girls?"

"Raynah and Lois won't go near it. They both think it's a health hazard now. Toxic or something."

Bev laughed and snapped a twig over her knee. "Well, the activist and the saint can kiss my contaminated ass. I haven't caught the flu bug since '87 and this skin stays as clear and smooth as black satin. Just think how long we've been using good ol' sassafras for tea and broth."

"Years," Justine said. "Never did us no harm." She didn't bring up the whispers about a handful of women they grew up with in Pruitt-Igoe. The ones who turned up pregnant and couldn't stand it. Ethel, the middle-aged nanny from Harlem who made moonshine in her bathtub and sold it to the tenants. Ida, the third floor's rising thespian-turned-waitress-turned-stripper, who threw the best record parties in the building. Or Margaret, the bully in their eighth grade class who once baptized a girl with Nair in the sink of the girls' bathroom. And others whose names Justine couldn't remember. All of them, desperately seeking the cheapest way out of motherhood, believed the rumor about downing a teaspoon of sassafras oil and suffered more because of it, in one way or another. Nerve damage, paralysis, even death.

"That's right," said Bev. She leaned in so close, Justine could smell the tobacco juice on her breath. "Maybe you can have Rich use the root in one of his good ol' Creole meals some time. I bet it helps a man with stamina, too, if you know what I mean."

"Shut up, wench." Justine bit down on her bottom lip to keep from smiling.

"You know he misses you at group."

"Let him miss me."

"It really wouldn't hurt to go out with him, Justine. Maybe let him see your birthday suit. That'll wake Wesley up in his grave!"

"Will you stop?" Justine hissed, bothered by Bev's suggestion. Was it just her making jokes again? When Bev arrived earlier, did she somehow see Rich sneak out Justine's side door to where he parked his Lincoln Town Car in the back alley? Had he mentioned anything at the elders' group in Justine's absence? She vowed never to see him again, if she found out he opened his mouth about them.

"You ain't no fun," said Bev, placing another piece of snuff in the side of her mouth. She told Justine about what she missed at the last elders' support group, which Rich had already told her, but Justine listened anyway, mostly to distract herself from the anxiety squeezing her.

Bev smirked and squeezed Justine's shoulder. "What are you doing for your big day, anyway, Ms. March Madness? Any plans yet, besides letting me dye those roots?"

Justine knocked Bev's hand away and eyed the fog as it started to clear. She didn't want to think about her birthday, much less talk about it. What good would it do to dwell on getting older? Especially when she hadn't pictured it would be this way. Sleeping with a man who wasn't Wesley, and liking it. Making funerals the highlight of her day. Allowing more snippets of the past to press into her system. "The kids are taking me somewhere later this morning. It's a surprise."

Bev narrowed her eyes. "All of them?"

"Yes, heifer. All of them."

They lollygagged in Myrtle's backyard for a while longer, picking at flowers and arranging seeds. Eventually, the day grew wide awake, giving them a bold sun. After Myrtle was put inside and made to take her blood pressure pills, they settled on the front porch steps of Myrtle's house and took turns drinking from a jug of ice water.

"Did I tell you I'm on the committee for this year's Pruitt-Igoe reunion in May?" Bev asked. She dug in her fanny pack for another piece of tobacco.

Justine looked at Bev. For a moment, she saw her best friend as the eleven-year-old girl she was when they'd first met in the housing project. Thin and bubbly with baby hair gelled to her forehead. Her chest lopsided and lumpy from the tissue she always stuffed inside her shirt.

"Now, why would you go and do a thing like that?" Justine asked.

"With all the shit going on around here, I felt it was as good a time as any to reconnect with folks we knew there. You know, catch up and reminisce. Why not? It doesn't hurt and we're not getting any younger."

Justine didn't respond. She was having a hard time shaping her feelings about everything into words, and the nonsense coming from Bev's mouth just made things worse. How could Bev want to return to something so grievous? She was dead wrong about it not hurting. Truth was, it did hurt to reflect on certain things. It hurt so much that some people, regardless of their fake success stories of how much they'd overcome, could clearly never escape. They'd always find an excuse to be suckered by the pain of their past and hold trauma parties with others who could best relate. No amount of liquor and laughs and soul music inspired Justine to want any part of it.

"What's wrong?" Bev asked. "Why do you look like that?"

"Like what?"

"I don't know. Like that. Like hell."

Justine released her breath, hoping that it would dispel some of the uneasiness that clawed at her. It didn't. She handed Bev the jug of ice water and unzipped her jacket.

"You ever just feel gutted?" she asked. "Like, past empty. Just depleted?"

Bev threw one of her legs over Justine's knees. "Honey, you're talking to the queen of depletion. Which sob story do you want today?"

Before Justine could respond, a maroon sports car with big shiny rims whizzed by, its stereo blasting rap music.

Another one with a two-toned white and green paint job and bigger, shinier wheels followed it.

Justine scowled and rubbed her ankle. If Wesley were alive, he would've surely called the police, as he had on many occasions, to file a noise complaint. The nerve of these young people, she thought. Parading their behavior around as if it were something to be proud of. People like them were helping to turn the neighborhood into what it was becoming: a cesspool of ignorance that made it bad for everyone. The whole reason she and Wesley had moved to the suburbs in the first place was so they could get away from all that.

"Girl, give me a story that doesn't involve one of these racket street folks that don't know how to act in public."

"It's 'ratchet,' not 'racket,'" Bev corrected. "Look, your husband's dead, but don't forget, mine ran off and left me with seven kids to raise. And, mind you, seven kids who I don't see or hear from unless somebody gets shot or needs a babysitter."

"You're a good person." Justine told her.

"Everybody thinks they're a good person."

"Unfortunately." Justine looked up into Wesley's bedroom window of what was now Raynah's house, across the street from them. There her daughter was, cleaning the pane with a duster and peering back at her with stony eyes.

Bev followed Justine's gaze and waved, but Raynah walked away from the window without returning the greeting.

"Was I that much of a bitch at her age?"

"Yep." Bev took another swig of the ice water. Justine snatched the jug from her and sprinkled water over her hands.

"You know she's turning that house into some kind of social justice museum? Lois told me that she plans on opening it up to the public on the weekends soon. The other day, I got nosy when I saw one of those Salvation Army trucks out front. Turns out this heifer got rid of all the damn furniture. The house isn't even a house anymore. Just all these clippings, posters, and nonsense books on the history of old demos and whatnot."

"At least she's not hiding herself away anymore like some loon in the attic," Bev said. "She's finding ways to reconnect with people here."

"She's wasting her time," Justine told her. "If she really wanted to start over fresh, she'd leave all that back in California where it belongs. Keep her decent job and stop stirring up trouble over nothing with these street hooligans."

"A boy died again, J. Is that really nothing?"

"You know what I mean. And don't talk to me about kids dying, okay? Let me tell you, the real ones who are suffering aren't out here trying to save the world. Look at Myrtle. Jesus, look at Lois. With all they've lost, you don't see them out here protesting."

"Maybe they should be." Bev picked something out of her teeth and took back the jug. "Sounds to me like she's just trying to be there, in her own way, for those who can't or won't speak up. I'm not all for everything this generation does, but at least they're trying."

"What are you, her publicist now?" Justine asked. "The problem is she's not of this generation. She can't go around talking smack with a bunch of silly rejects like she did in the Bay Area and using those same tired tactics they did in her heyday. It failed there and she's half-crazy because of it. Not to mention broke."

"Well, it's cool to be poor now."

"Not at her age."

"We were."

"No, you were."

Bev chuckled and pushed back a shock of red hair falling into her face. Justine knew she'd get that back. Maybe not right away, but soon enough. Best friends aside, the two of them had their differences that sometimes spilled over into small hostile acts. Justine's jabs at Bev's unapologetic life as a single mom and C-rate hairdresser. Bev somehow forgetting to pick Justine up for Sunday service, or slowly washing out a burning relaxer on Justine's head so she'd think about her offense while she scratched at the scabs left on her scalp. Then they were normal again like nothing happened, until the next time.

Justine had to give Bev credit, though. As bad as they could be to each other, Bev never went too far, like muttering things about how Justine got along with Wesley or didn't. It's not like Justine cared that much anymore. Folks could think what they wanted. The fact was, she never let Wesley move out; she wanted him to. Of course, Justine didn't know it at the time. It ripped her to shreds like it would any wife, but it was better than having to deal with his moods, his other women, or worse, one of those street clowns he called friends. Almost none of them could hold a job, much less their liquor.

The only one Justine had a soft spot for was Bev's husband, Beans. He owned a car, and more often than not, he was employed. Without him, they wouldn't have made it out of Pruitt-Igoe. Wesley would've never had his first legit gig working alongside Beans at the factory on the East Side and they would've never been able to save for the down payment on their house in the suburbs away from the madness they knew. Even after Beans had the breakdown and left Bev for broke, Justine kept the soft spot for him, knowing he'd tried his best with what he was given.

She'd never tell Bev, but sometimes Justine wished Wesley would've lost his mind too. Maybe he would've been easier crazy than evil. Too bad he hadn't been the abandoning type; Wesley's pride kept him around. Still, working so hard over the years to get—and keep—them ahead, made him mean. Not cruel or cold mean. Empty mean.

Justine remembered seeing him sometimes and he'd look back at her without really looking at her, but through her. If she did the same to him, she would've caught all kinds of hell because one thing Justine had learned is the worst thing to do to a Black man was to try not to notice him. After years of praying and hoping things would change, she realized only death could save Wesley. He was a man who'd known too much struggle to ever enjoy the fruits of his labor. Not surprisingly, one of those fruits—now, a sour lemon—was their eldest daughter who lived to outdo Wesley in needling Justine.

"Raynah's like you in more ways than you'll admit," Bev said, rising from the porch steps. She handed Justine the last of the ice water and went inside Myrtle's house. Justine held the container against her mouth, not drinking, just letting its coldness settle over her to numb the burn of Bev's words.

*

When Justine arrived at the nail salon that afternoon with Raynah and Lois, it was chilly again with big, gauzy clouds that competed with the sun. She wasn't in the best mood; Lois spent the entire time chatting about everything and nothing during their drive across town to West County. She talked about the latest March protests in the news, following the resignation of Ferguson's chief of police. Her move from full-time realtor to part-time consultant. And then, as she opened Justine's door, about the birthday gift that she swore her mother was going to adore.

"You can't be serious," Raynah said from the back seat. "We're celebrating slavery today, too?"

"Get off your high horse for once," Lois told her. "These women in here make some serious cash doing what they do."

"We can't do brunch? Or bingo?" asked Justine, both flattered and peeved. "What about your brother?"

"We can do those things anytime," Lois said. She helped Justine out of the car. "Let's get pedicures today. You deserve to be pampered. Besides, it's just us three. Theo couldn't make it."

Inside, the nail shop had the feel of a classic movie, with glass chandeliers, hardwood floors, and indoor water fountains. The bleachy smell in the air was strong, and shelves of nail polish lined the cream walls.

"You're so full of shit, you know that?" Raynah told Lois once they were seated in the pedicure chairs. "Mama doesn't even go to places like these and you know I don't."

A technician tapped one of Raynah's sneakers, signaling for her to remove them. The look she gave the nail tech quickly sent the woman away.

"Excuse me, Ms. Big Ideas," Lois said. "I didn't hear you coming up with anything better."

"You didn't ask me."

"You don't take my calls. I don't chase people."

"Enough," said Justine. She fiddled with her chair's massage remote control and glanced at the nail technician seated at her feet, a gangly girl who looked to be in her twenties. Her long hair, dyed blonde at the tips, was pulled up into a messy bun.

"Talk to Rich lately, Mama?" Lois asked.

Justine looked at her, ready to breathe fire. She and Rich had been careful up until a few weeks ago, when Lois came by the house just as Rich was leaving. They made small talk about the weather and Justine's progress since the day of her breakdown at the supermarket, and although Lois didn't outright ask Justine about his reason for being there, Justine noticed the smirk on her daughter's face during her entire visit.

"What?" said Lois. "He's into you, right?"

"Who's Rich?" asked Raynah.

"This white man that Mama's seeing."

"I'm not seeing him," said Justine. "And he's not white. He's a mulatto."

"Mama, don't say that word," Raynah said.

"Why not? That's what he is."

"It's a derogatory term, that's why."

"Since when were you interested in being politically correct?"

"Well, whatever he is," Lois said, "he sure is good-looking."

"Ow!"

Justine jerked her foot out of the tub and watched the technician scramble to adjust the bowl's temperature. The water wasn't really that hot, but she figured it was a way to keep the nail tech distracted from listening to their family business. The technician apologized and tested the water in the refilled tub with her hand before she guided Justine's feet back inside.

"You're giving her the deluxe, right?" Lois asked, and the blondish girl eagerly nodded.

"I don't need all that," said Justine.

"Mama, this'll be great, I promise." Lois gave their technicians a tight smile like she was advocating for a small child. "You're getting the works."

"Speaking of the works," said Raynah, "I found some papers in Sir's basement the other day. They were hidden behind a fake brick wall down there. Seemed interesting."

Raynah's steely gaze from earlier that morning returned, as well as the growing knot of anxiety in the seat of Justine's stomach.

"What papers?" she asked her daughter. "And, why are you snooping around down there?"

"Well, it's not snooping if it's my house now. I figured the basement might be useful with this new community project that I've got underway. That's when I stumbled on these newspapers under the staircase. Most of them are dated December 1972 and have something to do with the VP Fair, or the Veiled Prophet ball and parade, as it was called then."

Justine absently stared at the toe jam being removed from one of her big toes. The nail tech wiped the gunk on the towel underneath her feet. It lay there on the cloth, defiantly noticeable for all to see.

"Go ahead and say whatever it is you're saying, Raynah," Justine told her.

A steady stream of tension eased its way up Justine's body as she closed her eyes to the stains made on the towel from her own filth. It wasn't like Raynah to beat around a bush. Justine could tell her daughter was enjoying the suspense and trying to see how far she could push, or how much she could pull out.

"If it wasn't for the content of those articles, Mama, I would've sworn it was you in one of the photos. Anything you want to tell us?"

"What are you talking about?" Lois asked.

"You know exactly what I'm talking about," said Raynah. "That stupid Veiled Prophet parade we watched on TV as kids. The one where all those rich white men marched downtown in those ugly KKK-like robes before they had that secret invitation-only ball."

Justine watched Lois look at her, then Raynah, then at her again. A glint of recognition showed on her younger daughter's face before it was replaced with suspicion.

"So?" Lois said, readjusting in her salon chair. "And this is being brought up now because why?"

Raynah's nostrils flared the way they always did when she was about to lose her temper. Justine could all but see smoke rising from the fuzz on her shaved head.

"Because I think Mama was part of a shakedown that tried but failed to get rid of the annual spectacle, that's why. She was involved in a plot where an activist slid down a power cable—yeah, a damn power cable!—and un-masked the fool on the throne. And, she never told us anything about it."

The nail tech ran a foot file along the back of Justine's feet. It tickled horribly. She squirmed in her chair and pretended not to see the woman exchange looks with Lois's nail tech.

"'It don't take all that,' remember?" Raynah said to Justine. "'Racism's everywhere and who are you to stop it?' That's what you said when I told you I was thinking about quitting UC Berkeley."

"Don't you dare try and blame Mama for dropping out," said Lois defensively. "You left because you wanted to leave, not because of what she or Sir did or didn't do."

"Lois, stay the fuck out of this, okay?" Raynah pointed at her sister. "You're only making yourself look more clueless than you already are. But I'm glad you brought up Sir. What did he have to say about all this, Mama? How'd those papers wind up in his house?"

Justine held her breath as the nail tech massaged between her toes and around her ankles. She couldn't believe this was happening, and so fast. She could hear her head trying not to think. Turning down every corner and somehow still ramming into a twenty-two-year-old young woman that kissed a screaming baby before handing her to Bev and leaving in a crowded black van.

The woman rehearsing the plan again with her comrades and eating marijuana brownies to keep her hands from shaking. The woman wavering between giggles and paranoia with another "seamstress" in the back seat on their way to the Kiel Auditorium. The woman rolling down the window closest to her in hopes that December's frosty air would smack more courage into her.

The woman, once inside the venue, rushing through one of the rear corridors, past a sea of talking faces, into a dressing room filled with glittery gowns and boxes of tiaras, corsages, cosmetics, hair rollers, bobby pins, and pantyhose. The woman moving fast, following months of instructions pounded into her and not daring to look at the other "seamstress" as she resisted vomiting from the smell of mixed perfumes.

"You can ignore me all you want, Mama," Raynah said. "It's not going to take the clippings out of Sir's basement."

"No one's ignoring you, girl. Let me relax a little. This is my day."

"How many days do you need, Mama?" Raynah asked, her voice cracking with emotion. "The way I see it, every day's been your day. For forty-some odd years, you had everyone believing you were this lonely housewife who never had options. Must've been nice to make Sir into the bad guy when it served you, and in the next breath, go around praising his hard work for helping us keep up with the Joneses. Respectability, my ass. Tell me, when exactly did you forget you were part of the same struggle? Was it before or after you moved out of the housing project you refuse to acknowledge?"

"You don't even know Mama," Lois told Raynah. "There you are, right up under her, living in a hand-me-down house that we all know you can't afford, and you don't even know her."

"Based on what's in that house," Raynah said, "I know she's a hypocrite."

Someone dropped something breakable, maybe the TV's remote control or one of the manicurists' table lamps. Justine sat dazed and helpless. She could nearly hear Wesley shouting at her, demanding that she take control of the situation unfolding before her. That no child of his, not even Raynah, had the right to speak to her parent that way. He'd order Justine to do something. Anything! Was she really just going to sit there and let this happen? Why the hell wasn't she moving?

But the acid in Raynah's words were eclipsed by the young woman in Justine's mind who prepped the Sears seamstress uniform a day before the planned raid. All the shirt needed was some ironing, but the woman snuck downstairs and hand-scrubbed the skirt in the middle of the night, not so much because her nerves kept her awake or because the real seamstress it belonged to hadn't cleaned it before loaning it to her, but because Wesley was a light sleeper who couldn't stand hearing the gargle of their old washing machine. And, a little because it gave the young woman more time to practice in her head and find answers to everything that could go wrong. Things like being too high and too scared to respond quickly enough to the debutante whose gown the woman accidentally tore when it came time to fold the hem. And the young woman, just standing there, eyes closed with a sewing pin between her lips, after the angry debutante pinched her hard like she was a bad kid acting out in church. The girl, seeing the debutante's face twist with hate and disgust before she demanded new long white gloves that didn't have "nigger dirt" on them. The young woman, squinting in surprise as the camera's snap appeared from an onlooker who came out of nowhere.

"Raynah Jonelle Holmes," Justine said, pulling herself out of the memory. "I don't care if you ever like me enough to understand me, but you won't go calling me a hypocrite or any other names. If it wasn't for me sacrificing and living the way you say I chose to live, you wouldn't have half the opportunities you like to hear yourself complain about. Really, what struggle do you know, other than what you caused yourself? You walk around here with your butt on your shoulders and barely have a pot to piss in. You're the one who had the choices and, being Raynah, you squandered them. Don't bash me like I'm the loser when you never learned how to play the game!"

Snickers and whispering came from the waiting area. Justine counted the grooves in the hardwood floor and waited for her cheek to stop its twitching. When she looked up, Raynah's chair was empty and she was sitting on the curb between two parked cars with her back to the salon's window, a steady stream of cigarette smoke floating around her.

"I didn't mean that," she told Justine once they were all outside.

Justine's hands and feet were clean, but they looked more wrinkled and ridiculous with lavender nail polish. The yellow foam flip-flops given to her didn't help much, and if it wasn't for the bird poo sprinkled on the sidewalk between her and Raynah, Justine would've taken them off and smacked her with them.

"Raynah, I know you," she said. "You mean everything."

Justine got in the car and pressed the lock button before her eldest daughter could open the back door.

"Mama ..." Lois gave Justine that look, like she should be the bigger person.

"Shut up, Lois. Just drive."

But before they could pull away, Raynah bent down to look at Justine one last time through the open window.

"The facts are there and you can't change history," she said. "You can't wear two faces, Mama. Someday, you have to choose."

Raynah

Sir's house was cracking its knuckles again. Loud, earthy pops that shot through the ceilings and walls. Raynah cracked her knuckles back at the house, a little game she'd conjured up when she first moved in.

The place was a crumbling mess—chipped tile, faulty outlets, bad plumbing—that Sir hadn't been able to keep intact after his health failed. Raynah thought of the house's creepy sounds as her father having the last word; his permanent smirk. A scowl, sometimes. His revenge for her being a no-show in his final days and at his funeral.

It was a strange comfort hearing Sir have the last word. Even with little contact with her father during the final years of his life, Raynah sensed he had been waiting to die for a long time. Their last phone conversations were fascinating. Something in Sir had opened. He was never a talker, but he seemed more expressive and generous. His voice, once deep and placid, barely climbed above a whisper as he shared snippets of himself with Raynah that she had never seen or heard before, like what it was like being a factory worker in the same barge manufacturer for decades. He asked her opinion on things—sensitive topics that he'd never shown an interest in before: abortion, climate change, postslavery reparations for Blacks. He had random things mailed to her, like dental floss and a five-pack of fly swatters.

"It's the meds," Justine would say. "They're making him loopy."

But Sir's loopiness helped prepare Raynah for the inevitable. When news of his passing came in August— coincidentally the day after the infamous shooting in Ferguson—Raynah was more relieved than sad, more accepting than defeated, which was why she didn't jump to attend his funeral full of folks she didn't like, or barely knew, just because it looked like the right thing to do.

She also didn't participate in the Ferguson protests. Raynah knew it was something that was expected of her, a person that some folks at home—including her own mother—viewed as the longtime activist who ranted about progress from her soapbox in the Bay Area. She refused to let Justine accuse her of returning only to be part of St. Louis's publicized happenings and not because her family needed her.

The phone rang. Raynah stared at her landline on Sir's kitchen countertop and clutched the receiver with her sweaty palm.

"Yeah?"

"Hi, I'm calling about the internship ad at the social justice museum."

Raynah was stunned that someone actually read her recent Craigslist ad and decided to call. The woman's voice on the other end of the line was hesitant but calm. Raynah's breath quickened as a wave of excitement gripped her. She repeated the words "social justice museum" back to herself in her mind. The argument with Justine at the nail salon about her mother's hidden past as an activist had sparked even more of Raynah's interest in the history of Black activism in St. Louis. Working part-time at the history museum also brought on feelings of curiosity and deep regret about how the civil rights movement in St. Louis was rarely honored or shown to her, in school or at home, although it clearly existed and was rooted in every fold of the city's social landscape. Raynah ached to learn more, to devour and share all that was hiding in plain sight, especially with natives and residents who typically didn't have access to information that was public but hoarded and shaped by the city's select few. What better way to do it than by creating a home museum where people could learn St. Louis civil rights history? Everyone could feel safe and warm and welcome when visiting, instead of feeling intimidated by what they didn't know.

Raynah had quickly immersed herself into putting things in motion for her project. She applied for grants and asked for donations that could help her compile photos, books, and other diverse forms of memorabilia. She studied people and organizations, near and far, with similar plans. She applied for nonprofit status. She donated the furniture in her living room and dining room to the Salvation Army. Lastly, aware that she'd need help with marketing and promotion, Raynah put out an ad on Craigslist in search of an unpaid intern. After two weeks of no calls for inquiry, this was the first.

"You interested?" Raynah asked the woman.

"Yes. Is the position still open?"

"You see the ad's still there, right?"

"Yes."

There was an awkward silence on the phone before the woman on the other end cleared her throat. "So, should I send my resume?"

"No," Raynah said. "Can you write and keep things clean?"

"Yes, ma'am."

"Are you a student?"

"I start college this fall."

"My sympathies."

"I'm sorry?"

"Are you social media savvy?" Raynah asked.

"Yes," the woman answered.

"Not that I care about that, either. No one's changed the world with a hashtag yet, but it's the best way to get a message to the masses and draw people in right now."

"Got it."

"Come tomorrow at two," Raynah said into the phone. "Be here on time or don't bother."

"Yes ma'am. I mean, yes—wait, I didn't get your name."

Raynah hung up and lit a cigarette. She paced Sir's bare living room as she tried to organize her thoughts and plan her next moves for the project. The house seemed even bigger and more vacant than before. Its shapelessness was petrifying.

There was so much to do and it wasn't going to be easy. Having a single candidate interested in interning for a plan that was still in its infancy was encouraging to Raynah, but it wasn't even half the battle. She worried about how difficult it would be to get all the dots connecting. How would she sustain the home museum once she got it off the ground? Although Raynah's vision aligned with those seeking real change in St. Louis's underrepresented communities, the reality was that she was still a fortysomething outsider readjusting to her hometown. Who would trust her with funds to take her vision to the next level when she didn't have enough rapport with the local activists and changemakers?

Next door, Theo's white Lexus SUV was pulling into Justine's driveway. Raynah hadn't seen her brother since the end of last year, and that was only from afar as he was leaving their mother's house. That was typical; it wasn't like Theo to stay in touch, especially while he was in the last days of his campaign for alderman. Raynah suspected he was using Justine again to revamp his public image which had faltered during the Ferguson crisis. Either that, or he was in some kind of trouble.

"Hey stranger," Raynah called out from the opened living room window. "Let me guess. Trailblazing St. Louis alderman halts his campaign for reelection to comfort his widowed mother?"

Theo gave a wry smile and signaled for her to join him in the SUV.

He looked thinner than Raynah remembered. His chocolate, chiseled face needed a shave, and the boyish sparkle in his eyes was gone.

"So, what's the special occasion?" Raynah asked, closing the SUV's door behind her.

"Just thought I'd check on Mama."

It was a lie, Raynah knew, or at least not all of the truth. "Did she tell you we're not on speaking terms?" she asked Theo.

"No, Lois did."

"Figures." Raynah rolled her eyes. The mid-April sunlight spilled over her through the vehicle's windshield. It was unusually warm for spring, but the heat felt refreshing and reminded Raynah of their childhood. She saw herself racing her brother and sister to Sir's Oldsmobile when he let them go with him to buy beer and lotto tickets at the neighborhood mini-mart. They'd race each other back to their father's car after buying snacks and wait on him while he socialized and played his numbers inside the store. Raynah loved winning the front seat in the summertime. She liked being alone in Sir's sweltering vehicle before her siblings returned, inhaling the oily tar smell in her father's seats. She enjoyed the heat that softened her Starburst candies so they melted in her mouth.

"You and Mama are hilarious," said Theo, lowering their windows.

"What's that mean?"

"It means what it means. You two are so much alike and have no clue."

"Oh, stop," Raynah said. "You haven't seen the photo I found yet. Let me show it to you and then you can decide for yourself who's fucking clueless."

"No thanks, sis," said Theo. "I don't care."

"Well, you should."

The newspaper clipping Raynah found in Sir's basement burned in her memory. Dated December 1972 and yellowed with age. The girl on the front page was definitely Justine. Raynah hadn't intended on coming back from California to expose their mother as an underground activist. But she didn't regret it. Raynah didn't care if she wasn't permitted to use the old photo as part of a social justice exhibit in her home museum; she just wanted answers about Justine's untold history. She couldn't believe Theo and Lois were giving their mother a pass on something that was this valuable.

When Raynah first came across Justine's whispering past, she couldn't forget the way beads of sweat dampened the collar of her T-shirt and how her heartbeat thudded through her ears as she uncovered the old shoebox in the crawl space under the basement's staircase. How the photo in the newspaper article sitting at the top of the pile in the box screamed at her in the silence of her own confusion.

Raynah had seen enough photos of her mother in her youth—never smiling, with eyes that always looked ready to escape out of their own sockets—to recognize the girl in the Sears seamstress uniform kneeling before the debutante in the article. Still, the idea of Justine being an undercover activist in a scheme to take down a ring of elitists was wildly unbelievable and tantalizing. This was the same woman, Raynah remembered, who despised tambourines being used in church because she thought they sounded too obnoxious. The same woman who commonly shared her disapproval of Jesse Jackson's presidential bids in the 1980s on the basis that the idea of Blacks attempting to wield that much power in America was dangerous and unnecessary.

Between the time of Raynah's discovery and this point sitting in Theo's SUV, she'd combed through memories of their mother, desperately trying to find some opening in Justine's personality and actions that would've been a missed clue. Some sign that was overlooked, strange, or not fully understood in Raynah's youth. But she kept bumping up against the same version of Justine—stubbornly repressive, with little regard for anything that didn't fit into the status quo. Failure to detect anything else fueled Raynah's obsession until she memorized every crease, every fade, every curve, every angle depending on how the light hit the thin, faded photo.

"I'm meeting with Ms. Bev later to discuss everything," she told Theo.

He laughed and let his head fall back on the seat. "You're talking about Mama to her own best friend? You really don't have a clue."

"Maybe Ms. Bev knows something. I just want answers."

"Why?" Theo asked.

Raynah glared at her brother. "What do you mean, why? Because it's only right."

"Right for who? For Mama? Or for this little history project I hear you're trying to start in Sir's house?"

Raynah slumped against the car door and tried to remain calm.

"Look," said Theo, "all I'm saying is people have their reasons for why they do whatever they do." His voice was hard and resolute, but his eyes skittered across Raynah's sweatpants. "Some reasons, you have to be okay with never knowing. It was a long time ago, and at the end of the day, you really can't blame Mama for giving it up and wanting better than that."

"This is about more than wanting better," Raynah told him. "Mama shouldn't have to hide who she was. If anything, you two sound the most alike."

Theo traced the inside of his steering wheel and shifted uneasily in his seat. Raynah knew she'd said too much. Secrets or not, who was she to make her brother relive his first love's unresolved death?

Raynah closed her eyes and saw herself standing among the crowd in Ms. Myrtle's front yard again, watching her brother shake uncontrollably as he held on to the stretcher that carried Pete as it was rolled into the back of an ambulance. She smelled the strong metallic odor from the blood on the stained sheet covering his broken body. She heard the reports from police talking among themselves about how Pete was found on the train tracks, his body in one place and his head somewhere else. She witnessed the movement inside her own house across the street: her parents' shadows moving around in front of their bedroom window upstairs against the television's glare. The sight of Sir and Justine looking down at the scene in front of Ms. Myrtle's house from a distance—safe and unaffected—had split something inside of Raynah.

In the driver's seat, Theo pulled out a wad of bills from his wallet.

"I don't want your money," Raynah told him.

"Take it," he said. "No one ever thought you'd be dumb enough to come back here and move into Sir's house. In case you haven't figured it out yet, you're in for a lifetime of routine maintenance and safeguarding against some of these hard-up neighborhood thugs."

Raynah reluctantly stuffed the money inside her jeans pocket. The bills felt rough against her skin. She thanked her brother by giving him the middle finger and smacked him hard across his shoulder.

*

"Sweet baby Jesus," Bev muttered when Raynah showed her the old newspaper clipping of Justine that afternoon. They stood outside the Goody Goody Diner on Natural Bridge Avenue. Bev preferred to be in the restaurant's parking lot until a table became available for them. She claimed the small waiting area contained too many people who could see that she wasn't wearing makeup or a bra. She stroked the purple bob wig on her head which, to Raynah, favored the freshly spun cotton candy once sold at Skate King down the street.

Just thinking of the legendary roller rink in Pine Lawn calmed Raynah's anxiety, replacing it with warm, happy thoughts of the laughter and good times she had there as a kid, thanks to Bev. Despite Justine's insistence that the area had become unfit for her family, Bev always found ways to sneak Raynah and her siblings to the skating hub whenever she took her own children. The place often smelled like an armpit and had its share of neighborhood drama, but that never stopped anyone from showing up. Loud, sweaty summer nights usually left Raynah hoarse from screaming in excitement and her bare legs bruised from falling countless times on the wooden rink. At the end of the night, she and Pinch would exchange "yo mama" joaning sessions with the local kids, usually some rowdy boys, while cleaning their scraped knees with a bottle of turpentine.

Bev tsk-tsked, her eyes still on the old clipping. She gently removed it from Raynah's hands as if any carelessness would cause the article to dissolve before them.

"It's her, right?" Raynah spluttered. She was dying for a smoke but felt compelled to hold back in front of Bev. She didn't know why. Of all people, Bev was always the last to judge.

"You know there used to be a drive-in movie theater right next door to this place?" Bev pointed behind her. "The Thunderbird, they called it. 'The Bird,' for short."

Raynah shrugged.

"Of course you didn't know." Bev winked as if she'd read Raynah's mind.

Behind them, the door to the restaurant swung open. Several people trickled out and scurried to their vehicles, pushed by the sudden chill taking over the afternoon.

Raynah hugged herself and pulled her hood over her head, trying to get more heat from her UC Berkeley alumni sweatshirt. In California, she always felt like such a fraud for wearing clothes from a school that wasn't technically her alma mater. As if at any moment, an actual graduate of the institution would confront her on the street for laying claim to something that wasn't really hers. Here in St. Louis, she hadn't given much thought to being called out, not even by her family. No one blinked or gave her a hard time. The unconcern instilled more pride in Raynah, and made her feel more comfortable and deserving. There was a freedom that came with not having her past questioned. She could be anyone she needed to be here.

"Summer of '72 was the shit, honey." Bev smiled and ran a finger over the photo in the clipping. "You were just a baby then, no bigger than my two hands put together. Pinch was fresh in my stomach, but that didn't stop me and Beans from double-dating with your parents to see the Blaxploitation flicks playing at the Bird. We all had a crazy good time, considering all that had happened."

"All that had happened?"

"Yeah. Pruitt-Igoe, the housing project we used to stay in, got destroyed earlier that year. Straight blown up to bits on national television." Bev looked off into the distance and shook her head.

"It was a mess, chile. A total fucking disaster. In those days, our housing project was just that—a project. The place we called home was something of an experiment. I guess it got so bad, with us poor people living on top of each other, somebody decided to pull the plug on the whole thing. Problem was, nobody really saw to it that everybody being pushed out could get help relocating first.

"A lot of damn people got displaced. Folks left to sink if they couldn't swim. Some friends I grew up with, living out on the streets. Or worse, nowhere to be found. My own Mama ended up needing a place to stay because she was too sick to be on her own by then. Fortunately, before the razing, Beans and me had moved to a place in Hyde Park where we took her in to spend the last of her days. And your parents, of course, had already resettled out in the suburbs."

The clipping in Bev's hand looked smaller than before, like she had somehow reduced the size without tearing it or scrunching it up. Raynah peered at the fragile piece of paper, more out of desperation than curiosity. Keeping it within her view felt safe and necessary. She couldn't look up at Bev who now seemed more like a stranger telling a story than someone she'd always considered an auntie, a second mother.

"I can't believe nobody ever told you this," Bev said. "Justine oughta be ashamed. Anyway, if I remember right, the demolition happened early that spring in '72, so come next season, we were more than ready for some Shaft and Super Fly down at the Bird. It was then that I could tell your Mama was ... changed.

"For the most part, she was still the same fuddy-duddy you know. But more and more, Justine was talking some different shit. Hard and mean. Spot on, but too naked for me to hear at the time. Shit like sticking it to the man and going after elite power structures and whatnot. It was clear some other kind of folks had got all up in her ear. How, with Wesley and his tight-ass leash around her neck, I really don't know. I'm not sure he did, either. Maybe he thought it was just some silly phase that would pass.

"Your mama was never really straight with anybody, not even me, when too many questions got asked. One day, she begged me to babysit you but wouldn't tell me where she was going, or with who. Only that she had something important to do. Next thing I know, there's talk around town the day after the Veiled Prophet Ball was raided by a group of radicals. Some old bigshot who was a leader at one of St. Louis's biggest corporations was that year's hooded messiah and got his cover blown when one of the misfits snatched his head covering off.

"Well, you know, it was interesting news but really, most of us didn't give a shit. That ball had always been mysterious and swanky. Something strictly for rich white folks who didn't want our kind up in there, you know what I'm saying? But, it just struck me right away. In my gut, I knew your mama had something to do with the shit as soon as I heard about it. Justine has a streak in her. Always did, no matter how she puts on. There are sides to her, and this—"

Bev closed her eyes and held the clipping to the center of her chest.

"To her, this was revenge for Pruitt-Igoe," Raynah said.

"No, no. Not revenge." Bev waved the words away. "She didn't go burning down nobody's gas station to get back at the city for a wrongful death, if that's what you mean." She pointed to the photo in the clipping.

"All this, I think, was some kind of bandage for her. What happened at Pruitt-Igoe cut folks deep. Bruised souls, you know? On top of that, not many of us were getting decent jobs. Even if the role your mama played in the shaking up of some fancy ball for blue bloods was tiny, she ended up being part of something that hit back. Something meant to stir the pot and let folks know we weren't about to keep being nobody's silent sufferers."

Around them, the wind gained strength, endorsing Bev's words. It ripped the hood off Raynah's head and sent chills through her scalp. She was numbed by thoughts of a veiled figure being exposed in a similar way—unmasked over forty years ago, by a faceless radical swinging down a line cord in front of a shocked audience. Meanwhile backstage, her mother, in on the takeover all along, knelt at the feet of a debutante.

Bev moved to replace her hood and Raynah pulled back, aggravated. She felt her face growing warm, her eyes misting.

"This sounds way off from the woman I know," she said to Bev. "All these years of making me feel like I was some crazy person for wanting to be part of something bigger than the bubble she raised us in, and she did this? Why'd she switch up like that? Why the hell would she just give up?"

"I don't think she ..." Bev's voice trailed off. She leaned against the side of the building. "Her system probably just wouldn't let her digest any more of the shit that was going on, you know? Some folks get so tired until all they want to do is forget."

"You mean, fall into denial."

"It's called survival," corrected Bev. "You're the smart one. You should know that."

Another cluster of people came out of Goody Goody. They moved through the space that separated Raynah and Bev.

"Your mama wanted a life," Bev said when the crowd was gone. "She wanted a life with your father, who wanted nothing more for her than to be in that house together rearing you and your sister and your brother. Couldn't have been me but yeah, really, all she wanted was a chance to make a life for you that had been denied to her, just like the rest of us."

"Running up behind some man is not any kind of life."

"Speak for your damn self," Bev told Raynah. "It became her life, and that's just how it was."

There was more Raynah wanted to say, but she fought the urge to keep talking. Bev had already shared more than she really had to. Pressing for more information would only put her on the defensive out of allegiance to Justine and send Raynah further down into a dark maze of mixed emotions.

"Look here." Bev pushed the newspaper clipping back into Raynah's hand. "You didn't hear none of this from me. And if you say you did, I'll flat out deny it and come hunt you down later. Don't think you're too old for an ass whooping."

Minutes later, when they were seated inside the diner, Bev ordered salmon croquettes and dollar cakes. Raynah didn't touch her menu. Stomach tight with frustration, she knew she wasn't going to be able to eat for the rest of the day.

*

The mystery intern candidate's name was Claire Framer. The next afternoon, she brought her resume anyway, along with a list of references. She was albino with a freckled nose and lips. The nest of hair on her head was beige and woolly, cascading down her back in cornrows.

"Where's the social justice museum?" she asked.

"You're looking at it," Raynah said, leading the girl into the empty living room. "You come to all your interviews thirty minutes early?"

"I'm not familiar with this area and didn't want to risk being late."

"You're not from St. Louis?"

"I am, but I live in Ladue with my folks."

"Ladue."

Raynah sighed and plopped down on the floor. She motioned for Claire to sit beside her. "Nice times you're living in."

"Well, it's not the inner city, but it has its issues."

"I suspect none that have to do with spotty incomes, police brutality, or high crime rates."

"No," Claire said, "just good old-fashioned racism."

Raynah sat on her hands. She decided she already liked this girl who wasn't a ditz or easily ruffled. Claire was plainspoken with a quiet, comforting presence. Her powder skin and wire hanger frame showed she'd never been on popularity's good side, and the regal way she carried herself suggested she'd never cared.

"What interests you most about working here?" Raynah asked.

"I want to help change things around here," Claire answered.

You can't hate her for wanting better.

Theo's words found their way back to Raynah. Maybe Justine was right about some things that determined the way she chose to live her life. After her meeting with Bev, Raynah was coming to understand how liberated and in control her mother must've felt, in terms of her hidden history. But the "better" Justine wanted clearly didn't match with what Raynah had in mind now. Raynah didn't want to be that person who became jaded, patronizing, and frightened of her own community. She had to resist letting what she saw diminish her. Staying who she was meant everything, especially in front of this bright-eyed girl with tremendous care and hope in her voice, who reminded Raynah, in a lot of ways, of her younger self.

"You can start by doing me a favor," she said as she handed Claire a W-9 form.

"What's that?" the girl asked.

"Don't stray from that type of thinking. Always, always remember you said that."

Lois

When they were done, Lois and Ahmad sprawled out on the living room floor, a mess of skin, limbs, and sweat. It reminded Lois of when they were kids at church on the sanctuary's raggedy carpet, picking off wads of gum underneath the pews. She felt safe and comfortable watching the yolky sun set as it cast warm shards of light through the window onto their bare bodies.

"I called Quentin the other day," she said to Ahmad.

"You called him?"

"Yes. I called him."

"And what happened?"

"Busy signal."

"Don't do that," Ahmad said. "Somebody's gonna answer one day. It's been nearly three years and—"

"Don't tell me to stop. If I want to call, I'll call. If I get someone, I'll just hang up."

Lois felt Ahmad staring at the side of her face, his warm breath thumping against her temple. It was like a long dream. Everything was happening so fast and at full speed. All these years apart, and now she and Ahmad were together. Talking. Making love. Holding each other. And, on the verge of an argument when they drifted into the painful territory of their son.

She closed her eyes, wishing she'd never brought up Quentin. It was too soon. And words always got in the way. She played with Ahmad's chest hairs stubbornly sprouting in different directions across his torso.

"How's your mom?" Ahmad asked. He kissed her collarbone and shoulder.

"Okay. Still learning how to exist without Sir."

"All these years and you all still call him that."

"What else would we call him?" Lois asked.

"Pops? Daddy?"

"He never let us. You know how he was."

Lois dodged the rest of Ahmad's kisses as an image of her father surfaced. She cringed, remembering him as a younger man, handsome and commanding, before his appearance was defined by bones and bedsores.

The living room became smaller and airless. Sir was never a person; he'd always been more of a force before he was ghost of a man tortured by his own secrets. When he entered a room, his energy seemed to soak up everyone else's. Lois hated the way he treated her mother. An expert at saving face, Justine made sure what went on inside their household stayed there. She normalized everything in front of Lois and her siblings. The years Justine spent living inside her own bubble had soured all of them. As far as she was concerned, Sir was the best thing that ever happened to her. Lois and everyone else knew better.

"How's Ms. Myrtle?" Lois asked Ahmad.

"Same," he said. "Out of her right mind."

"Has she recognized you yet?"

"She called me Pete." Ahmad pushed his face into Lois's hair. His breath smelled like spearmint gum.

Lois started to ask if he'd seen Theo, or planned on dropping in on him anytime soon. Instead, she pulled away from Ahmad and played with one of his ears, hoping to lighten the mood.

"I see these are still big as hell."

They both laughed, filling an unwanted silence.

"You never could leave me alone about my ears. If it wasn't you, then it was Raynah. That smart-ass mouth of hers."

"Raynah who?" Lois asked, narrowing her eyes.

"Uh-oh. Looks like I hit a nerve."

"It's okay. We're just not really gelling right now."

"Why not?" asked Ahmad.

"We're just not. Nothing to talk about, as far as I'm concerned."

Ahmad chuckled and shook his head. "With Raynah, there's always something to talk about."

Lois bit her bottom lip, considering what to say. "She tells lies about our mother. To me, that doesn't call for a conversation."

"Lies?"

"Yes, lies. Let's just drop it."

Lois picked at a curled edge of her shag rug underneath the coffee table. It had been six months since Ahmad's move back to St. Louis and almost three months into what-ever they had going. The accusations Raynah made about Justine's past were one thing, but it also bothered Lois that her sister may have known about Ahmad being back in town before she did. Lois started to ask him outright, but decided she didn't really want to know. Things were better than they had been for her in a long time. Why mess that up now? As it was, Raynah had lived closer to Ahmad for years. Those years, Lois thought, should've been hers.

"Looks like you're finally getting some color on you again." Ahmad rubbed Lois's thigh. The inside of his palm felt hot and smooth. "You looked so pale the first time I saw you last year."

Lois made a face, remembering her three-day shut-in be-fore she ran into Ahmad at the mall.

"Of course I did," she said. "I couldn't go outside for a while. Not with all the protests. Hell, I could barely go online. I'm still thinking about deactivating my Facebook until all the gripes about what went down in Ferguson goes away."

"It's not going away," said Ahmad. He closed his eyes and pinched the bridge of his nose.

"Well, it should. It's 2015 and people are still taking sides. I don't know which makes me madder: the whiny we-shall-overcome posts from us or the subliminal finger wagging posts from them. And, why is it still an us versus them?"

Lois thought of Dawn and her flock of frauds. She hadn't seen or heard from her since they hung out last November, but Dawn was bound to come back around when she got bored or curious.

"Took me a long time to realize it goes deeper than race," Ahmad said. "Sometimes it's a character thing. Add personal issues, outside circumstances, and a whole lot of fucked up history. Now, you got war. Ghosts and cyborgs."

"Don't forget us do-gooders who do nothing," said Lois. She expected Ahmad to laugh at her self-mockery, but saw the bones in his jaw as he ground his teeth.

"You should come to California with me," he said. "I need to go back and tie up some loose ends next month and—"

"Oh, is it time I got enlightened?" Lois asked him.

"That's not what I meant."

"I know."

"I miss home, but I'm never here when I'm here."

"I know," Lois repeated, not sure of what else to say. The last time she'd seen Ahmad return home was for Quentin's funeral. She figured the trip must've been awful and equally amusing for Ahmad. Lois's family only knew him as the guy who'd left her to move to Oakland with relatives and get his head straight after his brother's tragic death. In Quentin's lifetime, they only saw Lois, the single teen mother struggling to maintain a decent GPA on less than three hours of sleep each night. She remembered how most people who'd never met Ahmad stared at him when she introduced him before Quentin's ceremony.

"Just Ahmad," he'd told Lois the night before after she sorted through the last of the paperwork at the funeral home. "Make up something. Anything."

They both knew Lois couldn't weasel her way out of talking. She cared too much about how others reacted, what they would say. People ambushed her with all kinds of crude questions and she, unable to bear the guilt of deflecting, never changed the subject. She ended up lying as Ahmad instructed.

Everyone understood anyway. Ahmad may as well have been the one in the casket. Aside from the obvious age difference, the resemblance was clear. That copper skin. Those bushy eyebrows. The same plucky ears.

Before the viewing of the body, Ahmad lost himself in the back of the sanctuary away from the immediate family's designated pews. He cried the longest and the loudest until Justine requested someone escort him out. Echoes of his raw screams in the church's basement sent a familiar bestial passion through Lois. Harold, her boyfriend at the time, had held her hand while she dabbed at her eyes, knowing that, if given the chance to be alone with Ahmad again, she'd saddle him without shame. To Lois's relief and disappointment, it never happened. Ahmad vanished before the burial, leaving no trace of a working phone number or an address to send a thank-you card.

Lois turned over on her stomach and rested her head on her folded arms. She stared at Ahmad, now resting on his back with his eyes closed. So many times, she'd planned out in her mind what she would say to him if ever given the chance. The anger and pain she'd unleash after years of being without him. She hadn't said any of the things she'd intended, and instead of wishing she'd wrote it all down, Lois found herself praying to God that Ahmad wasn't getting it in his mind to move back West again. She wouldn't let him leave. Not this time.

*

The trains weren't really in sync. They were a few minutes apart, despite the schedule on BART's digital display screen. Lois tuned out the Fremont train roaring down the station's tracks and the late Richmond-bound train opposite it. She couldn't remember what side of the platform Ahmad told her to be on when he left the hotel early that morning to run errands, so she stood in the middle near the elevators, not sure what to do next without drawing attention.

"Yo, where are you?" Ahmad asked her over the phone.

"I'm here at the train station."

Lois hated when Ahmad tried to sound younger than he was, using slang words like they were still a high school item from thirty years ago. He started doing that as soon as they boarded the plane in St. Louis. She figured it was his way of introducing his other side, a hipper version of himself that he'd grown into after moving to Oakland.

"Which one?" asked Ahmad.

"The one you told me to be at."

"Fruitvale?"

"Yes, if that's the one you told me to meet you at. I'm on the platform."

"Is there a big-ass coliseum within view?" Ahmad asked. "If so, then you're at the Coliseum station."

Lois gripped her purse, feeling foolish as she stared at the arena across from the station surrounded by sports team emblems and stadium lights.

"It wouldn't be like this if we'd just rented a car."

"No," said Ahmad. "It wouldn't be like this if we weren't staying in some ritzy four-star hotel that stopped us from renting a car. I told you my uncle and aunt would've been happy to host us."

Lois sighed. It was happening again. Her: helpless and jealous of a city, like it was some secret girlfriend of Ahmad's she discovered. Ahmad: smearing her insecurities in her face. Them: arguing over the pettiest things.

Maybe it was a mistake visiting the Bay Area. Besides a random BFF retreat to the Bahamas with Jillian a few years back, Lois had never travelled outside of Missouri. She tried reminding herself how this was an enviable vacation, but after getting the long-awaited tour of San Francisco's hotspots, she felt like loosened yarn under Oakland's claw of scathing artists and revolution junkies. She and Ahmad hadn't been in California for two whole days and already, Lois was tired of the dog fetishizing, anti-Walmart rants, and the overexaggerations about rain.

Here, she learned fast that hair relaxers and designer clothes weren't a priority. No one cared if you were a condo-owning PhD graduate or a room-renter who delittered the streets for a living, so long as you were a fan of independent film, never color-coordinated your clothes, and had tried yoga at least once.

"I'm uncomfortable, okay?" Lois told Ahmad. "Don't expect me to mingle so fast."

The patch of dead air on the other end lingered. Lois could tell he had stopped listening.

"I'm hanging up now," she said. "Come find me later at the ritzy four-star hotel."

"Just turn around, woman."

Lois did, and she saw Ahmad walking toward her at the other end of the platform. She tried to contain the excitement gushing through her. Ahmad's Raiders cap hung low over his boyish face and for a moment, Lois saw Quentin all over him. She looked away before the memory of their son could break her.

"How long have you been over there watching me look like an idiot?"

Ahmad playfully nipped at the tip of her nose with his front teeth the way he always did when he wanted to stop an argument between them. To Lois, it was a raunchy habit, like squeezing a nipple or yanking on a belt buckle in public. She wondered, envious, what kind of lover he had learned that from during the years they were apart.

"You call anyone yet?" Ahmad asked her.

By "anyone," he meant Lois's mother. Ahmad didn't seem capable of saying Justine's name anymore.

"Keep that up," Lois said, "and I'm going to make you call out her name three times in a mirror with the lights off."

"You didn't even tell her, did you?"

"I'm not a kid. She doesn't need to know everything."

Lois shrugged off the guilt rising in her. Why should she feel obligated to tell Justine about her getaway? It was already a given that her mother wouldn't approve, if she knew Lois was away with Ahmad. Besides, the trip was only for the weekend and then she would have to return so she could check on Justine and run errands for her through the week like the dutiful daughter she was. Just thinking about her weekly routine back at home gave Lois confidence in her decision to join Ahmad in this place where nothing seemed off-limits.

The Richmond train came and slowed to a stop in front of them. They boarded the first car and stood against the bike rail near the doors. Ahmad removed his hat and scratched his bald head. Lois stared at him, pleased with his decision to cut the thinning dreadlocks that marked him as the ranting bohemian everyone in St. Louis wrongly assumed he was, including her mother.

"Any of your old friends here say something about this?" Lois ran the tips of her fingers over his head. Finally, she could enjoy a piece of him left untouched by the women she imagined he had dated, possibly loved.

"It's the first time I've been called snazzy, if that's what you mean," Ahmad said.

"Isn't that a compliment?" asked Lois.

"Who cares?"

"Clearly you do, the way you said it."

"My boy Fisher's a storage property manager, not a style advisor. Besides him helping me clean out my unit, I didn't expect much else."

Lois cocked her head. "Is this the same guy who claimed it was cheaper to ship your belongings home instead of driving back in a U-Haul?"

"Guess you and him break even when it comes to saving money," Ahmad told her.

Before she could respond, Ahmad covered Lois's mouth with one of his colossal hands. His signature cologne—crisp and woodsy—warmed her. She imagined her insides glowing like one of those lava lamps Ahmad kept in his room back when he used to live with Ms. Myrtle. Lois remembered the nights they cuddled together on the floor instead of Ahmad's top bunk so his grandmother wouldn't hear the creaks in his mattress when they fooled around. Together, they watched globs of color inside the lamps embrace, dismantle, and reshape as the two of them lay in the dark, listening to *The Quiet Storm* on Magic 108 FM.

As the train neared its next stop, Lois dipped under Ahmad's arms and pressed herself against his back, burying the side of her face into the safety of his muscles for the duration of the ride.

*

"Where are you? I've been trying to call you." Justine's voice sounded hoarse and nasally, like she'd been crying.

"Mama, I can't talk right now."

"Why not? You can't be at work. I thought you said no more weekends. It's Saturday."

Lois left Ahmad in the mini-mart and went outside to block any chance of cross talk.

"What is it, Mama?"

"You're not with Ahmad again, are you?"

"Mama, what's wrong?"

Justine blew her nose into the phone. "Theo hung up on me, that's what's wrong. I swear, him and your sister are plotting against me. Next thing you know, she'll have him accusing me of being a bad mother, too."

Lois sucked her teeth. If she was there with Justine, she could've just nodded her head the way she'd learned to do when she wanted to politely shut her mother up. Justine, always confusing acknowledgement with agreement, would then drop the subject to rant about more important things, like the art of mashing Ms. Myrtle's pressure pills into her oatmeal when the woman wasn't looking. Or how Raynah's silent treatment after their spat at the nail shop was tempting Justine to disown her firstborn.

Raynah claiming their mother, the Blackest June Cleaver on Earth, was an underground activist in her twenties was beyond ludicrous. Her nerve to take things further and drag Justine into the Veiled Prophet scandal, based on a tattered newspaper photo in Sir's basement, was pure slander. But Raynah was just being Raynah: a hotheaded has-been who resorted to making up stories when she couldn't accept her own failed reality. No one believed her, least of all Lois.

Still, as more time passed, Raynah's fight with Justine conjured up things Lois hadn't thought about in a long time. Things like eating Cracker Jacks while braiding her dolls' hair as she and her siblings watched the Veiled Prophet parade on their family television. Or, competing with Raynah and Theo to see who could point out more Black faces in the sea of bystanders that viewed the hooded figures marching through the streets of downtown St. Louis in proud silence. Or, Justine skittering in and out of the living room, avoiding the screen as she busied herself with housework and grumbled at them for minor offenses she'd normally let pass. Or, the tube getting shut off once Sir was home, no explanation given and no backtalk allowed.

"No one's accusing you of being a bad mother," Lois said into the phone, more gruffly than she'd expected.

"Speak for yourself," said Justine. "Don't forget the monster Raynah's been to me. And Theo, well ... I haven't always seen eye to eye with your father, but at least we agreed on one thing."

"And what's that?"

"Do I really need to say it?" Justine asked. "Not my fault he couldn't get reelected. No one's going to vote for him, or one of those do-funnies he hangs with."

Lois hadn't dwelled on the outcome of her brother's reelection. She didn't see much of him as it was—no one in the family did. And last month's crushing poll results were enough to assure her that Theo would lay low throughout the rest of the season, maybe even well into the summer.

Who Theo was laying low with was the real question on everyone's mind. Lois tried not to indulge the thought for too long. What her brother did in his personal life, and with who, wasn't her business. It wasn't anyone's place to judge, something Lois knew their mother was privy to doing, especially when she didn't get her way.

Lois chewed on her bottom lip, trying to mute her giggles.

"What the hell's so funny?" asked Justine.

The idea of being this far out of Justine's reach for the first time in years ignited a giddiness that was hard for Lois to hold down.

"Are you on drugs?" Justine demanded.

"What kind of question is that?"

"Don't make me ask you again."

"Mama, stop it. You're being silly."

"You giggling like a little high school girl doesn't change the fact that Ahmad's damaged goods, Lois. Leave him alone before it's too late. I know you miss Quentin, but—"

Lois's stomach tightened at the mention of her son's name. She couldn't let Justine shift the conversation again. "I thought you called about Theo."

"Don't get fresh," warned Justine.

"Just let him breathe for a while, will you?"

"Child, please," Justine said. "Your brother's had more time to breathe than anyone I know. Always away for something. Always needing his space. No wonder Beth left him. Hell, the only difference between him and Ahmad is the continual fool Ahmad makes out of you."

Across the street, a fuchsia cardigan flung off a clothesline, its powerlessness pronounced against the forceful breeze. A sickly swirl entered Lois's stomach as the sweater blew into the street and silently landed. Holding back tears, she looked the other way.

Through the convenience store's window, Lois saw Ahmad tuck his wallet into his pocket and take a bagged bottle of sangria from the checkout clerk before moving left and then right, through a pocket of people to reach her. Sometimes he moved with so much caution, like he was preparing himself for the next unforeseen blow.

"I'm in Oakland," Lois told Justine. She'd wanted to say it more firmly, with more defiance, but the words came out small, almost clumsily.

"California?"

"Yes. With Ahmad."

"I knew it. Why—"

"Sorry about Theo," Lois cut in, "but there's nothing I can do right now. I'll call you when I get back."

*

Ahmad's relatives' house was a festive orange with Zapp & Roger funk music pouring out of it.

"Two hours tops, and you can't leave me alone." Lois held up her finger to show she meant business. She trailed Ahmad onto the front porch and smoothed down her hair in front of one of the windowpanes. Her mouth was dry and her teeth pasty from sitting cramped and close-mouthed on the bus ride from Jack London Square to the Lower Bottoms.

Surprisingly, Justine hadn't called back. Lois knew she should've been relieved, but her mother's silent disapproval made her fretful.

"Motherfucker!"

A fortyish lanky man flung open the screen door and bounced onto the porch. He was dressed in a tank top and flip-flops.

"Say it ain't so, cousin!" The man ran his hand over Ahmad's bald head.

"Not so!" Ahmad exclaimed, pulling the man into a bear hug. They geeked out like schoolboys before Ahmad raised his bagged bottle of sangria in Lois's direction.

"Yo, is this her?" the man asked.

Lois stiffened. Her body always clamped shut when it was time for introductions with Ahmad. To say he was her child's father was inappropriate. Technically, it was also inaccurate. She hoped Ahmad knew he couldn't get away with calling her his lady friend anymore which, to Lois, was like being reduced to somebody-I'm-sleeping-with status. Someday, being known to others as his fiancée or wife would be nice, but right now, it was too soon and too dangerous.

"Jermaine, this is Lois," Ahmad said. "Lois, Jermaine."

"Nice to meet you." Jermaine kissed her hand and held it against his chest. Lois wondered what he knew about her. Did he need to be so dramatic? Maybe he was confusing her with someone else in Ahmad's vault.

They went inside where the air was thick with the scent of beer, barbecue sauce, and marijuana smoke. Adults, kids, and in-betweens filled the living room and blended with the busyness of Afrocentric paintings on the walls, shouting over the big-screen TV to hear themselves.

Jermaine disappeared and reemerged with a busty chocolate woman wearing metallic purple lipstick and a checkered head wrap. She looked like an older, warmer version of Raynah. Her silver bracelets clashed loudly on her meaty arms as she embraced Ahmad.

"You must be Lois," the woman said, hugging her tightly. "Call me Auntie Kit like everyone else around here." Something about the woman was hopelessly genuine. Lois could feel herself trying, but failing, to pull away from her magnetic energy. She looked at Ahmad, who looked at the floor, and back at Auntie Kit.

"And this is Uncle Earl."

"Uncle Earl, I am," said the squat, fair-skinned man approaching them.

He led Ahmad and Lois into the backyard where more people sat clumped together on the patch of lawn beyond the patio. Con Funk Shun's "Love's Train" floated from the stereo. Under a palm tree, a buffet-style table showcased ribs, hot dogs, burgers, pork and beans, potato salad, plasticware, napkins, condiments, and a cooler full of drinks.

"How's Myrtle?" Auntie Kit asked Ahmad once they settled at the table.

Ahmad poked at the beans on his plate. "She's alive."

"I've been trying to get your uncle to visit his big sister."

"With what money and what time?" Uncle Earl asked, irritated.

"He just doesn't think he can see her like that," explained Aunt Kit. "It's been awhile since we ... well, you know, since Pete."

"She doesn't bite," Ahmad said. "She's pretty stable most of the time, as long as someone's around to make her take her meds. Lois's mom helps her."

"That so?" Uncle Earl asked.

Lois took a swig of her lemonade, trying to decide how careful she should be with the information she shared. "Yes," she said, "my mother and Ms. Myrtle have lived across from each other since Ahmad and I were little."

"So you're childhood sweethearts," Auntie Kit said. She grinned.

"Something like that," answered Lois.

"How do you like California?"

"It's not bad."

"Not bad?" The woman leaned forward, clearly amused, her nose ring twinkling in the sunlight.

Lois stuffed her mouth with potato salad. She'd already given up on the ribs, which were just sweet sauce over undercooked meat, a disgrace to her Midwestern barbecue standards.

"I can't say I've fallen in love," she told Auntie Kit after swallowing. The dish wasn't awful, although she'd had better. "But I'm charmed."

"Just wait," said Auntie Kit, "it grows on you in ways you'd least expect."

"So I've heard."

"You have such a cute drawl," said a twentysomething girl sitting opposite Ahmad. "Where are you from again?"

"Missouri."

"Misery," someone said within ear's reach. A flurry of laughter rose and fell under the music.

"She's from St. Louis, like me," Ahmad said, a pinch of defense in his voice. "Ignore Sasha and the trolls, Lois. They're anti-America except for Cali."

"Pro-NorCal," said Sasha. "LA can kiss my ass, too."

"You ever been in a tornado, Ms. Lois?" Jermaine asked.

"No I haven't, fortunately."

"I bet they're worse than earthquakes," Sasha said.

"Except for that one we had in '89," recalled Jermaine.

"Oh, that was pure hell." Aunt Kit shook her head in disgust. "Sirens everywhere. Power shut off for hours. Earl was still driving trucks in Sac and Jermaine was on fall break from school. Thank goodness I was on maternity leave, nursing Sasha at home, or else I would've been stuck on the twenty-seventh floor of an office building in San Francisco."

"Yeah, I heard about it," Lois said. "My older sister was living here at the time."

"You all remember Raynah," Ahmad injected. "The one who went to UC Berkeley."

"Oh, right," said Auntie Kit. "Smart girl!"

"Your sister went to UC Berkeley in the '80s?" Sasha's face flushed with excitement. "That's pretty impressive."

"Late '80s," Lois said, "she flunked out." She smiled, hoping to veil her envy.

"She's not the first or the last," Auntie Kit said. She lit a joint and inhaled deeply.

Sasha's eyelids fluttered with feigned innocence. Lois braced herself for more foolishness.

"And what college did you attend?"

"I didn't," Lois told her. "I had a kid and then I went to real estate school."

"Yeah, she's built a pretty large clientele back home," Ahmad added. "Now, she's into consulting on her own time."

"Nice," said Sasha, "considering no one really buys property anymore."

Lois squeezed and dented her empty ginger ale can. Technically, the girl was right—there were more folks renting than buying, especially in North St. Louis County now, and it had forced Lois to cut her hours and transition into consulting. Fortunately, Lois had enough money saved to fill in for the slower seasons. All of this, however, was none of Sasha's business.

"Maybe not in California with the ridiculous cost of living," Lois told her.

"The best views and good weather year-round don't come cheap," said Sasha.

"Puny yards, no basements, clueless young professionals …"

"… which still beats cheap coffee, bad wine, and cow tipping."

"Cow tipping? Really, cuz?" Ahmad asked. "We tackle bison in the M-O. Check your facts."

He cackled at his own joke with Uncle Earl and Jermaine as they clinked their beer bottles together.

"There's more to the South than farms and cattle, Sasha," Auntie Kit told her daughter.

"Actually, Missouri is the Midwest," Lois corrected.

"Same thing, if you ask me. Damn shame what happened there in Ferguson last year. Is that close to where you stay? Did you know Mike Brown?"

"Come on, Auntie," Ahmad said, irritated.

"What?"

"Did you know Oscar Grant?" he countered.

"Well, we knew a friend of his family's. They were such nice folks, I hear."

"Are such nice folks," Uncle Earl said. "He's the one dead, not them. Bastard pigs."

Lois excused herself from the backyard gathering and found an empty bathroom upstairs. She locked the door and sat on the toilet lid, a familiar solace overtaking her as she scrolled through her list of phone contacts.

The warm device's battery signal turned yellow. Lois landed on Quentin's name, her eyes devouring every letter. Thanks to Ahmad, she'd stopped the calling and hanging up, but the entry would never be deleted.

"I know you're in there, Lo."

Ahmad's robust, deep voice was now a whine as he knocked on the other side of the locked door. "So, you're just gonna hide out up here?" he asked.

Downstairs, speakers blasted the bassline intro of George Clinton's "Atomic Dog." Stomps and shouts promptly echoed throughout the house.

Lois remembered the house parties her parents hosted the few times things between them were okay. How she and Theo once found the nerve to ask Sir if they could dress up in dog and cat costumes like the actors in Clinton's colorful music video.

Who would be the dog, her father had questioned, because the last thing he needed was two damn cats running around his neighborhood. What he said still stung, as did the image of Theo sucking the insides of his jaws the way he always did when he tried not to cry. Lois sympathetically did her little brother's chores, along with hers, for nearly a week until Theo caught her taking out the trash one night and—in an impulsive rage—elbowed her in the face and broke her nose.

Lois, nose immediately swollen and bleeding, was glad about the timing of the whole thing; no one was home except the two of them. She knew Sir would deal with Theo if he ever found out. Maybe not as bad as if her brother messed with Raynah, his do-no-wrong favorite child, but their father still would've dished out a brutal punishment.

With Theo's help, Lois snuck towel-wrapped ice into the room she shared with Raynah. She lay in bed for days, a bedspread covering her smashed face, and pretended to be debilitated by stomach cramps. Of all people, Lois couldn't believe her mother bought a ten-year-old's claim of having her first period. Raynah, she knew, didn't care enough to out her lie. Maybe none of them did, if it meant keeping what little peace there could be at the time.

"I'm on the phone," Lois lied. She ran a finger along her nose's healed bridge. It felt straight, but she always noticed the difference and was mildly offended when no one else did. Being branded the beautiful sibling—both in appearance and behavior—had its drawbacks. People, it seemed, pitied her for living up to her blandness as the middle child. Even her imperfections became unseeable.

"Who you talking to?" Ahmad probed. The twinge of jealousy in his voice was deeply gratifying.

"Theo."

Up until then, Lois was careful not to mention her brother—not out of concern for what Ahmad would do, but in fear of what he wouldn't do since he'd returned to St. Louis last year, which was love her. She tried not to blame Theo for Ahmad's leaving. She reminded herself that Theo being in love with Ahmad's brother wasn't what attacked Pete or left him dead on those train tracks. The incident was what it was: an unsolved murder that cracked Ahmad enough to sever ties with his best friend and disappear from his own son's life.

"Okay," Ahmad said, "I'll be downstairs."

"He says hi," Lois offered, feeling the words rush out of her.

There was silence, followed by what sounded like an exaggerated swig from a beer bottle.

"Tell him I said what's up."

Lois texted Theo's number to Ahmad before the yellow light in her battery signal could turn red. Then, she texted Ahmad's number to Theo and typed *Ahmad says call him.*

"He says tell him yourself." She dropped the phone inside her purse and wiped the skin underneath her eyes. Suddenly, she felt fatigued. She didn't know why. She wasn't crying, but somehow, the tears felt as if they were there. She stood and glared at her dry-faced reflection in the mirror above the bathroom cabinet.

"Is this what you and my sister wasted yourselves doing here every day?" she asked Ahmad when she opened the door. She pointed to the beer bottle Ahmad held close to his chest. His eyes looked clouded and bloodshot from smoking.

"Who, Raynah?" he asked. He smirked and tugged at his beard. "Hell no. Tough as she is, she's still a square."

"Yeah, except for when it comes to those damn cigarettes." Lois grabbed the nearly empty bottle, swirled it around to dissolve the backwash, and took a swig. She followed Ahmad to the end of the hallway. Neither of them said anything, but she knew he was showing her his old bedroom.

The room was small, much tinier than the space Lois shared with Raynah when they were young, but larger than Ahmad and Pete's room at Ms. Myrtle's house. It smelled ancient—like mothballs, used books, and years of leftover food eaten in silence and sadness, away from concerned but easygoing relatives at the dinner table.

Some of Ahmad's articles and writing awards were still pinned to the walls. There was a picture of a young woman holding him and Pete as toddlers. Lois presumed it was the boys' mother and wondered if it was the only picture Ahmad had of her before she succumbed to drugs and left them with Ms. Myrtle. On the ceiling, above Ahmad's old bed, was a picture of Lois holding Quentin as an infant. Raynah, she realized, must've given the photo to Ahmad.

Everything seemed to shrink as Lois heard Ahmad's anxious breathing behind her. Or, maybe it was her own breathing. She was no longer sure where her tension ended and his began when they were alone together.

"I was a bad mother," she said.

"Lo—"

"I was. All those years of listening to Mama and keeping him away from you. I was worried about what people would say. What they would think. I'd rather you be dead than seen as some Afropolitical nut in poverty." Lois flinched at her own honesty. She waited for Ahmad to spit something back. He wrapped his arm around her waist and fingered her navel through an opened button on her dress.

"Sometimes there's no one to blame," he told her. "You get that?"

Lois shrugged.

"How you know things would've been any different if he was with me?" Ahmad asked her.

"He would've had more options. You've seen some of the kids in St. Louis."

"Have you not seen some of these kids in Oakland?"

Lois didn't say anything. Her tongue was growing thick and doughy inside her mouth. Her chest tightened; the weight of words snapped in her throat. Standing there, Ahmad seemed to sink without moving. She could feel him crashing down on her. Wondering about a child—a life—he couldn't have.

The heaviness between them felt nauseating, endless. Downstairs, Lois heard "Atomic Dog" fade on the stereo as another classic came on. She couldn't stop her fingers from tapping against the beer bottle. She needed to get away. She needed to dance.

*

Auntie Kit had a smile as big and infectious as Chaka Khan's while she sang "I'm Every Woman." She merrily waved a chicken bone in her hand like an ethnic deity. Her jewelry slapped against the heads of excited children surrounding her in the backyard. Between verses, she'd pause to rub her bum against the back of her husband's dashiki, or turn around to kiss him on the top of his head.

When she saw Lois, she dragged her onto the patch of grass that was the dance floor. Lois's knees buckled beneath her jean dress. Her hands hung passionlessly at her sides. She felt like one of those acne-scarred kids attempting to blend into the walls at one of her old high school dances, only there was no wall to cling to. No punch bowl to hover around.

"C'mon, girl!" yelled Auntie Kit over the music. "Shake those hips!"

Auntie Kit held Lois's palms up above her head. The woman's hands were hot and damp. She reminded Lois of one of the sweaty women standing on either side of her then eight-year-old self in her childhood church. The women spoke in strange tongues and closed themselves around a newcomer who'd caught the Holy Ghost during a Sunday night revival service.

At the Oakland yard party, Chaka's song faded, replaced by Parliament's "Flashlight." The sound system's ruthless snare tore into Lois and vibrated through her, one limb at a time. The more she tried to contain herself, the less control she had. Everything tingled, and then she felt herself rippling. Her body shuddered, like it was weeping to the beat. Struck like a cymbal, with nowhere to go but out.

In the distance, through the cluster of people on the dance floor, Lois caught a glimpse of Ahmad standing over a group of men playing dominoes. He turned, as if he sensed Lois's attention on him, and looked back at her, his face lighting up as she moved.

The quilted sky, with its peekaboo sun, opened out to her and, in that moment, she was no one's angel, or devil, or daughter, or sister, or friend, or lover, or aching once-mother. She wasn't a neighbor, or boss, or worker, or guest, or hostess, or congregant, or citizen, or race, or sex. She was no one, but she was hers. She was all hers.

*

The next morning, Lois woke up feeling sore and severely lightheaded. Ahmad was already gone, probably somewhere complaining about Missouri to people as his way of apologizing for not staying in California. He'd already sent her a text message, promising to return to the hotel by noon before checkout.

"You're drinking beer now?" Jillian asked Lois over the phone. "I thought Californians were wine snobs."

"So ladylike of me, right?" Lois joked. She swallowed an aspirin and turned on the television. Already, there was coverage of a brewing demonstration on the local channels.

She heard Jillian suck her teeth.

"God, is protesting all they do there? I'm not even in the room, but from the sound of things on TV, folks just wake up angry and take to the streets. Does anyone have a real job?"

Lois laughed, mostly at the absurdity of her best friend's judgment. If their conversation had happened earlier, she would've entertained Jillian with her own similar thoughts of people in the Bay.

What bothered Lois was not being able to make her best friend understand how coming to California wasn't the romantic getaway she hoped for, but a hard awakening into who she really was, or wasn't. How she returned to the hotel room last night, wishing she was drunker, to numb a persistent darkness that couldn't be outdone with good manners or a quick lay. How she pretended to watch television from the sofa until Ahmad, expectantly naked between the bedsheets, dozed off so she wouldn't have to explain why she needed to be alone with her thoughts. Or how, somewhere in all of that, she was slowly beginning to wrap her mind around the complications in her parents' rocky marriage and how they'd grown worlds apart from each other until their lives could no longer be contained in the same house.

But, the past was the past. Some things didn't matter anymore, not in the same way they'd mattered before. This wasn't 1985; she and Ahmad weren't silly sex-starved kids with endless possibilities at their feet. A lot of things had happened, including Pete and Quentin.

Where that left Lois was anyone's guess. She felt like such an in-between. In the middle, where she'd been all her life. She was shapeless, capable of anything and nothing. A pixelated image that no one could make out. So much of yesterday had left Lois confused enough to want to share how she was feeling with someone and yet, speaking too soon about her experience seemed to cheapen it.

"I need to finish packing," she told Jillian. "Call you when I get home."

The solitude was stifling. Lois turned up the volume on the television and changed the channel to a sitcom she couldn't name. She giggled absently with the syndicated audience, trying to shirk the cloud of desperation that followed her on the plane ride home with Ahmad and into St. Louis where they unpacked in a drowsy, wordless daze.

"What kind of a greeting is that?" Lois asked when she arrived at Raynah's house later that day.

"I'm working," said Raynah. "What do you want?"

Lois heard the faint sound of keyboard-clicking and glanced over her sister's shoulder, curbing the resentment that rose in her. The evening sunset's glow sprinkled over glass encasements of memorabilia and scribblings in what used to be Sir's living room. How Raynah was managing to pull off turning their father's home into a free-for-all community project in the heart of a dwindling neighborhood baffled Lois, but it was clear she was closer to finishing.

Raynah rolled her eyes and stepped aside. Lois trailed her sister into the kitchen that was still a kitchen. A college-age albino girl in dungarees rose from her laptop at the table and introduced herself as Claire, the new intern. She offered Lois coffee which Lois politely declined. She sized up the girl and decided she was good company for her sister. Claire said very little, but her gentle nature seemed to pacify the tightness in the air. Lois almost wished the girl would've stayed instead of excusing herself.

"Sir would draw blood if he saw how you gutted this place."

"I'm sure he's having his say somewhere," said Raynah. She leaned against a cabinet, her eyes cutting into Lois. "Mama put you up to reporting on my latest failure? Next time, tell her if she's that concerned with how I'm bringing down the property value, she should bring her nosy ass over here and see for herself."

"You tell her," Lois said, easing into a chair at the table. "I just got back from Oakland."

Disbelief washed over Raynah's face.

"For you." Lois handed her sister one of Auntie Kit's head wraps. Raynah held the cloth to her nose and inhaled. She stared Lois down again.

"Don't tell me you and Ahmad eloped unless you're ready to bury Mama, too."

"I just broke up with him." Lois traced her mouth with her finger, not believing she'd found the words to describe what happened. "I mean, we're on standby right now," she said, "until there's more reasons than not, why we should be together."

Raynah turned the head wrap over in her hands and looked down at the floor. "Something happen out there to make you mad?"

"I don't know what the hell I am anymore," Lois blurted.

They both let out hard, soulful laughs that sounded more like shouts.

Raynah smiled at her, a sad recognition in her eyes.

Suddenly, she became the sister who barged in on Lois's thirteen-year-old self, bawling softly in the bathtub over a pair of bloodstained drawers on the tile floor. The one who hid the soiled underwear at the bottom of their joint laundry basket, tossed Lois one of her maxi pads, and closed the door without a word.

Now, as Raynah poured Lois a glass of wine, the clock's ticking on the wall above the fridge grew louder. Lois took her glass and swirled the wine, feeling on the edge of something.

"Show me those clippings of Mama you found."

Theo

Theo arrived at the café two hours before he was to meet Ahmad. He wanted to be prepared for their talk. No sooner than he had ordered his Americano, he saw the only other customer in the place, hunched over a newspaper at a table in the window. Even with a Raiders hat covering half the man's face, his penny-colored skin, pronounced ears, and beefy build were instantly recognizable.

Theo started to leave and return later, but he knew once he stepped outside he wouldn't go back in. He took his time dressing his coffee in the corner and thought about all the times he'd played out this scene in his mind. Him, being overpowered by a rush of nostalgia. The lump in his throat. His legs nearly caving under him. All that cinematic shit.

But he felt nothing. Ahmad was now an acquaintance in Theo's stockpile of emotion. A person who'd fallen out of touch.

Theo sat at a table on the other side of the larger than average café and observed Ahmad's movements. The way he glared at the sun, adjusted papers, ate his bagel. He seemed normal. Not the liberal boogeyman everyone had reduced him to.

He was rounder and his lips were darker, maybe from smoking too much West Coast hydro, or whatever they called the weed over there these days. But he was still handsome. Not Pete's unsettling handsome, but Ahmad had managed to maintain a noticeable spark. Circumstances aside, it looked like California had been good to him.

The wind chimes on the door jingled. A tattooed man in khakis backed in, pulling a dolly full of boxes. After unloading the supplies behind the counter, he turned to exit, when he noticed Theo.

"Oh shit, Theo Holmes! My man!"

The man was loud, but not loud enough for Ahmad, who didn't look up from his paper. Theo stood and grinned, fishing in his head for the practiced humble rhetoric he'd fed constituents over the last couple of months. The skin between his eyebrows quilted into a declaration of apology.

"Bruh, you look a lot taller on TV," the man said.

Theo shook his hand.

"I get that a lot. What's your name, my friend?"

"Darrius. Damn shame about the reelection loss. We rooted for you. But, you know how it goes."

"Hey, we tried," Theo said. "And believe me, your support is what matters in the end. I really appreciate you all showing up at the polls."

Theo glanced over Darrius's shoulder. Ahmad had barely moved, except to cross his ankles. His not noticing them was a relief, but it also made Theo a little self-conscious. Being a constant in local media, Theo was used to standing out, and it was dawning on him that he'd grown into someone who welcomed that entitlement. Maybe he was the one who'd done all the changing in a way that dulled him to nonresidents like Ahmad.

"You know we got you, bruh," Darrius said. He leaned in closer to Theo.

"Actually, I don't feel too bad for you. Women love it when you lose. Gives a lot of 'em some purpose. They wanna be the one to stroke that big, long ego, you know what I'm saying?"

Theo forced a laugh. "Nah, I don't get as much play as you'd think."

What Darrius said was true, to some extent. Theo was still getting business cards from women, often in front of their spouses, with personal messages scribbled on the back. He received the occasional thong in an envelope delivered to his office. It was shameful how tasteless people could be for a dose of what they considered fame.

Although his general distrust of women was at an all-time high, he'd started seeing a woman again after his spat with Alex about the book. Her name was Tangela. She was quick, spirited, and inhumanely pretty, with two school-age kids from a previous marriage.

As a political science instructor at a community college, politics was Tangela's passion, but what most attracted Theo to her was an appetite for God rather than the limelight. Religion wasn't Theo's idea of comfort anymore, but Tangela's relentless devotion to scripture had somehow coaxed him back onto a church pew beside her on some

Sundays, in hopes that whatever rapture she received would rub off on him.

Justine might've liked Tangela, had Theo introduced them. Instead, he had abruptly ended things when Tangela called him perverted—not because she knew he liked men too, but because according to her, he was a mama's boy who got off on injecting Justine into most of their conversations.

It wasn't possible, or so Theo thought, given the embarrassingly low number of times he visited Justine each year. But, the longer he had a chance to wrestle with Tangela's claim, the more it registered he was attached to Justine in ways that reached beyond distance.

Nothing weird ever happened between Theo and his mother, as far back as he could remember. He never walked in on her naked or she, him. There was that one time he'd heard Justine and Sir having sex in the middle of the night and had his first wet dream, but it could've been coincidental.

He remembered Ahmad's admission to seeing Ms. Myrtle's bare crotch once when she fell on ice cubes in their kitchen. Even then, it was more of a laughing matter to pass the time during vacation Bible school and not his ex-best friend's account of some sexualized adventure.

Still, Tangela was onto something. Theo wondered if her accusation about this secret obsession for Justine was the reason his brain and hormones worked against him. Maybe it was what led to his deep repulsion of other women. And, maybe growing up with a father like Sir—detached and volatile—complicated things even more. The thoughts noodled Theo so much that by the time Justine phoned him to offer her sympathies for his reelection loss, he let out a rage he didn't know was there and hung up on her, cutting off communication.

"You cool, bruh?" Darrius asked.

"Yeah, I'm alright. Just had a long night. Hence the double shot."

Theo raised his mug, regretting the purchase. One side of his face was already starting to twitch.

"Stay up, bruh," Darrius said. "I'm heading out before my boss starts with the bullshit." He retrieved his empty dolly in front of the café, where a steady stream of people were now entering. Theo absently watched the man fling the equipment in the back of his truck, secure the sliding door, and drive off.

"You look like you've seen a ghost."

Theo whipped around and saw Ahmad beside him, a sad smile in his eyes.

"Man, ghost or not, I haven't seen your ass in thirty years," Theo said, grinning and holding his arms out. "Let me in."

They embraced in a quick, awkward hug. Then, it was the painful game of figuring out who would speak first and what about. Ahmad broke by motioning for Theo to follow him back to his table.

Once seated, Theo set his cell phone and his coffee mug down on the table before Ahmad could notice his hand shaking. He felt the talkative nature of his professional side pulling at him but was reluctant to use it. This was too fragile a situation to waste on meaningless chat about the weather and sports.

"What are you reading?" he asked Ahmad.

"The newspaper," Ahmad replied. He grinned at his own wry humor, and Theo noticed one of his front teeth needed to be looked at, possibly pulled out. Theo wondered how long he'd be able to keep glancing at it, using the discolored tooth as a distraction away from bigger things, like his thought about what Ahmad would say if he ever read Alex's book. The ugly things that had been written.

Not that it really mattered at this point. Alex published his trashy tell-all memoir before the reelection, which to Theo's surprise and relief, went nowhere. The book never made it on any chart, probably due to premature release and poor promotion. According to Theo's assistant, who he'd ordered to keep tabs, the book had no readership outside the pocket of St. Louisans who personally knew Alex, or were friends of his friends. To date, the book was a big flop—a fucking embarrassment. The last Theo heard was that Alex, unable to cash in his own broken heart, had relocated with his family to Atlanta.

"I see you still have jokes," Theo told Ahmad. "Really, what are you reading in there?"

"Stuff, man."

"What, the Cardinals' hacking investigation?" probed Theo. "Post-Ferguson protests? The funnies? My reelection loss?"

Ahmad sat back in his chair and folded his arms over his chest. The level way he looked at Theo reminded him of Pete. "Sports scandal, a little. Haven't touched the funnies since Calvin and Hobbes ended, and I don't want to hear about another protest right now."

"Get out. You, of all people?"

"Yep," Ahmad said. "I don't really follow politics these days either, so I didn't know about your reelection loss. Sorry things didn't work out."

Theo knew better than that. Ahmad had to know about his run again for office if he was involved with Lois. He was in no mood to play games, especially not with another grown man, one that had once been closer to him than blood. But, if this was where they had to restart, Theo could act clueless, too.

"So, what brings you back this way?" he asked. "You just visiting? Or you have other plans?"

"I had plans on staying before last week. Now, I don't know."

Theo stared blankly at Ahmad.

"Your sister broke up with me. She didn't tell you?"

Theo looked down at his hands. He didn't want to show Ahmad how unphased he was. The thing about this breakup was that it wasn't much of a shocker. To Theo, and nearly everyone else, Lois and Ahmad were on completely different planets. Always had been. Quentin was the only thing that bound the two of them together. And apparently that wasn't enough, even when the boy was alive. Now, with no son between them, it was obvious that both of them had been trying to rekindle the carcass of a love that was gone.

"I'm sorry, man."

"Fuck you."

Theo winced, bucked his eyes. "Excuse me?"

Ahmad's eyes turned hard and hateful. "You heard me," he said. "Everything always gets shitty when you come into the picture. So fuck you."

The way Ahmad's jawline jutted out from his face made Theo think about a gigantic T. rex exhibit the two of them had seen together as kids at the Science Center, either during a church outing or school field trip. Lois, being the sister who was hard to get rid of, had pried her way into their adventure. Theo could still see her grass-stained jeans and long, stiff cinnamon-colored pigtails sticking out from the sides of her head as she flung herself around them.

Her once-broken nose that Theo couldn't stand to look at and the annoying whine it left in her voice—it was as if she talked more just to remind him of what he'd done. The anger he took out on her face since he couldn't take it out on Sir.

"Fair enough," he told Ahmad. "I can't hate you for feeling that way. But Lois was the one who set this up, not me. Frankly, I wouldn't have minded staying dead to you."

Ahmad knocked his empty paper coffee cup off the table. He sat back in his chair again and folded his arms, shoulders heaving.

"Okay," Theo said. Ahmad's reaction was surprising. Even for Ahmad. He had always been a little impulsive, but never this aggressive. Theo glanced around the café at a few patrons who'd taken notice. Not a good sign. "Clearly, wrong choice of words. Look, man ... I'm sorry. What else do you want from me?"

"I want it to be you, not Pete."

Theo concentrated on his ex-best friend's Adam's apple bobbing up and down in an effort to swallow his tears. Ahmad most resembled Pete—deeply intense, but restrained—when he didn't mean to. It was hard to think that if Ahmad had his late big brother's popularity and tall athletic physique back then, Theo could've easily fallen for him instead of Pete. But the feelings wouldn't have been reciprocated, and Theo wouldn't have acted on those feelings, and maybe everyone would still be alive or at least okay.

"And, don't give me none of that 'I'm already dead' bullshit," Ahmad continued. "You seem to be doing a whole lot of living here, man. And you got your family. They might be a little fucked up, but you've got them."

"I get it," Theo told him. "You want a pity party. Is that it? Let me make it easy for poor Ahmad, who's lost everything and fell out of touch with everyone because he stays thinking the world owes him a new life. Bitch-ass Ahmad, who thrives off his own misery by scapegoating and judging others and running off to other cities to be in the company of those just like him."

"Just stop, man." Ahmad held up his hands. "I'm so tired of hearing everyone's shit around here. What is it with you people and the guilt trips you all love to put on anyone who's explored anything outside of this damn city?"

"It's not a guilt trip," said Theo. "It's owning up to your responsibilities. Not running from them."

"Says the undercover fag. Please help me because you know so much about being open and true to who you really are."

Theo looked around again to make sure no one had overheard. He couldn't help it. Showmanship was part of who he was and had been for a long time. If someone caught a whiff of their conversation, he'd be given no other choice but to improvise his way out of potential disaster.

"Just tell me you never looked at my son that way," said Ahmad.

"Your son?" Theo repeated, sneering. "Well, now that you mention it, there was that one time … "

Theo let the rest of his bad joke hang in the air between them. He knew it was wrong for those kind of words to fly out of his mouth. He saw the malice flash in Ahmad's eyes. It left as soon as it came, but it was enough to show what he was capable of if pushed too far.

"He was my nephew, man. I can't imagine how it felt to lose him as a son, but he meant a lot to me, too."

All this talk about Quentin forced Theo into a cruel wave of nostalgia. The boy was nurturing like his mother, and willful like his father. Fate's savagery had outdone itself in taking him away from the two people who seemed the most deserving of his light.

It occurred to Theo that he could tell Ahmad about his own failed marriage and the baby he and his ex-wife almost had. Maybe it would help Ahmad understand he wasn't alone. He let the thought go; it wasn't his duty to match or quench Ahmad's pain. And it would be opening something in Theo that he didn't have the energy to neatly repackage.

"So, what's the point in this little reunion?" Ahmad asked. "Why'd you want to see me after all this time? What, you wanted to brag about how you made a name for yourself here and the election you're so down about losing? You thought we could just gloss over the bad shit, or pretend it never happened and laugh at things we did as knucklehead kids?"

Theo held up his hands. "Like I said, Lois set this up, and she told me it was you who wanted to see me. I didn't have any thoughts on how this thing would go, man. I'm too old for expectations."

"Good," Ahmad said. He rose from the table and gathered his belongings. Theo watched him exit the café. His own legs felt unusually heavy and plastered to the floor. He no longer wanted to be here, but he didn't want to leave, either. He kept sitting, looking at nothing, until his cell phone rang on the tabletop, Lois's name appearing on the screen.

*

Midmorning was soggy and abrasive. Cold pellets of rain stung on the arm that Theo hung out of his open window. He had ignored Lois's third call since he'd left the café but now listened to her first voicemail, asking him to meet her at the woods at Cass and Jefferson. Once he pulled up, he realized she'd been careful to leave out what was there: the remains of the Pruitt-Igoe housing project.

Her Benz was parked on a vacant lot across the street from the large, abandoned patch of property that bristled with trees and shrubbery. Next to the vacant lot was a church Theo visited on a whim before the election at the urging of one of his colleagues. Theo's first thought was that Lois meant to surprise him about her new membership there: subtle encouragement for him to follow suit. He figured it could've been her attempt at finding solace in something other than real estate or Ahmad's companionship. But something was off. It was Monday, the beginning of the work week, so the church lot was empty. Even so, why not just park at the church?

Nearing the vacant lot's entryway, Theo saw a second head with short flat twists emerge from the passenger side of his sister's car. Raynah.

"What's this about?" he asked, slamming the car door behind him. "And why's she here?"

"Hello to you, too," said Lois. "Thanks for coming on such short notice." Her eyes were puffy and her nostrils flaky, like she'd been crying the previous night. She leaned in to hug Theo. He backed away.

"What's wrong?" she asked.

"One, I'd like to know what the hell this is about. Two, you didn't tell me that she was tagging along." He pointed at the camera equipment Raynah was removing from Lois's car. "Three, does she have a permit to do that?"

Raynah stopped what she was doing, her eyes blazing into Theo. "Okay, one and two, you should quit talking about me like I'm not here. If you'd answer your phone, or listened to Lois's second voicemail, you'd know I wanted to take pictures for my community social justice exhibit at the home museum. It was Ms. Kumbaya Sibling Solidarity's idea to invite you. I didn't really care who came or not." She started removing more equipment and stopped again. "Oh, and three, I do have permission to be on this property. Not like that's any of your business, considering you don't really have a say-so in zoning anymore."

"Do you mind?" Theo asked. "I was actually addressing my sister."

"So I'm not any kin now because I see through your bullshit. Got it."

"You want that role, you have to act like it."

"Don't go there with me on roles," Raynah told him. "You're not winning in that department, either." She stuck her tongue in the side of her mouth until her cheek jutted out, implying fellatio.

"Stop it, both of you," Lois said. "Theo, I didn't tell you why I wanted you to meet me here because I didn't think it'd be a big deal."

"You seem to leave out a lot of stuff lately," he said. "Your breakup with Ahmad's not a big deal either?"

"That's between us."

"Not when you arrange for me to meet with him after you quit him," Theo said. "Dude wasn't exactly shitting lollipops when we talked."

"Was it that bad?"

Theo didn't answer. He turned to get back in his SUV and drive away, but he was already there. What else would he do now, after such a depressing meeting with Ahmad, but go home and drink? Or worse, end up somewhere in a secret rendezvous, doing things he was trying to keep from doing? If the day was to get any shittier, he preferred it to be that way with family.

He walked ahead of his sisters, crossing the street when traffic slowed, and waited for them at what appeared to be the wide plot's dusty entrance. Together, they cautiously trudged down the damp dirt pathway in silence, human specks among the river of trees.

"Imagine Mama, Sir, Ms. Bev, and her husband Beans here during their childhoods, years ago." Lois said. "Must've been hell on so many levels."

"Why? Because they were poor?" asked Theo. "I suggest you do your homework on Pruitt-Igoe. Not all tenants considered living in a housing project a bad thing at the time."

"Right," Raynah said, opening her camera's tripod. "That's exactly why it's been called the 'poor man's penthouse.'"

"When it was first built, yeah," said Theo. "But that's actually because it was nicer than what a lot of its original tenants were used to. We're talking single beds for everyone, doors, elevators, all this stuff we take for granted now."

"Yep, right in the middle of a postwar decline in people, jobs, and employment," said Raynah. "Those city planners sure knew what they were doing, with all that urban renewal talk. Sound familiar?"

"I'm sure they didn't foresee a train wreck."

"It's too bad they didn't," Lois interjected. "We're talking about a big failure that eventually led to other failures, like Section 8 programs, all across the city. As a realtor, I've seen the ripple effect of this, you start handing out decent properties for less to folks who know they can't afford the upkeep."

"You're kidding, right?" Raynah said. She pulled a camera out of a double-vested case and adjusted it on her tripod. "You're placing blame on the oppressed, not the oppressor. That's just how these officials want you to think. If you don't want run-down neighborhoods, then give underserved neighborhoods the resources that teach them how to maintain these so-called decent properties in the first place. Who really expected a thirty-three-building complex full of Black folks from the slums to miraculously amount to anything good?"

"It wasn't just made up of Black folks from the slums," said Theo. "There were a lot of whites who were living there, too."

"Yeah, and they bailed, as soon as their Buicks and bank accounts allowed them to. It's called white flight. So, who do you think were the ones most affected?" Raynah asked. "Come on, little brother. You're the big-time expert in politics. You should know these things."

"My goals in politics have always been about redirecting the conversation to building sustainable neighborhoods for the future, not dwelling on the past."

"And effectively building for the future means recognizing and understanding the past so you know what pitfalls to avoid."

The muscles in Theo's neck grew tense. He tried to keep himself composed as he watched Raynah reposition her camera at different angles and snap several photos. He didn't like the way she carried on about Pruitt-Igoe, like it was little more than a subject in a sociology class. She was so caught up in her social justice dogma that she didn't seem to understand, or care, that his parents—their parents—were part of a living, breathing community who dwelled there. Ugly fate aside, these grounds were once a place that housed warm memories and a rare tenderness.

"Look, whatever," he said to Raynah, "I don't really get where you're going with all of this. Your focus shouldn't be on turning Mama's life into some history lesson that fits your agenda for a homegrown exhibit that frankly, I don't think benefits anyone."

Raynah gave him a scourging look, one that he could feel pulsing through him like an explosion of pent-up emotion waiting to happen. She took her hands off the camera and motioned for Lois to do something. Theo didn't understand until Lois brought out a yellowed newspaper clipping from the inside of her trench coat. She handed it to him.

"Oh, come on," he said, looking it over. "You two can't be serious. Is this supposed to be Mama?"

"You said it without either of us having to," Raynah said. "And Ms. Bev confirmed it."

Theo turned over the thin, fragile paper and studied it. The innocent, surprised expression on the youngish woman's moonlike face. The pronounced mole on her broad nose. A mole that was hauntingly identical to the one he remembered playfully poking with his index finger as a child, when Justine held him in her lap. It became their little inside joke, especially around Halloween, because to him, she warmly resembled the likes of a witch. Now, the spot on the subject's face in the photo sneered at him like a devilish cackle bouncing off the article.

"The Veiled Prophet scandal in December 1972," Lois explained. "It happened after Pruitt-Igoe's razing in the summer of the same year."

"And?" Theo asked.

"The point is, the demolition of Pruitt-Igoe must've really took a toll on Mama," Raynah said. "She needed to find a way to fight the system back, to let people know that leaving her community abandoned and alone, to fend for themselves in that type of situation, wasn't okay. What better way to do that than to try and overthrow the tradition held by a group of local elitists who represented some bullshit societal order?"

Theo massaged his temple. His head was starting to hurt. Even with all the stress and pressure that came with being in the political limelight, he'd prided himself on never having his body physically take it out on him. He marveled at how a peek at a stupid photo and this bizarre claim by his sisters was quickly changing the way he processed things. Their mother, a fighter? It was too much to take in.

"The only question that's still out there," said Lois, "is how Mama got involved in a scandal like this to begin with. Ms. Bev and her other friends from Pruitt-Igoe weren't ever part of the radical crowd. And you know Sir wouldn't have allowed it."

"I think it's safe to quit calling him Sir," Theo said, anger leaping out his throat. "Our dad's dead, Lois. Kind of sad you're still that scared of him."

"I'm not scared. If Raynah's still calling him Sir, then I'm calling him Sir."

"Don't put me in that," said Raynah. "Regardless of what either of you think, living with him was never sunshine for me either. Why do you think I left when I did?"

"Because you thought California was all sunshine," Theo said.

"Fuck you. I had an opportunity and I took it."

"Yeah, and you failed," he said. "Came back with your tail hanging between your legs just to turn your nose up at the folks who've been here and made something of themselves. Like Lois and me. Here, take this shit." Theo tossed the clipping in Raynah's direction. He watched it quietly descend to the ground, light drizzle falling over it. Lois picked it up, brushed it off, and placed it back inside her coat.

"Says the man-child too scared to stand up to his father or go past the state line," Raynah shot back. "Yeah, let's talk about people making a life for themselves—"

"Raynah, drop it," said Lois.

"Shut up," Raynah told her. "He needs to hear this, being the son our father always wanted and all."

She got in Theo's face and flashed him a dry, ironic smile. "You talk about folks making a life for themselves since I've been gone, but all I see is façades here, people trying to hide who they really are, or want to be. What kind of fucking life is that? You're walking around here leading a double life, playing two fields, and have the nerve to say I'm the one who failed. You're a conniving fraud who deserved to lose that reelection. At the end of the day, people like you need people like me, so you can sleep at night and tell yourselves how fucking practical and good you are when you wake up every day. The reality is you don't serve the people; you only serve yourself. So great job, little brother. Sir and Pete would be proud."

The rain was beginning to fall in sheets. Wet as he was, Theo had never been more thankful. The water tempered a growing wildness inside him. For the first time in his life, he wanted to hit a woman.

Then, he heard the snap of several twigs close by. Male voices floated into range. Nearly blinded by the sudden downpour, Theo shushed the panicky exchange between Lois and Raynah as shadows emerged on the ground. Shadows that didn't belong to him or his sisters.

Two men appeared on the opposite side of the pathway. One, skinny, tall, and fair-skinned. The other, plump and short with a deep brown complexion. Their clothes looked too small for them and clung tightly to their scabby bodies in the rain.

"Hey there, folks," said the plump one, exposing a bottom row of greenish teeth. "Some weather we got going, ain't it? What y'all doing out here?"

Theo steadied his gaze on the vagrants. Out of the corner of his eye, he saw Raynah and Lois struggling to push the camera back inside the equipment case.

"Yeah, some weather," Theo repeated. He herded his sisters behind him and forged ahead on the path opposite the vagrants. "We were just leaving."

"Don't go," said skinny vagrant. "Say, that's a nice camera."

He advanced toward Theo and nodded to his partner who rubbed his hands together.

"Can I see it?"

"No, you can't," said Raynah, force and fear filling her voice.

Something of a sob and groan escaped Lois. Theo tried to stay calm in front the vagrants.

"Gentlemen, I don't really think that's a good idea," he said. "If you'd step aside, we'll be on our way."

The plump vagrant licked his lips and laughed.

"It's the camera or these bitches," said his skinny partner. He tugged at the zipper on his scant pants.

The rain wasn't letting up. A sharp oak odor had been released into the air and made Theo's stomach queasy. In one swift move, he turned and pushed his sisters in the opposite direction, his eyes urging them not to make a sound.

He saw Lois's mouth twist before she screamed, and he felt an unbearable sharpness in his lower back. Then, there was weight on top of him as he collapsed to the ground, his face meeting wet mud.

He wrestled with the plump man, their bodies rotating on the pathway. He bit and hit and kicked until the vagrant fell off him. He pulled himself back to his feet and hobbled over to the skinny man who had Lois on the ground beneath him and Raynah on his back.

Theo slammed into the vagrant, and the two of them rolled into shrubbery, small puddles, and gnarled tree trunks. Something dark and vile rose up in Theo, and swelled over him like a thick, tarry mass of poison.

Amidst his sisters' wails, Theo swung and swung at the man's face, now a pulp of blood and skin. He kept swinging his hands and punching, willing the mass of poison off of him, one limb at a time, until he could feel himself disappearing like vapor into the day.

Part III

Justine

Justine promised herself this really was the last time. Funerals were getting too risky to steal from, especially with no one to cover for her since Bev vowed not to go with her anymore. Justine knew she couldn't ask Rich. They were really close now—nearly inseparable—so much that it terrified her. It was good that he was away seeing his son, so she couldn't talk herself into asking him. The last thing Justine needed was for Rich to get a glimpse into this other world of hers, one that she was almost sure would be a deal break-er for him.

, it was necessary for Justine to do this last fu-rself. Today was exactly a year since Wesley died. called or dropped by the house to check on her. er kids. All of them stuck on stupid, banding to-nst her over some nonsense.

from being overtaken by the throes of self-pity, ured herself that this last funeral was how it was supposed to be. From the moment she came across the judge's obituary in the newspaper, on a break from cutting coupons, Justine knew she was meant to face the first part of the day alone and inside the walls that now housed Sonya's spouse.

Wesley, she knew, wouldn't agree. He'd be downright beside himself. Justine could hear him now in her head, calling her every name but her own for having the nerve to show up to the wake of his mistress's husband. And, maybe she deserved that. Maybe she was a little crazy to go and to steal from an innocent dead man. A rich, innocent dead man.

Justine walked into the funeral home and slipped past the growing line of people waiting to sign their names in the visitors' book at the entrance of the judge's chapel. Inside, a stubby man wearing a tan fedora offered her an obituary which she politely rejected. The flower-filled room was bitterly cold and dark, like someone had forgotten to turn on all of the lights. Only a handful of people sat scattered throughout the space, all of them at least three rows away from the casket. Sonya was nowhere in sight. The stiffness in Justine's shoulders loosened. This might be easier than expected, if she moved fast enough.

She sat in an empty pew towards the back of the chapel and slid one of her sandals off. Now, her left pinky toe was bruised and swollen from rubbing against the inside of her shoe. Even after catching two buses, Justine still ended up walking a bit to get to the funeral home in Creve Coeur. From the looks of the chapel, Sonya got the two-story dream house, built from the ground up, that she'd talked about at the bridge party she hosted all those years ago.

Envy swelled in Justine. She squeezed her eyes closed, trying to get rid of old memories. Something bumped into the back of her pew, followed by whispers from women who'd eased into the row behind her.

"This must be the place."

"Girl, yes it is. Doggone shame about Herbert. Such an upstanding man. You know about it, right?"

"Something about a blood disease, I heard?"

"Uh-uh. Massive heart attack, girl. They say he was found in his study in the wee hours of the morning, slumped over his desk, glasses still on."

"Girl, shut your mouth."

"Dog wouldn't stop barking and neighbors finally called the cops. No telling where his wife was."

"Heifer was probably out screwing some new joker. You know her last one croaked around this time last year. Honey, she messed around with him for decades. Some retired factory worker, of all people. A drunk, if you ask me. Had a wife and kids, too, but you wouldn't know it, the way he liked to prance around with Sonya."

"My God. The wife must've known. They always do."

"Probably did. I met her once before, years ago during a bridge party at Herbert and Sonya's old house. Timid little bumpkin with no style or education. Nothing going for her at all, poor thing."

Justine turned around, pretending to look for someone she knew coming in through the chapel doors. She had to find out who the two women were behind her. Out of the corner of her eye, she saw long braids and gleaming jewelry but not much else. Curiosity made her want to keep sitting, listening, but anger spattered her interest. She rose and neared the casket in the front of the chapel, her legs on the verge of turning into twigs as she walked.

Herbert was a handsome man. Even better looking than Wesley. A short, neat graying afro with a matching beard. Smooth skin as fair as Sonya's. Small nose and full lips. But he was big around the middle. A bloated fish, minus the scales. The bottom of his bulging stomach nearly collided with the closed door of the casket that housed everything below his waist. To make things worse, the mortician had the bright idea of placing Herbert's hands on top of his belly, which put more attention on its bigness.

Justine zoomed in on the large wedding band on his left hand. Even under the dim lighting, she could see it was real gold. The sight of it brought her back to Wesley and the way he would sometimes trudge into the house long after his shift at the factory ended, his left ring finger free of any indication of their marital vows. As Justine would reheat his dinner, she always thought about how long it took Wesley to finally be able to afford a ring for her. How, up until the time he settled into the house next door, he claimed there was never enough money saved for him to buy himself a band.

Herbert's doughy fingers were tightly locked together.

The saliva in Justine's mouth thickened. Her heart nearly thumping its way out of her skin. She clamped her eyes shut again before her vision blurred from tears. She wanted to hit something and hit it hard.

Behind her, people's movements and chatter grew louder. Justine knew she didn't have long to decide. What was there to decide anyway? Herbert didn't need the ring anymore. Sonya could care less, and if she did now, her concern came many years too late.

The gold was colder than Justine expected. She took her fingers off the ring and balled her hand into a fist. She could hear Wesley laughing. Mocking her fear.

Quickly, she clasped the ring again and dug into the body's stiff fingers as she tried to remove it. The hand wouldn't budge. Its resistance stirred panic in Justine. She tugged harder until the strap of her purse fell to her forearm.

"Hey, what are you doing?"

The voices behind her rose as feet pushed against carpet, but she couldn't manage to let go of the ring or the hand. She wanted to. Lord knows she did. But, she just couldn't.

Justine felt a heavy grip around her arms. Hot, sour breath on the back of her neck. More words spitting out as someone pulled her from Herbert's hand just after she yanked the ring off.

Two tall men in matching dark suits dragged her away from the casket and nearly tackled her to the floor. She spotted Sonya in the scuffle, instantly recognizing the woman's long neck, as she tried to wriggle away from the men.

"Give it here!" one of the men demanded.

"Let go! I don't have anything!"

Both men kept struggling to pry open Justine's hand, but she clenched the ring tight between her fingers and held her hand close to her bosom.

"Easy, guys." Sonya held up her hands. The two gossipers from the back row, Justine noticed, stood next to Sonya, murmuring things in her ear as if they were now her best friends.

In the midst of the scuffle, Sonya removed her from the men's hold. Justine stood looking into the eyes of the woman who she'd competed with for so long. The skin on Sonya's neck sagged now. So did her cheeks which looked like the jowls on a dog. Her wavy hair was thinning, now amber instead of blonde. Justine had dreamed of the day when she would see Sonya again—what she'd say, how she'd give her hell for taking what wasn't hers. Now that the time had finally come, all Justine could think to do was clasp Herbert's ring tighter until her hand ached.

She watched the expression on Sonya's face turn from confusion to guilt, and then to pity. While Justine was a lot calmer now than she expected, she couldn't be responsible for what happened if the woman tried to pry the jewelry from her hand.

"Forgive them for bothering you," Sonya said, her eyes remaining on Justine's closed fist. She nodded, as if trying to convince herself that this was the right thing to do and pointed toward the chapel's entrance in the back of the room. The same stubby man with the fedora who'd tried to hand Justine an obituary shook his head at her in disgust.

"Thank you for coming," said Sonya. "Gregory will see you out."

*

When she returned from the funeral home in the afternoon, Justine placed Herbert's ring underneath her pillow. It didn't belong with the other thingamajigs that she'd taken from previous funerals and stashed on the living room console. A wedding band represented the most sacred union between two people, and it had been on the hand of a man who was once in love with a woman who was loved by someone Justine loved. That was enough to make her want to have the ring close to her, particularly when she slept, with nothing to separate it from her body but cloth and cushion.

Lois finally called and so did Bev, but Justine didn't answer the phone either time. She grew concerned about Rich not calling but then it occurred to her that he was probably giving her space to be alone on the anniversary of Wesley's death. It was so typical and considerate of him. Only Justine didn't want to be alone. Not when it gave her so much time to think. And remember.

A visit with Myrtle sounded like the closest thing to comfort. Justine let the front door whine shut behind her. She got that sickening feeling in the bed of her stomach that she'd locked herself out again. No lanyard of keys around her neck, or her cell phone. And Myrtle's new caregiver staring Justine down her throat from across the street.

"Behind you, in the keyhole!" the woman yelled, pointing her finger.

Justine yanked the key out of the door, wondering how long the woman had been outside watching her. She looked older than any of Myrtle's previous in-home care assistants. Ratty wig and clearly no girdle. B-cup bra for those D-cup breasts bulging out of her uniform.

"Happens to me all the time." The woman said as Justine climbed the stairs on Myrtle's front porch. "You can't win with keys. No matter where you put them, they always seem to come up missing or end up in the funniest places."

"She asleep?" asked Justine. She put her face up to Myrtle's storm door. The living room lights were off, and the lingering smell of old fried fish floated through the screen. A Johnnie Taylor record was playing in one of the back rooms.

"She's just listening to music." The woman held out her hand. "I'm Roslyn."

"Justine."

"You the hairdresser?"

"That's Bev," Justine told her. "I'm just the one who's been coming by to keep Myrtle company for the last forty-five years."

"Got it. I'll go get her."

"Make sure she's wearing socks. The thick ones. Her feet stay cold."

When Roslyn went inside, Justine removed lint from Myrtle's rocker and sat in the other chair near the side ledge. She always hated settling in this spot before sundown. Summer's savage heat nearly dried her into a human prune, and her curls turned into a frizzy mess. Plus, there was something mortifying about looking at her own house from a distance. A feeling that it would vanish if she stared at it for too long.

Justine told Wesley about that feeling when they first moved to North St. Louis County from Pruitt-Igoe. He just cocked his head and kissed her hard on the mouth before he assured Justine that as long as they could recall the first part of their penniless lives, she would always have that feeling. He said showers would never make her feel all the way clean and a pantry stocked full of food would never blot out the grief that came with once not having enough. Too bad he turned out to be right.

"Here she is."

Justine cut her eyes at Roslyn for speaking in a baby voice. The woman guided Myrtle out onto the porch and hung back, waiting to see if Myrtle would find her way to the rocker. Myrtle had that usual faraway look in her eyes. Hair tangled in mismatched rollers. Fish crumbs on her sunken cheeks.

She looked at Justine, not really seeing her. Justine kept her attention on her hands so Myrtle wouldn't get overwhelmed.

"What's that you got there, Missy?" she asked.

"She's into yarn lately," Roslyn said. She tugged at the teal-colored string clutched in Myrtle's fists.

"Best to let her answer," Justine told the woman. She already didn't like this caregiver. She could tell that she was pushy. The kind that never got married or had kids and devoted herself to a so-called passion of controlling her elders.

Myrtle shoved the ball of yarn into Justine's chest. Slowly, Justine took it and eased her friend into the rocker before returning the yarn.

"What number's this one?" she asked Myrtle once Roslyn was back inside the house. "Jesus, Myrtle. They're getting worse. If you weren't a little off before, you definitely will be by the time this Roslyn goes."

Myrtle stared down at her bare legs and then, her socked feet, stuffed in sandals. Like a cow, she had that habit of blinking hard to keep the bugs from settling on her face.

Justine wiped the crumbs from her cheek with the sleeve of her own housecoat.

For a while, they sat in silence. Myrtle, petting the yarn. Justine, watching the sunset's sherbetlike colors spill across the sky. Shades of red, purple, pink. Elegant golden hues that made everything sparkle. Justine snorted, feeling cheated. Why on Earth was growing old compared to such beautiful things? There was nothing elegant or golden about the sunset years of one's life. Just fear of not being seen and fear of being seen too much.

Justine dragged her chair closer to Myrtle.

"My kids are up to something," she said. "I know it. I can feel it. Theo and me are finally on the mend, but I almost wish we weren't. There's this new sympathy in his voice when he calls now. Like I'm too fragile for him to waste his words on. I can't stand it. He's the one with the problem; fighting homeless men in abandoned lots and whatnot."

Myrtle sighed wearily. Justine pet the other half of her yarn.

"What was he doing at Pruitt-Igoe anyway? That's private property, Myrtle. Every local paper had that boy headlined. Here it is August, and it's still popular news. I know it, because I read it."

Justine stopped to catch her breath and take in the subtle, sweet odor of Myrtle's sassafras tree. Even from the backyard, the tree commanded attention with its lemony scent that wasn't yet pungent, but warned of its full potential. She crossed her arms, dreading the way its leaves and its bark would eventually let out an overwhelming stench that didn't sit well on her belly each fall season.

"Lois isn't herself, either," she said to Myrtle. "Still helps me around. Drives me to and fro. Here and there, you know. But I feel her picking at something in me. Pulling, like I'm this doll she's trying to open and see if my stuffing's wrong or not."

A sudden rush of wind ruffled the bushes in Myrtle's front yard. She giddily pointed at the shrubbery and whispered something Justine couldn't hear. Her arm dropped down to her side when the bushes stopped moving.

"She's been like that ever since she came back from visiting California with your grandson," Justine continued. "I don't know what it is about that place. I haven't brought up the thing between her and Ahmad anymore because she gets all defensive. You know how it is. They have to learn on their own, right? Hopefully, before it's too late."

Justine searched Myrtle's face and tried to make out how hard the woman was listening. She didn't seem fazed about the mention of Ahmad. Justine had been so careful not to say things that could lead to memories of his brother, Pete. The death. Those train tracks. But it was hard not to let on what she thought about Ahmad. She didn't care what he knew or where he'd been. The boy was no good.

"I don't hate him, Myrtle. How could I? Some things you just can't take back. You and me both know that. We all deal with the past and what's happened in different ways."

Justine glanced at Myrtle again. A thin line of spit hung from her friend's bottom lip.

"Different ways," repeated Justine. "And I don't need to tell you about that she-devil, Raynah. Daughter or not, I still don't speak to her. She's the ringleader of whatever they have going. Miss Thing's got another thing coming if she thinks she can get one word out of me about some stuff she shouldn't be worried about.

"So what, if she never calls me again. It was the '70s. The 1970s, Myrtle! Veiled Prophet newspaper clippings, my behind. What was she, but the size of a doggone bucket anyway? Couldn't even talk a lick past toddler gibberish then. Now, she wants to come at me about owning up to some scandal that's supposedly part of my history. My history, not hers! Mine."

Justine realized her hands were shaking. She rubbed them together in her lap. She felt incredibly selfish for pouring out her woes to a woman who'd lost so much, including her own mind. For all of Raynah's shenanigans, she was still here. In plain sight, for Justine to see and deal with. When was the last time Myrtle had seen her own daughter, who'd done little good besides birth Pete and Ahmad? Was she still out doing Lord knows what with the devil knows who? Was the girl even still alive? No one knew, or dared to ask, least of all Justine.

"Say, Myrtle," she said. "You remember the first time we met? Me and Wesley hadn't been here for longer than a week, I think. Those were lonely times. Gainful times, but lonely. I remember you knocked on my door while Wesley was at work one day and handed me some watery potato pie. You had on those bleached overalls of yours and patent leather heels too big for your feet. Country as hell, and you had nerve to tell me that I looked like a tiny lost fool in that house all by myself, with all those pretty chandeliers and new carpet around me. I loved and hated you just the same, from that day on."

Myrtle looked around Justine in that way of hers that kept Justine wondering if she was really as closed off in the head as everyone had been led to believe. Or if she was somewhere in there having her fun, finally free from the life once thrown at her. Justine wanted to shake her and find out. Just once. Real fast, before Roslyn came back out.

"Anyway, enough about old times," she said to Myrtle. "Did I tell you the latest on Rich? No, we're not a couple yet, according to me, but we'll see what happens. He's away right now, visiting his son in prison.

"Don't give me that look. Yeah, I said his son, in prison. Thing is, he runs that elders' support group that Bev's trying to talk me into returning to this week. I haven't been in a while, not since the thing happened at the supermarket, because I don't want folks to catch on to whatever me and Rich are doing. But there's supposed to be a substitute running it in Rich's absence this time. With Bev working at her shop most days and the kids acting up, I've got nothing better to do than attend another funeral or hang around here with you. No offense, but that's not getting me anywhere."

Justine stopped talking, long enough to listen to Myrtle's shallow breathing. She'd tightened the grip around her yarn, like she was gesturing for Justine to get to the point.

"Guess what I'm trying to ask is, should I go back to the elders' group tomorrow or not? Let me know what you think. Grunt, stomp your foot, do something."

Myrtle kept looking straight ahead, her jaws tightly clenched.

"Forget it," Justine said. "Wonder what Bev would think about that Roslyn. Heifer just doesn't rub me the right way. I hope to God it rains and she gets caught in it, so those fake eyelashes of hers get stuck together while she's trying to drive home."

Sudden panic gripped Justine as Myrtle's face twisted like she was in pain. Then, before Justine could move, her friend's shoulders started shaking. A soft raspy cackle that sounded like loose change being rubbed together erupted out of the woman's mouth.

"Oh, Myrtle," Justine said. "You don't know how good it feels to hear you laugh again. I'm so glad they brought you back here and didn't let you stay caged in that place. All you're missing now is one of those Stag beer cans you used to lug around. We'll pretend for now."

Justine held the ball of yarn up to Myrtle's grinning face and made gulping sounds. Her lips twisted again. This time, there was fear and darkness in the woman's eyes. Justine leaned forward and looked her square in the face.

"What happened to you in there? The Myrtle I know wasn't scared of nobody. She'd kick your behind and hug you next."

Myrtle stared behind Justine at her house across the street. Her cheek quivered a little. Justine gave her yarn one last pet and rose, ready to call Bev and accept her invitation.

"Well, no use dwelling on things. Everyone'll get what's coming to them, good or bad, if the Lord says the same."

The moon was becoming its own silver ball of yarn in the sky. Justine rapped on the screen door to alert Roslyn that she was leaving. She got halfway across the street and heard thudding noises behind her. She turned around and saw Myrtle banging one of her socked, sandaled feet against the porch's floor. Reluctantly, Justine gave her friend a thumbs-up, wishing she hadn't opened her mouth at all about the elders' support group.

*

The next day, Bev picked up Justine for the elders' support group. During the drive, she gave Justine the latest updates on several participants. Grit's long-distance engagement to a big-time preacher in Chicago. Potbellied Phil's current stay in ICU following diabetes complications. Rachel Beth's sock monkey portraits after a feral cat stole Coconut from her. And some stuff about people that Justine hadn't met yet.

They arrived at the elder's center about an hour too early. If Bev hadn't reeked of burnt hair from her salon, they could've stayed in the car and waited. Instead, they wound up signing the guest log in the lobby with the redhead receptionist whose name Justine always forgot. When she and the woman played the fake-face game, seeing which of them could smile at each other the longest, she realized the redhead couldn't remember her name, either.

"So, what is it you had to say in person, that you couldn't tell me on the phone last night?" Bev asked once they'd made it upstairs inside the empty meeting room.

She sat down, readjusted her wig, and waited for Justine to settle next to her. Justine kept standing near one of the windows and stared at the view of downtown's buildings around the Gateway Arch, the trickle of brown river behind it. Nervous, she traced a water mark on the windowsill with her finger.

"You know Rich, right?"

"Of course I know Rich," said Bev. "What kind of question is that?"

"Are you going to shut up so I can tell you or not?"

"Go ahead then." Bev waved her hand at Justine.

"I've been seeing him."

"You've been seeing him."

"Uh-huh."

"So, you and Rich have a thing."

"It's not really a thing."

A froglike chuckle escaped Bev's throat. "I knew it," she told Justine. "You've been glowing and shit since your birthday. Can't believe you didn't tell me."

"I'm telling you now."

"How long, heifer?"

"None of your business."

"The kids know about this?"

"None of their business, either."

"It is, if you two get serious," Bev said. "What, you think they'll never find out their mother's been fooling around with another man?"

"You make it sound like I'm cheating."

"I wish. You should've known somebody like Rich a long time ago and gave Wesley a dose of his own damn medicine." Bev removed the wig and dug at her scalp through the hairnet. Her hair was longer and thicker than Justine remembered. A confused explosion of colors. The bold black strands now careful grays. Some yellows. Some whites.

"If you didn't miss him so much, you could remarry," Bev told Justine.

"If you didn't run your mouth so much, maybe you could, too."

The back door flung open. Staff members brought in food trays of baked chicken, garlic potatoes, green beans, fruit salad, and slices of pound cake. The wind outside shook the room's flimsy windowpanes. Justine held her breath for a while to keep her stomach from growling.

"My nine o'clock this morning showed me an article on Theo," Bev said after she fixed her plate.

"What article?"

"Don't play simple with me. The piece on him knocking the shit out of a homeless man on Pruitt-Igoe's property."

"There were two homeless men," Justine corrected. She wasn't big on Theo playing a tough guy, but knowing that he carried out an act of ruthless self-defense was starting to feel an achievement.

"Well, whatever," said Bev. "All I know is the woman sat her ass in my chair and nearly talked me to death about how much she's always had an eye for Theo and what a fool he was to throw away his public identity for a careless tumble in the grass. I should've nicked those kangaroo ears of hers with my flat iron. Uppity little wench. What was he doing at that site anyway? I know you said you didn't want to talk about it, but—"

"Then, that's just what I meant," Justine said. "I don't want to talk about it."

She tinkered with the fake pearls around her neck.

"Hello there, early birds."

A tall, medium-brown woman carrying a flip chart and briefcase sashayed in. She waved at Justine and Bev before placing the chart on an easel in the front of the room and raised her sundress to curtsy for them. She chatted with Bev about the weather, her background, and her weekend plans while yanking papers from her bag and scribbling on the flip chart.

Justine couldn't figure out the woman's age. No giveaway lines on her cheeks or forehead. No sagging skin in random places. She talked with her hands a lot and from the side of her mouth like some washed-up jazz singer who was used to being drunk and in love with her own voice. Probably had her name changed to something she thought made her sound more interesting, like Dynasty or Magenta.

"Hi, I'm Pat."

"Justine." She shook the woman's hand. She smelled like lemon tea and fresh-baked raisin bread. "I'm filling in for Rich today."

"Big shoes to fill," said Bev.

"Certainly. You all be easy on me."

"Listen at her, trying to be modest!" Grit said as she entered the room. "Don't let Ms. Pat fool you. She ain't no rookie."

Pat smiled, like she was too shy for words.

"Hey, I remember you." Rachel Beth pointed at Justine and beamed. Same wrinkled face, but she'd lost weight. Her Hawaiian shirt hung off her shoulder, exposing a rose-shaped birthmark, and the jeans around her waist looked ready to fall to her ankles if she moved too much. Instead of Coconut, she held a small notebook with a picture of her latest sock monkey drawings.

"Go find us a seat before they're all taken, will you, honey?" Grit nudged Rachel Beth away and before Justine could open her mouth, the woman had her in a death grip like they were long-lost kin. She thought about the extra laundry detergent she'd have to use that evening, washing glitter eyeshadow and pink lipstick stains out of her dress.

"So glad to see you again!" Grit said. "Lord, we've all been wondering. Don't you do that to us again, you hear?"

She pulled back and thrust her hand in Justine's face. The one with an engagement ring.

"Did Bev tell you? The man's got me glowing. I just don't know what to do with myself!"

"I can help you with that," said Phil as he sat down at the table.

"Shut up, Phil."

Grit turned back to Justine and playfully yanked her arm.

More newcomers came in and got their plates of food. From there, Pat directed them to the table and asked for people to check in. A redbone with a thick French accent sitting across from Justine, who she'd never met, cleared her throat and called herself Beatrice. She started talking about her issues with switching to a new geriatric specialist after not being able to smell or taste her food anymore.

The accent became an ear-hassle. Justine lost interest and fumbled with a handkerchief from her purse, dabbing it with her spit to blot out Grit's makeup stains on her blouse. She heard Pat ask the redbone the famous question, "How can we support you?" which usually meant, how can we make you act like you have some sense in public? The woman mumbled something, and then Justine noticed Pat's eyes were on her.

"Would you like to check in, Justine?" Pat offered an encouraging smile. Justine wanted to strangle the woman for putting her on the spot.

"It's Mrs. Holmes. Aren't we going in order?"

"Yes, we are, Mrs. Holmes, and it looks like you're next," said Pat, pointing to the number of empty chairs next to the redbone with the French accent.

Justine sunk back into her chair and folded her arms over the damp stain on her blouse.

"I'll pass."

*

"All you do is press down on the keys with your thumbs."

Bev tapped the keypad with her shears, her sculpted nails brushing against Justine. As soon as Justine tried to peck the little buttons, letters from the alphabet flooded the search box. Random tabs popped open that she couldn't make disappear.

"No, no, heifer. Like this."

Bev dropped the shears in the sink and yanked the phone from Justine. She punched the pad with her thumb nails, her fingers expertly flitting across the screen.

"Okay, okay."

Justine snatched the phone back before Bev could see Rich's message. If she couldn't control who got ahold of her past, she figured the least she could do was still have some say over her current private life.

"Still can't believe how quiet you were at group yesterday," Bev said.

"Get off my back. I went, didn't I?"

"Yeah, but the whole point is to talk. There's a reason we meet, you know."

"Well, you talked enough for both of us," Justine reminded her.

Bev passed on her check-in speech just like Justine did. But for what she held inside during the group wellness discussion, she plenty made up for afterward during their drive home. Talking up the good food Justine missed out on and warning her how she'd end up like Myrtle if she kept refusing to be social with folks.

By the time they pulled into Justine's driveway, she was ready to call it quits on their friendship, if just for a little while. Justine went back into the house with a dark cloud over her. Everything felt wrong, so she ended up doing what she did when she got that down. She read her Bible and smoked a joint. Flipped right to some of her favorite passages in Psalms and rolled up what little she found in Bev's glove compartment when they'd stopped to get gas. Then, Justine listened to some Bill Withers while she took a bath and played dress-up in clothes she hadn't worn in years. Decades. Stuff she couldn't believe still fit, with smells and textures that hurled old memories at her until she was nothing but a weak, teary mess on her bedroom floor.

Justine realized that nothing she'd stolen from funerals—flowers, jewelry, handkerchiefs—could compare with what she rehashed that night. Crucial moments she'd tried to bury inside of herself, or replace completely with other people's crucial moments, came back full force. Just thinking about it put her on the verge of imploding.

"Cut it all off," Justine told Bev.

She stared at her best friend through the mirror.

Bev put her hand on her hip. "Do what?"

"You heard me."

"Why?"

"Just do it."

The showerhead's drip seemed like it was getting louder. Muttering to herself, Bev disappeared and returned with a large towel.

"Thought you just wanted a quick, easy trim," she said, hurling the cloth on the floor around Justine's feet. "Took me six years to get your hair this long and healthy. Now, you want to go do something stupid."

"You sound scared," Justine said.

Bev knelt in front of her on the closed toilet, her slender palms hugging Justine's knees. "Justine, I know these past few months have been rough for you. I mean, hair is just hair, but still—"

Her voice trailed off and her gaze, too. Justine got the feeling she was being refused, bargained with.

"When Wesley died," she said to Bev, "all the neighbors came by, and they weren't just coming by to offer their condolences. The last thing I wanted was to be smothered in pity, but I found most of them just wanted to meddle, to see what all Wesley left me so they could try and take it. I wanted to tell them so bad, *not a damn thing*, but it was none of their business, so I didn't open my door for days. Not to you. Not to the kids. Not to anyone. No one belonged in this house but me and God. We were the only two I could handle, or trust, or—"

It was Justine's turn to trail off. She started thinking about things that had nothing to do with Wesley's death. Like her kids who'd taken pains to better understand the person she was before any of them were alive, or even thought of. And what the hell for? To dig at the root of what they saw as their father's ugliness? Or, worse, Justine's obedience? To get why she left her old life behind, never to speak of it again, to make things peaceful for their nosy, ungrateful behinds?

Justine remembered Ma once telling her the way a person treated their parents came back around to them. They'd had their differences, but Justine didn't recall giving her mother this much grief, outside of the endless worrying during Justine's little stint.

Things had happened so fast. Pruitt-Igoe's demolition in the spring of '72. The displacement of her family and closest friends. At the time, Ma was a wife and full-time mother, and had spent nearly two decades working in produce at the same grocer. And she was made to leave the housing project she called home before it was destroyed, with only a suitcase and the urn filled with Pop's ashes. There was no way she and Justine could, or cared, to talk about it openly, even when Ma was finally given a new place to live, only two years before she died.

What were they supposed to say to each other? *Gee, remember when that happened?*

Justine couldn't let it go, not in the way Ma wanted her to. Ma dealt with it her way, as did Wesley and Bev; Justine dealt with it differently. She did what she thought was right at the time. Months after Pruitt-Igoe was destroyed, she joined others in the crusade to unmask, and ultimately dethrone, the Veiled Prophet for the sake of winning back the dignity and basic rights of herself and the people she loved. In that moment, she finally recognized how her part in the scheme, as small as it seemed, recovered so much humanity.

But the plan backfired. They lost. Case closed.

When Wesley saw Justine in the newspaper after the scheme, he beat her for a week straight. Seven days. Up until then, he had never laid a finger on her, although they constantly argued. After feeling his wrath for so long, it was a wonder Justine still had all of her teeth. She remembered the sharp taste of blood in her mouth and how she willed herself not to cry out after that first night, out of fear of waking Raynah who, as a toddler at the time, was still adjusting to a regular sleep pattern.

So, Justine vowed to give up her days as an undercover freedom fighter. No more secret meetings with the group she'd forged a strong bond with while Wesley was away at work or tending to one of his affairs. No more nothing. In a week's time, Justine had let a man she loved more than life itself knock the will out of her. She dimmed her own spirit, and she learned to like it.

Thinking back, Justine couldn't believe she'd stuck around and allowed Wesley to change the course of her path. But it happened. And why Raynah had taken it upon herself to throw everything back up in her face now was outrageously ignorant. Folks loved to pick at the untold, sometimes simply because it was untold. Everyone always wanted to know why. But, sometimes, there was no why.

There was just the things people did, or didn't do.

"Please, Bev," Justine said aloud, "don't be one of those meddling folks. Do me this favor, just once, simply because I asked. I just want the ends gone, the relaxed part. My roots can stay."

Small puddles formed in Bev's eyes. She squeezed Justine's kneecaps.

"Then give me the damn scissors. I'll do it myself."

The shears wound up in Justine's hands and then, in her hair. Bev snatched them from her and began snipping until shiny black strands fell around Justine like black feathers.

Justine looked at nothing as one hand gripped the other in her lap. When Bev was done, she rose before her legs could freeze and stared at her reflection in the mirror. Her mind flashed unwanted snippets of a young woman, with her memories of televised blasts turning vacated buildings—once, her home—into mountains of gray powder on that fateful day in April '72.

She saw the young woman on that cold December day of the same year in the Sears uniform she borrowed—hot and red and mad and wanting room to spread. She was there, as instructed by her comrades, to keep tabs on the dressing room behind the Kiel Auditorium while she mended the gowns of those debutantes, all hoping to be crowned and dance with the hooded figure. The veiled one.

In the mirror, Bev stood behind Justine and sucked her teeth, hands on her hips. A mess of short, tough, uneven black hair sat like a halo around Justine's face.

There she was. Or, the person she was once becoming.

Raynah

Raynah pulled her old Camry into the lot of the gas station. She thought she'd spotted a familiar gray Prius behind her, but the car didn't have Claire's Mizzou license plate on its front. She parked in front of the station's convenience store and emptied her ashtray, preparing a mental checklist of all the things she needed to do today.

The work of maintaining the home museum's appeal had Raynah irritable and thinking in fragmented sentences. Already, there was talk of new protests against the Veiled Prophet Ball in December that she needed to document. But, with all of the demands on her as the museum's founder, she finally accepted that she could no longer be her own shutterbug and hired a photographer to keep track of the city's ongoing racial and socioeconomic rifts.

Agreeing to meet with Claire under these circumstances bothered Raynah. Together, they'd spent the entire summer preparing the social justice museum ahead of next January's grand opening. Claire was detailed, eloquent, and business savvy. She eased into her internship, spending countless hours with Raynah at the house as well as the Missouri History Museum and the Missouri Historical Society and Research Center, ironing out facts on documented events. She recruited renovation specialists and ordered bamboo plants for every room. She resized and framed old photos Raynah ordered, encased the exhibits, and developed the museum's social media following with posts that were timely and engaging.

Raynah was also moved by Claire's teachability. She quickly synchronized facts, blending bits of the past with pieces of current themes for crossgenerational appeal among community organizers. Raynah developed a deep respect for the girl's work ethic. She always demanded excellence, sometimes at the cost of Claire's weekends, but she wanted to drill into Claire the unique value of social reform.

Still, Raynah never liked to see herself as a mentor. The thought wasn't flattering; it terrified her. She dreaded failing Claire. In Oakland, all Raynah had was her world of ideals and soon realized she couldn't feed a child on grassroots pamphlets, and so she chose not to have one. Working with Claire caused Raynah to see the line between mentorship and motherhood was starkly thin. It also made her come to grips with eventually losing Claire in August, when the girl began her freshman year at Mizzou, two hours away in Columbia, Missouri.

As if things couldn't get any worse, Claire's last day had been on the anniversary of Sir's death. Raynah was forced to let go of someone who'd turned into a mentee, another little sister, a daughter, a special friend.

It wasn't for good, Claire claimed, but Raynah knew too well the thrill of undergraduate life. Soon the studying, extracurricular activities, after-parties, and dating would pull Claire away, regardless of her good intentions. Raynah could only force herself to find the bright side: Claire's experience would shape her into a person she could never break out of or away from, no matter where she went, who she returned to, or what she did. She wished Justine could see her own experiences that way, regardless of how secret or shameful they were to her mother.

The ash on Raynah's cigarette had grown long enough to fall off. She flicked it out the window and then turned the air-conditioning up as high as it would go. She inspected her fingernails. They were caked with grime and dandruff. The saliva in her mouth thickened when she inhaled her unwashed hair's sour smell, which she now routinely covered with the head wrap from Auntie Kit. She liked to think of the fabric as a symbol of protection and strength from an elder who was physically far away, but close within a heartbeat's radius.

The clock inside her car read 10:07 a.m. Earlier that morning, the conversation she had with Claire was short and strained. Raynah had immediately noticed the urgency in her old intern's voice. The high-pitched shrillness at the ends of her sentences. Nothing like her usual warmth and calmness

Before then, Raynah had heard of the wave of dissent and protests erupting on the Mizzou campus. In the last five weeks since Claire had been away in Columbia, she'd sent Raynah over a dozen emails, all of them summarizing her classes and teachers and dorm life and filled with details about her experience as part of the "fresh blood" minority student population that was becoming known for an unstoppable defiance. Claire's candor and excitement spilled out of Raynah's computer screen, laced with the sort of youthful mischief that Raynah missed and craved.

So, Claire's call wasn't a red flag. It was a complete throw-off. Raynah hadn't seen it coming at all, especially not in the middle of the week.

Something about the girl's panicky behavior was deeply disturbing. Claire's temperament was her gift. She could keep her cool when everyone else—including and especially Raynah—lost theirs. Holding it together was what gave her the capacity to accomplish what she'd already achieved at such a young age and do what she was doing now. Her being on the verge of a meltdown meant there was grisly chaos in Columbia.

Before Raynah could redial Claire's number, she saw the familiar Prius—Mizzou license plate included—pull onto the lot and go somewhere out of view.

Minutes later, Claire emerged from the side of the building, half of her ghostly pale face covered by shades and an MU hoodie. The girl's sneakers seemed to barely touch the ground, like she was afraid that stepping too hard would make her fall through the pavement.

"Well, so much for the freshman fifteen," Raynah said. She got out of her car and looked Claire over. "If those jeans of yours were any looser, you'd need a belt."

They embraced, and then Claire mumbled what sounded like something between a groan and a whimper. Raynah released her, aware of the embarrassment it could cause if she held the girl long enough to make her cry.

Claire sneezed, yanked off her hoodie and leaned against the hood of Raynah's Camry. The beige tufts of hair on her head, usually kept in neat cornrows, were scooped into a messy bun and packed with what looked like days' worth of old styling gel.

"You look like shit," Raynah told her. "Who are you and what have you done with Claire?"

Again, Claire mumbled a choked response, barely moving her lips. All Raynah heard was something about mounting tensions in the last few days.

Perturbed was the actual word the girl used.

But Claire didn't look perturbed. She looked plain sick and badly shaken. Raynah recognized the look as one of her own, developed after seeing and feeling too much at protests gone wrong. There were many during her freshman year at UC Berkeley, and for many reasons, but perhaps none like those that happened ironically after Raynah's time at her would-be alma mater.

"Things are a rocket at the museum right now," she said to Claire. "Curtis and Samantha are getting all their energy worked out of them before this new exhibit. Still can't believe I had to hire two people to be one of you."

A small grin spread across Claire's face. They both knew that it was the closest Raynah would get to complimenting her.

"I met a guy I like," Claire said. "I didn't mention him in my emails because I didn't think it was really a big deal."

"That's great, Claire."

"He's a junior and plays basketball. Kansas City native. We study together sometimes. Good kisser and very smart. My parents want to meet him. They're so old-school about that."

"Sounds like a good idea."

Claire narrowed her eyes. "No, it doesn't."

"Why not?"

"He's community."

"That's all the more reason. He sounds like someone I wish I'd met back in college."

"No," said Claire, shaking her head. "He's community. As in, he's been around. With lots of girls."

"I see." Raynah folded her arms.

"The other day, he told me he didn't want us to be complicated. I saw him at a party the same night, and then the next morning, it was Erica Bridges, queen of Black sorority life, leaving his dorm room in his jersey."

"Hmm," was all Raynah said, careful not to instigate.

"I know it sounds all high school. You're probably wondering why I'm telling you this. Sorry if I'm wasting your time."

"You're not wasting my time."

"It's just this is the same guy who warned me about the monsters on that campus," Claire said. "You know he's a third-generation Mizzou student? Said the racism he's dealt with doesn't sound too much different from what his granddad or mama went through when they were there. He's not down with what's going on right now, though. The protesting, or our talk of hunger strikes. He says it's just going to work against us because who are we to stop a whole system? He's always talking Lloyd Gaines and saying things could get realer than what we're ready for."

"The boy sounds like a punk-ass playboy to me," said Raynah, defensively. "You don't need some—"

"He's right," Claire blurted. "I think I'm done. This isn't what I signed up for. I shouldn't be living like this."

Claire removed her sunglasses and placed them on Raynah's car. There was a pool of red in one of her eyes from where a blood vessel had burst. Waves of pity, anger, and disgust ran through Raynah. She wanted to pull the girl close. The only thing that made more sense was to share.

"Before your time," she said to Claire, "I remember being at Berkeley for a Rodney King demonstration. It was spring of '92. I hated that damn campus by then, and all it stood for. But I had no car and hadn't caught a ride with some of my friends, other protesters, who'd left early to go block off the Bay Bridge. It wound up being a good thing since several of them were arrested and I was still paying off a debt to someone for posting my bail the year before."

Raynah stopped to light another cigarette and steal a glance at Claire. The girl looked interested in what she was saying, although tired and defeated.

"So I went to the standoff on campus and it was a nightmare. One of the worst I've ever seen or been in. It wasn't the first time I got pepper sprayed, or spat on, or nearly trampled. Hell, by then, I'd grown used to that and a whole lot of other things.

"But I think it was probably the first time I started letting all of it sink in. By the end of the day, my thoughts had caught up with what we were doing—the message we were trying to get across—and it crushed me more than any police baton.

"I kept thinking, 'wow, this is soul murder' and wondering how the hell I'd ended up there. Not there, as in back on the campus I'd flunked out of for a protest, but there, as in fighting against folks who didn't give a damn what was coming out of my mouth, so long as they could find a way to kill it.

"And that was it, for a while. I didn't march or do anything merely close to activism for a long time. I got deep into film and other creative outlets, anything that allowed me not to act much, but just analyze and record whatever was right in front of me. I took up running, too; in and out of the gym, because it let me release a lot of poison.

"Funny thing was, I couldn't outrun myself or the issues I was hot about. I'd walk outside after a mindless jog in the gym, or a long sit in the sauna to loosen my leg muscles, and everything would still be the way it was, whether I was in it or not. Me recognizing the effects of my absence started haunting me more than adding my little two cents in the civil rights pot. Me quitting because I didn't understand what was at stake got to me more than just wanting to be."

Raynah bit down on her tongue to stop herself from talking. She couldn't tell what Claire was thinking, or if she was thinking at all. The girl had absently started fiddling with her bun, tugging and pushing at strands that were loose.

"Look, this isn't about me. What do you want, Claire? What is it that you really want?"

The girl leaned forward, cradling her forehead in her palms. Then, she sat back up and looked at Raynah.

"I just want this to be over. I want to have fun right now and get my degree in peace and not feel guilty about it, like I always owe someone something. I want to study and dance and go to parties and live, without having to worry about being a target or laughingstock of some fucked-up system that keeps telling me I'm lesser. I want to not feel like I'm going crazy more than 85 percent of each day. That's what I want."

"That's what you want," Raynah repeated. Without wanting to, she thought of Justine. She envisioned her mother as a young girl in '72, after her part in the Veiled Prophet scandal. Vulnerable and tired, like Claire. Wanting an easier life, like Claire. She sighed, a pang of guilt filling her for the way she'd criticized Justine lately.

With Claire, she stared absently at a stubby woman with long crochet braids pumping gas a few feet away. The doors to her pea green minivan opened, and kids of varying ages in tank tops and shorts spilled out onto the lot.

One school-aged girl with an outie poking through her spandex had strayed the furthest from the parked minivan. She blew bubbles in the air with her wand while she skipped in a circle between the crowded minivan and Raynah's parked car. Her dimples cut into her smooth, tan skin as her face lit up, watching the iridescent water clouds pop against her.

"That's what I want," Claire said again, tears streaming down her cheeks.

*

Raynah returned home after dusk. Everything was as she left it. Curtis and Samantha, her new interns, scurried around the place, calling vendors, arranging artifacts, and instructing the movers they'd hired to transport the new encasings. But she didn't have energy to throw herself back in the work. Her throat was raw and her ears were still ringing from yelling and fun with Claire at a dingy arcade they'd found. By the time they left, they were both drained and sweating and reluctant to end what was probably the last time Claire would return before midterms.

Raynah resisted the urge to mother the girl with overzealous hugs and clichéd expressions on how things would get better. She did buy Claire a small cactus and a keychain shaped like a condom when they returned to the gas station's mini-mart. In the haze of people moving through her house, Raynah's mind still saw Claire's glassy expression when she mumbled goodbye. Her small figure swallowed by baggy clothes that looked too warm.

Upstairs, Raynah let the scalding pressure of the water from her showerhead wash away the day's mugginess and the heaviness she was feeling. She thought about the few friends she still had back in Oakland, how they were doing, and what most of them would say if they saw her now: a forty-three-year-old program assistant with hardly any savings left, consumed with transforming her dead father's rickety house into a social justice shrine before her mother's past suffocated them both.

She missed her network back West. The Bay Area had deepened her sense of self. That growth had eventually given her a greater respect for her origins and the willpower to do what she was involved in now. But the more Raynah dwelled on the life she'd built there, the more confused she felt about where she stood with people. Who she could trust and confide in.

The latest sporadic conversations with friends on the West Coast weren't always the easiest to digest. From the sound of things, they all thought Raynah was insane for going back into the belly of the beast. She didn't tell them much because even if she did, they expected her to be miserable. Several people were almost too sure that her hometown was only a pit stop or some placeholder in her life, meant to endure until something better presented itself. They kept assuring her that she'd soon grow bored with what many of them believed to be flyover country and eventually decide to return to Oakland or some other city that seemed to match her.

"What matches me?" Raynah had asked DeeDee, one of the few contacts she still kept close. She was somewhat reluctant to hear her friend's response. It had been close to 8:00 a.m. Central time, which was 6:00 a.m. DeeDee's time, but she, always an early riser, had called Raynah to check in.

"I don't know," DeeDee said, "Maybe Portland? Or Philly? I hear Austin's a riot these days. No pun intended."

Something about the way the woman laughed into the phone after her remark made Raynah realize that their friendship had taken a dive, and would possibly never recover, despite the attempts they both made to be cordial and keep in touch. Maybe they had never really been friends and had just bonded over being Midwest transplants, both Black and young and intellectual.

It was possible that DeeDee really hadn't known Raynah, a pass that she was willing to give because it had taken decades for Raynah to begin knowing herself. Still, sitting with DeeDee's mocking giggle hanging between them was disappointing. Cities, Raynah understood, weren't merely tools to be fiddled with for social justice propaganda, and then dropped and abandoned for a new place on America's radar for cultural awakenings and cool happenings.

As much as she loved seeing a miscarriage of justice being called out in mainstream America, Raynah wasn't thrilled that St. Louis had turned into the country's antidarling overnight. That kind of limited recognition brought with it media hogs and misplaced attention under the guise of fake outrage. It was what made the skeptics in this world—people who saw most activists as nothing more than opportunists with bullhorns.

*

By half past midnight, Raynah had given up on trying to sleep and found herself back at Pinch's bar.

"Put that shit out." Pinch waved off the smoke from Raynah's cigarette. "You trying to get me written up?"

"Shut up. This is Missouri."

"No, bitch, where you been? Cali may have been the first to ban indoor smoking but since then, most states did, too."

Raynah rolled her eyes and dropped her cigarette in an abandoned cocktail on the counter.

"You need to quit anyway," Pinch said. She poured cranberry juice in a glass and placed it in front of Raynah. "What brings you here at this hour? No cranberry juice at the crib?"

"Couldn't sleep."

Raynah gulped down the juice and played with the water droplets on her glass. She glanced around the place, which was less crowded than the last time she was there. Clumps of people moved with the music instead of dancing on the small dance floor. The few patrons at the other end of the bar quietly hovered over their cocktails.

"I've been there." Pinch poured more cranberry juice in the empty glass. "Some days, I'm still there. I just don't have the time or energy to do nothing but cope like I've been doing."

"And it's enough?" Raynah asked.

"Nah, but I'm here. Thank God there's a God."

"And gutter bars for insomniacs."

"And good dick," Pinch added.

They both giggled, shoulders heaving.

"Let me ask you something." Raynah leaned forward. Pinch's revelation the last time, about her missing Sir, haunted her in ways she hadn't been able to express. It frustrated her to live in her father's house and rarely be able to recall his appearance without the help of old photographs. To Raynah, that was the cruelest thing about him being gone. She needed to know if she was alone in that feeling. Or if Pinch could somehow relate, after being without Beans for so long. "You remember the way your dad used to look?" she asked.

Pinch sighed and ran the ball of her tongue ring over her lips. "Sometimes," she said, "even when I don't want to. He wasn't half the man I'd like to remember when we were growing up. Not physically. Definitely not in the head. Everybody thinks the issue was too many kids and not enough money and all that. It wasn't. Mama's been doing hair in her sleep since before any of us was born, and Daddy was never the type of man to feel bad about his woman working."

"Then what do you think happened?" Raynah asked.

"It's not what I think," said Pinch, "it's what I know. He saw something. Whatever the hell it was, maybe we're all better off not knowing. Then, he stopped working. Didn't call in or nothing. Just wouldn't go no more. I remember hearing him scream in the middle of the night one time. Sounded unreal, you know—not like a man. Not human. His skin was gray, like the color of a pot, and Mama couldn't get him to stop shaking. After that, I overheard her tell one of her most trusted clients that she thought it was drugs. I thought that was the stupidest shit, but hell, looking back, it was the eighties—crack was on and popping. Next thing I know, he started leaving home for days and Mama would go looking for him. I always feared she wouldn't find him. One day, she didn't."

Raynah tried not to look into Pinch's grieving face. She couldn't help it, though. Her eyes landed on Pinch's flushed cheeks.

"It hadn't been the first time anyway," Pinch continued, sniffling. She looked off somewhere at something behind Raynah. "Whatever had him back in the early '70s took him again, and for good."

Raynah raised her eyebrows and folded her arms. "Early '70s?"

"Yeah. Mama thinks it was some woman or the bottle. I'd like to think it was more original, more interesting than that. I know my Daddy. He might've been too nice for his own good, but he was no imitator. He did things his own way, and in his own time. You can bet he was onto something that wouldn't let him go all the way without giving himself up in return."

Raynah's mind shot off in different directions. The image of Justine in the Veiled Prophet clipping came hurling into her thoughts again. She crossed her legs to keep them still and gulped down the last of the juice in her glass. She didn't quite know how to handle the idea of someone else being in on the scandal with her mother. Someone Justine trusted but kept at arm's length. Not too close, or else it would've made it easier to track, to ruin plans. And, who else but Bev's husband, someone—a man—from her own community to aid her in doing the unthinkable?

The weight of it all surprised Raynah. Maybe she was reaching. Then again, what if she wasn't? The timing felt right. And she felt ready to jump through her skin. She had to get out. To break free and get to Lois and Theo before anything else could happen.

"Pinch, love you." Raynah hugged the woman as best she could with the counter between them.

"Bitch, okay stop," Pinch exclaimed. She laughed and waved her off. "Get outta my damn lounge."

Raynah grabbed her purse and slid off the stool. All at once, she wanted to call Lois, and do cartwheels, and scream, and hug Pinch again. She turned around to wave at Pinch before exiting, but the woman was already taking a drink order for her next patron.

*

It took two days for Raynah to get in contact with Lois and Theo, and then another day to finally meet them. And when she finally did, she immediately wished she'd kept her mouth shut.

Theo's apartment looked deeply unlived-in. Since her move back home, it was the first time Raynah had been to the high-rise nestled in the heart of the Central West End. The neighborhood was all bookstores and hookah lounges and college exchange students. All those years of her brother sticking his nose up at the person she was, only to witness him living in a replica of California.

Inside, Theo's foyer was overly air-conditioned, too clean, devoid of warmth. The color scheme was white on white, with specks of gray here, a dark-hued piece of furnishing there. John Legend's "Ordinary People" playing softly in the background.

Raynah removed her sneakers at the door, not out of respect, but to silently confront the way Theo already assumed she tainted everything. She held the shoes in her arms, glad she'd put on fresh, matching socks with no holes that morning, until Lois took them from her and set them next to her sandals in a corner near an umbrella holder.

"You hungry?" Lois asked her. "We just returned from Soulard Farmers Market."

Lois had never been a stick figure, but she was noticeably fleshier to Raynah. The split with Ahmad certainly had its side effects.

"So wholesome of you two," Raynah said. "I already ate, thanks."

She trailed her sister down a long, narrow hallway with her arms crossed tightly against her chest. She wanted to look at everything, touch nothing. The walls were filled with paintings of famous landmarks, certificates, photos with

Theo shaking the hands of constituents and local celebrities. No visible family photos. Or any trace of his ex-wife.

There was an urge to veer off into an office, or the patio, maybe a bathroom. Raynah didn't know what she expected to find. Surely, there'd be no smiling man with a towel around his waist waiting for Theo on his balcony. Or gay porn in the magazine rack next to the guest toilet.

My dear baby brother, she asked herself, eyeing an opened custom-made box of vintage Cuban cigars on a hall-stand. Just who are you trying to be?

"You made it," Theo said once they entered the living room. He sat forward in a broccoli-colored recliner and dipped a pita chip in hummus. The chair, Raynah noticed, was near a window, just like it was in their mother's house, and her house, and Lois's house. None of them could get away from owning that memory of their father. The chair was so Sir-like.

"You eat in here?" Raynah asked.

"I do," said Theo. "We're adults, right? You stain, you buy."

Lois sprawled across the couch in the middle of the room and motioned for Raynah to sit down.

"Look, I won't bore you with small talk," said Raynah, leaning against a wall between her siblings. "I hung out with Pinch a few nights ago at the bar."

"I haven't seen that girl in ages," Lois said.

"She's still bartending?" asked Theo.

"Yeah, why not?" said Raynah. "It's a respected trade in some worlds. Anyway, like I was saying, I talked to her and somehow, we got on the subject of dads. You know, how tight Sir was with hers. How Beans went nuts and left, yada

yada yada. Well, turns out Beans was into something back in the early '70s, too. Pinch claimed he gave it up for a while, for reasons still unknown, and tried to relive whatever that was in the next decade. Well, I don't have to tell either of you that didn't work out because—"

"Raynah, Raynah, Raynah, Raynah." Theo held his palms together in front of him like he was starting a prayer. "As much as I want to believe you, I can't do this today. Do you have any idea about the things running through my head right now? Why you're really here?"

"What?"

"Sit down, Raynah," Lois said, hardly audible. "Please."

There was a throbbing trying to beat its way out of Raynah's chest. The air suddenly wasn't breathable. She did need to sit down, but wouldn't.

"What is this?" she asked. "What's going on?"

Lois stared at Theo, who stared at the hummus on the end table.

"Mama's missing," he murmured.

"Mama's what?"

"She went missing."

Raynah smacked the sofa with her palm. She hoped she'd smudged it with remnants of a Snickers bar she'd had on the drive over.

She and Justine still weren't talking, but over the past month, Raynah noticed something seemed off with her mother. The spacey look on her face when she caught Justine staring at the house from next door whenever Raynah grabbed the mail or the morning paper. The extra-short haircut. Things were tricky. Stranger than usual.

"What the fuck do you mean, she went missing? For how long? Is she at Ms. Myrtle's? Did you contact Ms. Bev? And why the fuck are we whispering?"

"Language, Raynah," Lois said, still whispering.

"When was the last time anyone saw her?" she demanded. "Someone answer me in a regular tone!"

"We've tried everything," said Theo, his voice rising and echoing under the high ceiling. "There's been no sign of her for the last twelve hours or so."

"Did you call the police?"

"No, crazy," Theo said. "Getting paranoid and way too suspicious isn't going to help. Why are you asking so many questions?"

"Same reason why you almost never ask any," said Raynah. "Not the right ones, anyway."

"We just need to think." Lois rubbed her temples with her fingertips. "Theo and I have been trying to backtrack. Who, out of us three, saw her last?"

"Well, you know it wasn't me," Raynah said.

"You live right next door to her," said Theo. "And you have museum assistants now. You mean to tell me you can't pop your head up from that social justice mumbo jumbo you have going on over there and check on Mama, despite your differences?"

"Or, at least, see her poking around outside or something," Lois chimed in.

Raynah's mind went blank with rage. The room was spinning into something unknown. Collapsible. "You know what? Fuck both of you. Call me when you find her."

She stormed back down the hallway towards the door, their protests on her back.

Lois

Lois followed Raynah to the doorway of Theo's apartment. She shouted and tugged and pleaded. She forgot how physically strong her sister was. Chasing Raynah's thin build and grabbing her pencil-sharp shoulders wore Lois out by the time they'd made it to the street's curb.

"You have to help us," she told Raynah. "For once in your life, stop thinking about yourself!"

Raynah turned around, balancing her sneakers with car keys in her arms. She threw one of the shoes in Lois's direction. It landed in a nearby bush. Lois returned it, her own bare feet burning on the street's hot pavement.

"I see you're ready to be an adult about this."

"You could've told me about Mama over the phone," Raynah said.

"A missing person isn't casual conversation, especially when it's your mother."

"And you two munching on fucking pita bread and hummus from your morning excursion at the farmers market isn't casual?"

Lois marched over to the patch of grass on the other side of Raynah's car and cooled her feet. Nothing she could say would explain the mental agony she'd experienced in the hours leading up to Raynah's arrival at Theo's. How being around her brother and seemingly happy strangers at an outside food market felt like it was keeping Lois breathing. How her body needed to keep moving in order not to break down under what could be another misfortune, like losing Quentin. How eating, even when she wasn't hungry, was equated with not remembering.

Justine's forty-year secret as an accomplice to what some would say was more of a petty crime than activism wasn't the only thing hanging over Lois's head these days. Since the breakup with Ahmad, she'd become preoccupied with stories. All kinds of stories, but mostly personal stories. Unlike Raynah, she'd never been an avid reader, but she found herself piecing together the words that weaved together scenes out of people's lives.

Maybe the images and captions from Raynah's hand-me-down newspaper clippings had opened something up in her. Still, Lois preferred online articles that were more recent and relatable. In between consulting appointments with rookie realtors, she'd fiddle with her tablet in an office corridor, or library, or café, sometimes not even making it out of her car in a parking lot.

Then, Lois learned she was pregnant. She was eating anything within reach these days, sometimes without even tasting it at all. Fruit, peanuts (preferably dipped in vanilla ice cream), fried chicken, meat-filled salads, chop suey, any-thing that was filling. To date, Red Hot Riplets were her favorite because she could actually experience their flavor; the spice on each potato chip seared her tongue and hurt so good, it kept her alive.

Despite her therapist's explanation, Lois suspected crav-ing for almost anything edible was more than a coping tool. While web surfing one day, she read somewhere about a mother losing her sense of taste after the death of her son. The upset was rare, but understandable. You lost, and then your body took it out on you by losing again, to make up for that loss.

It was part of the woman's grieving process and alt-hough the condition was surgically fixable, Lois couldn't imagine the toll that the postoperative recovery period took on the psyche. She dreaded the complications of a vicious cycle and ever since reviewing the article that day, she was determined not to let fate win again. Food would be her soul guide. She could deal with a little weight gain. An extra gut. A larger shoe size. Her breasts being heavier gave her an unexpected comfort. She could deal with a little human forming inside of her again and what it meant for her and for Ahmad. The only thing she couldn't see herself manag-ing was another possible loss in her family.

"You're the only one who can find her," Lois told Raynah. "You know that, right?"

"Me?" Raynah stabbed her chest with her finger.

"Yes, you. You're the one who helped get her lost, digging up stuff you damn well know should've been left where it was: in the past. So, now, you go find her."

"No, if anyone, it's you, Lois," Raynah said. "You two have been joined at the hip since forever. She listens to you."

"Not anymore. She thinks you're poisoning me."

"Why? Because you spent a weekend in Oakland? You left Ahmad, didn't you? What else could a mother ask for? I didn't turn you out with my politics. You did it to yourself."

Lois knelt down in the grass and rested her elbows on her knees. She wished Raynah hadn't mentioned Ahmad. It was bad enough that he still took up so much space in Lois's mind, especially now, when there was a baby involved. Hearing his name upset her stomach.

"I just tried Ms. Bev again," Theo said from the doorway. "No answer. Someone should probably go by Mama's house."

Lois rolled her eyes and stood. "I told you I checked there this morning before coming here. No sign of forced entry, everything inside looked normal—"

"Well, go again," he said. "Maybe she'll turn up soon."

"Why don't one of you go?"

"You're the only one with a spare key," Raynah said to Lois.

Lois pulled her set of keys out of her shorts pocket. She slid Justine's key off the ring and held it above her head for both Raynah and Theo to see. "Which one of you is doing the honors this time?"

The awkward silence of her siblings was deafening. No one even looked at the other.

"I'll make some more calls," Theo finally said, looking at the phone in his hand. "If there's no luck within the next hour, I'm going to the police."

Lois knelt again, the blades of grass beneath her feet now wet, worn, and squishy. She heard her brother's screen door close behind him. The sucking sounds his feet made against the tile in his hallway as he retreated back into his cave.

Raynah got inside her car and started it. She looked straight ahead, but let the passenger window down as if she was debating on what to say and how to say it.

Lois took her time putting the spare key back on the ring with the rest of her keys. The way it gleamed in the sun made her eyes and head ache.

*

Dozens of fire ants marched along Justine's front porch. Their tiny red bodies also filled the spaces between the bricks near the house's exterior doorframe. Lois shoved her spare key into the keyhole, inspecting her feet and then the patches of yard around her.

"Make sure you stomp on the mat before you come all the way in," Justine said, pointing. She was sitting on the living room sofa with a Schnucks coupon booklet in her lap.

"I don't want those pests taking over this house."

Stunned, Lois wiped the backs of her sandals on the door mat inside the house. She stared at her mother, who was still barely recognizable with her short, grayish afrolike hair growing around her full face and now matting at the ends. The house was how it had been left: stuffy and clumsily arranged in the way Justine liked it. Everything hidden to all who entered and findable only by her.

The strong, spicy scent of boiling sassafras root struck Lois as she closed the front door behind her. She wanted to be angry, but the lingering smell only made her hungry. And nostalgic.

She saw herself and her siblings when they were little, running in and out of the kitchen to watch Justine crushing the root bark from Ms. Myrtle's backyard sassafras tree and steeping it in boiling water before she combined it with the bone broth she made for them. It was a rare meal in their house; because of its lengthy cooking time, her mother only made use of the recipe when someone was sick or in danger of getting sick. Justine swore that just a tiny dose of sassafras, along with the medicinal quality of bone broth, could reduce a fever and dislodge mucus. For that reason, Lois found coming down with a head cold or the flu to be a bittersweet experience. She loved the taste of bone broth. How the liquid's thin components soothed her and slowly opened her up as she sipped it down with a spoon, or drank it straight from the bowl. It was like she could feel herself healing. As upset as she was at her mother, she was tempted to try the broth now, even if the pregnancy wouldn't let her enjoy the flavor.

Still, Lois wondered why Justine had decided to make the broth now. Today. She thought about what she'd once heard about sassafras root, probably from Raynah. If consumed excessively, it was thought to poison the insides. The result could be fatal.

"Where have you been, Mama?" Lois didn't wait for Justine to answer. She plowed through the house and into the kitchen, where a large pot of sassafras roots was boiling on the stove. She looked inside the freezer where there were packaged neck bones and bags of chipped ice. She searched the refrigerator, which still had the Kool-Aid she'd made last week for Justine, as well as a bunch of raw vegetables, unopened pudding containers, and leftovers covered in aluminum foil.

Suddenly, her throat was terribly dry. On the top shelf of the pantry, Lois found a six-pack of bottled off-brand soda.

She took one, popped it open over the sink, and chugged it. Still not much taste, but she enjoyed the warm, carbonated burn going down her throat and spreading through her chest. She took another bottle and returned to the front room.

"The water in that pot look brown yet?" Justine asked, not taking her eyes off the coupon booklet.

Lois stood in front of her mother. "Everyone's been looking for you. We were about to file a missing person report."

Justine looked up and stared at the soda bottle in Lois's hand. "Lord, I didn't even know that was still in there. You can take the whole pack with you when you leave. Been trying to stay away from soda. Gives me too much gas."

"I know you heard me, Mama."

"Yes. I did. You knuckleheads have been looking for me and almost declared me missing. Who told you to go and do a thing like that?"

Lois drank to keep herself from shouting. She held the liquid in her mouth until it lost its fizz, swishing it between her cheeks before swallowing.

"You disappeared and no one could reach you," she said to Justine. "I came by yesterday and again this morning, and you weren't here. We tried your cell phone, we tried Ms. Bev and then Ms. Myrtle's house ... nothing."

"Who is 'we'?"

"Me, Theo, and Raynah. Your kids."

"Lies." Justine waved her hand. "Raynah would never do that."

"She was concerned. We all were. And, really, that's not the point. The question is, where were you and why didn't you tell anyone?"

"Well, a few minutes ago, I really was at Myrtle's. Where do you think I got all the sassafras from?" Justine slammed her coupon booklet against the coffee table and went into the kitchen.

"Where were you before that?" Lois demanded, trailing her mother. She played with the open bottle in her hand as Justine stirred the boiling roots in the pot and turned the stove off.

The phone rang. Lois watched her mother fumble for the cordless phone in one of the pockets of her housecoat. She motioned for Lois to follow her downstairs into the laundry room.

"What, son?" Lois heard her mother ask as she pulled linen out of the dryer. She held the soda bottle against her lips, even though it was long empty. She'd never felt such hatred toward Theo until this morning when he failed to step up and physically check on their mother. It was all she could do not to snatch the phone from Justine and scream every low, rotten thing that came to her mind. Insults that she'd prided herself for being mature enough to avoid over the years. Things that she ignored when everyone else resorted to being nasty about their understanding of the way Theo lived his life.

Justine hurled the full laundry basket onto the folding table. She signaled for Lois to help her, which Lois reluctantly did.

"I'm over here being questioned by your sister right now. The one who still speaks to me." Justine stretched out a towel and began folding it. "Boy, don't you start with me, too. What is this, 60 *Minutes?* Look, I'll call you back later. Better yet, you call me again."

She hung up and tossed the phone onto a pile of clothes hangers in the corner of the room.

"Damn shame it takes me to come up missing for him to call and check on me, like any normal son."

"So, are you going to tell me?" asked Lois, shaking out a fitted sheet.

Justine's lips curled into a scowl and for a moment, she looked painfully indecisive. She stood there, stroking her folded towel. She looked like she might cry, and then smile, and then, like she would march back upstairs without saying anything else.

"I went with Rich to see his son in prison."

"Prison?"

Lois held a wrinkled sheet to her body as if trying to shield herself from her mother's revelation.

The signs were all there; it was so obvious. Why hadn't she remembered her mother's man friend who Justine refused to talk about?

All this time, Lois was worried about her mother collapsing under the grief of missing Sir, and her funeral scavenging, and the pressure of having her children throw her involvement in an embarrassing stunt back in her face, and somehow getting herself hurt or killed in the latest elder abuse crime. In truth, Justine had been carrying on with this guy Lois knew nothing about, other than that he was the facilitator for a grief support group.

"Prison," Justine repeated. "We went yesterday. You know Jefferson City's the farthest your mama's ever been outside of St. Louis? Rich was pooped after the visit so we stayed the night there and rode back early this morning."

The smell of fabric softener was starting to make Lois nauseated, but she couldn't bring herself to lower the sheet in her arms. She clenched the cloth harder, trying to block out any horrid imaginings of Justine alone with another man.

"Well, you might as well stop looking ugly," her mother said. Justine folded another towel and snickered to herself, which inflamed Lois.

"Is this really a joke to you? You're doing this to get back at me for not telling you I was going with Ahmad to Oakland, aren't you?"

"Girl, please. No one's thinking about you. This was for Rich. And, in a lot of ways, for me. It's something how people are repentant. I know it sounds crazy. I'm not talking apologetic in the churchlike sense, either."

They stared at each other, not blinking until the kitchen refrigerator's smug hum vibrated against the ceiling above them.

"You know you two are only a year apart," Justine said. "Blake's cute too, in a lonely sort of way. Well, in the picture Rich showed me, he is. I didn't go with Rich inside the prison. Isn't that a nice name? Blake."

"Mama ..."

"What? Everyone deserves a second chance."

"You hated the father of my only child, but you're okay with trying to play matchmaker for me with a guy in prison? We're really not going to have this conversation."

Justine's obvious anger caused the skin on her forehead to ripple. "Lois, I'm your mother. You don't get to tell me what conversation we can have. You're sounding more like your sister every day."

"Oh, now I'm like Raynah again," said Lois, "because I'm not going to let you control my life? We've always been two different people, Mama. She's her and I'm me."

Upstairs, the refrigerator coughed and went silent. The frantic chirp of someone's car alarm went off outside.

"But, since you want to drag Raynah into this, I think it's time you two have a little sit-down on those old clippings she found of you in Sir's basement. You not talking to her has gotten way out of hand; I'm sick of being the go-between for you two."

"Girl, shut your fool mouth," Justine hissed. "I don't have to explain myself to you and definitely not to her. If she spent half as much time and energy worrying about her own shady past as much as she did mine, she'd be a much happier person."

Lois's pulse raced. She felt her blood beat against the skin on her ears. "So that was you in the Veiled Prophet scandal photo."

Justine pointed to the sheet in Lois's arms. "Drape the sheet over your hands first before you tuck in the corners. How many times do I have to tell you? Here, give it to me."

"All this time, I didn't really want to believe it," Lois said.

"I can just hear your father now. He'd say this is what happens when women decide they're better off working outside the home. You end up failing at the simplest tasks."

"So, it's true that Beans was in on it too?" asked Lois.

"Look at you, so bent on being a little diva—"

"God, is that why he ended up leaving Ms. Bev? Her poor babies ..."

"—and you forget about what's actually important."

"He never could shake the events of that day and how it went wrong, could he?"

"Stop it!"

The terror and rage in Justine's voice bounced through the small room. She stood by the dryer, her shaking hands on its top for support. Her shoulders bobbed, slowly and then faster.

Lois froze at the thought of bringing her mother to tears. Then, she heard the woman's fragile cackle.

"You're a bigger fool than I thought," Justine said over her shoulder. "You come over here like you're all concerned for my welfare and have the nerve to stand there and talk at me in my own house. What you should be doing is counting your blessings. Had I stayed out there trying to be a hero, your sister would've lost a mother and you and your brother wouldn't even be here. Me and your father, we may not have been the best for each other at one time, but we had a responsibility to you and we saw to it that we kept you in a world that was as normal as we could get it to be."

"What's so normal about us, Mama?" Lois asked. "Tell me, did you end up getting the cookie-cutter life you and Sir always wanted? Was that part of the whole love and duty package? Where is it? Because I don't see it. Open your eyes. Look around you."

Slowly, Justine turned around. To Lois, she now looked to be ten, maybe fifteen, years older.

"You don't know nothing about nothing." Justine took her time climbing the stairs and left Lois in the laundry room feeling confused. She listened to her mother bang pots against the stovetop, and then, the clicking sound of the stove's electric ignitor sparking the burner.

*

After her ultrasound, Lois went to see Ahmad at Ms. Myrtle's house. He had his own place, but according to Ms. Bev, the in-home care assistant situation at Ms. Myrtle's still wasn't working out. As a way of making up for her sworn silence on Justine's disappearance, Ms. Bev told Lois about Ahmad's indefinite stay with his grandmother while they explored other options for a new assistant.

Lois hugged the shoebox filled with several of Quentin's old childhood photos that she'd had copied as she trudged up the walkway. It pained her to see the front yard's brown patches of lawn where a vibrant garden used to be. Several of the spots were filled with newer, darker dirt from an opened garden soil bag propped against the end of the porch rail, a shovel's handle poking out the top of it. Strips of masking tape, dirtied and curling at the corners, still covered the doorbell next to the front door, so she knocked.

"You look hot," Ahmad said when he opened the door. He was shirtless with shaving cream spread over his cheeks. He barely looked at the shoebox offering in her arms. Relieved he'd called her hot instead of the obvious, fat, Lois wiped sweat from her brow with the sleeve of her shirt and closed the door behind her with the back of her foot. The late afternoon's scorching heat released her from its grip as they walked past the empty living room, where a soap opera on the TV blared, and up the stairs, past sounds from another TV coming from behind Myrtle's closed door.

Lois giggled and then pretended to cough, unable to contain the gush of warmth when they entered Ahmad and Pete's old room at the end of the hall. She felt oversized and clunky in the space that still housed the two brothers' bunk beds. Pete's bed on the bottom bunk had a crisp, bare mattress on it. Ahmad's top bunk was a mess of his old Cardinals linen, faded red birds and baseball bats covering the sheets and pillows.

Sunlight from the window sprayed across the walls' puke-green paint, a color Lois relentlessly teased Ahmad about when they were teenagers. No one had bothered to repair the hole in the drywall across from the beds, from when Pete's punch missed Ahmad's head the day they fought over something so stupid, Lois couldn't remember. Next to the wall's depression, a worn double cassette deck sat on the nightstand, and the framed photo of Ahmad's mother. Returning to this room as an adult, Lois finally realized how young and innocent the woman looked—she couldn't have been any older than fifteen in the picture, with soft eyes and baby fat still framing her cocoa-colored face. No signs of the drug use that would eventually pull her away.

"I see you still like the nosebleed section," Lois joked, tilting her head toward Ahmad's top bunk. She started to set the shoebox on the bottom bunk, but decided not to. Instead, she placed it on the nightstand next to the cassette player and stood against the wall. She ran her hand over its enormous dent. It felt slippery under her caresses and she noticed how her hands were sweating and trembling. Her throat felt like it was closing up. She tried hard to ignore the anxiety building inside her, which only seemed to add more anxiety.

"Yeah," was all Ahmad said, and he retreated into the bathroom down the hall. The soft buzz of his electric shaver was surprisingly soothing to Lois. She stared at what was once their favorite spot on the floor to cuddle and fool around whenever Ahmad had the room to himself. She thought of everything that had happened between them, back then up until now. Little moments, and the big moments. Ways Ahmad had shaped and misshaped her existence. Not only the memories they shared, but also the people they shared. Regardless of what happened, or what state Lois left this house today, it was safe to say no one person had stained her life with such uniqueness, color, and emotion.

To pass the time, Lois was tempted to tell Ahmad about the fiasco surrounding her and her siblings' manhunt for Justine the week before, now that it had ended on a safe, but not completely favorable, note. What would've happened if she, Theo, and Raynah had ended up filing a missing person's report after the scare with Justine. What local headlines may have been crafted in online and print newspapers to garner sympathy from Theo's dwindling fan base after his failure to get reelected. How nosy neighbors—minus Myrtle—and shady extended family members would've reacted, or not reacted, once they realized nothing was up for grabs at her mother's house during her absence.

But with that, Lois knew she'd also end up sharing the discovery of her mother's more complicated and outlandish history. Ahmad, being Ahmad, would probably find the story of her mother's old adventure amusing, if not admirable. Without actually spelling out Justine's hypocrisy, he'd probably point out more of the stench of St. Louis's glamorized conservative culture, the one that folks like he and Raynah caught slack for calling out.

To some extent, Lois knew Ahmad was right. She wasn't above realizing she was raised to be part of that culture. Unlike Ahmad, she belonged here. She'd been just another sad mother. Maybe that's what St. Louis was and had always been: a wounded, grieving woman. And why not? What wasn't there to grieve?

Lois decided against giving away the family secret that was still taking its time to unfold. Picking it apart with Ahmad would only make her directly confront the cause of their breakup, which wasn't what she intended to do while the wounds from the split were still fresh. Plus, she'd have to own up to the fact that trying to reunite Theo with Ahmad had only made the rift between them worse, another thing that didn't deserve her energy right now.

"I don't see how your grandmother can sleep with all that TV racket," Lois shouted, hoping Ahmad would answer her.

"She's a hard sleeper."

Ahmad reentered the room, wiping his face with a towel that covered most of his protruding naked belly. He looked more agreeable and hauntingly boyish without his beard.

His bold, fixed chin made Lois reach for her face and shift her gaze toward the shoebox on the nightstand.

"She wasn't always," Lois said, forcing a smile.

Ahmad stood stone-faced in front of the dresser's mirror across from her, no sign of recalling the nights he and Lois locked their bodies together on the floor to keep Ms. Myrtle at bay.

"Your mama send you over here to steal the rest of my grandmama's sassafras tree?" he asked, applying cologne.

"No."

"Good, because there's not much left. She's been sneaking them for a while. Roots and all. I'm getting ready to have that tree cut down and plant regular do-nothing bushes out there, so tell her to grow her own."

"Maybe she needs to hear that coming from you."

"Maybe," said Ahmad. "Believe it or not, Ms. Justine's a lot nicer to me now. She actually smiled at me the other day when I asked if she could cover this evening and stay with Grandmama while I went out on my date. Scary."

Lois's breathing quickened. Through the mirror, she saw the spite in Ahmad's eyes, his lips curling into a grin. She looked away, numbed by a sudden exhaustion. She willed away the jealousy and nausea and the blood draining from her body, determined not to give Ahmad the satisfaction of seeing her do something stupid, like faint.

"Well, I'll get going," she said. "I just wanted to bring you some things to look at when you have time."

"What is it?"

"More photos of Quentin."

Lois picked up the shoebox and then, placed it down again. She started for the door, figuring Ahmad wanted his privacy for the occasion, but he put the box on Pete's old bottom bunk and started fingering through the photos.

She watched him for some kind of reaction but his face showed no emotion. One brown block of freshly shaved skin. Full, dark lips shining with his saliva when he licked them, a habit of his that Lois loved.

"I'll go get them enlarged tomorrow," Ahmad said.

"Good idea," said Lois. "I had some frames, but I couldn't find them. Or else I would've brought those, too."

"It's all good."

She continued watching Ahmad repeatedly sort through the photos. He laid them out on the bed before him, one by one, and made a quilt of his son's images that hardily shined against the whiteness of the bare mattress. Then, as quickly as he sat down, he rose and went back to fiddling with things on the dresser.

While she still had the nerve, Lois hugged him from behind and stared at him through the mirror. "Thank you."

"For what?" he asked.

"Not allowing anyone to make you feel obligated. For doing exactly what you felt you needed to do to heal yourself. We're better off because of it."

Ahmad met Lois's eyes through the glass, a startled look contorting his face. Lois pulled back and stood beside Ahmad. She reached in her jeans pocket, surprised by how calm she'd grown, and pulled out an ultrasound photo. She placed it on the dresser between her and Ahmad.

"I don't want anything from you. Just thought you should know."

Ahmad snatched the photo. He held it so hard, Lois thought he would tear it. She saw a wild glee in his eyes that made him look like his old teenage self.

"Nothing from me? Lo, I want to be there. I have to be there this time.

"That's fine," she said to him. "Actually, that's wonderful. I just don't want you to think we have to be a traditional couple to make things work. We can stay friends and co-parent. We can be whatever feels right."

Ahmad's face held a stern, settled look that Lois found refreshing. "How many weeks?" he asked.

"Almost twelve."

"Is it healthy? I mean—well, you know what I mean—is the baby healthy?"

"Why? Because I'm over forty and this doesn't seem normal for folks our age?"

"No." Ahmad vigorously shook his head. "Well, yeah. Kind of. Look, I'm just saying—"

Lois welcomed the concern. "The baby's fine. Everything's alright."

Ahmad nodded and returned to Pete's old bottom bunk. He leaned forward with his elbows on his knees and blinked hard. He breathed in long and hard, exhaled, and then leaned forward again.

"Thought you said you had a date."

"I do," Ahmad said. He licked his lips and continued arranging Quentin's collage on the bare mattress.

Lois licked her lips, too, and tried to contain her joy.

Theo

Theo dialed his ex-wife's number with shaky fingers and a head clouded with booze. He hoped no one would answer. He didn't think he could take the sound of Beth's voice, but he missed hearing her breathe.

After several rings, an automated message declared her voice mailbox full. Theo turned over the bottle of brown liquor in his hands and took in the familiar stench of brown river just miles away from his parked car under the moonless sky.

He was still adjusting to his new gray Malibu, the car he got in return for trading in the SUV he loved. He didn't want to, but he needed something he could drive and go unnoticed.

He decided he would try Beth again later, while he still had the nerve. Fortunately, he was calling from an unrecognizable number, which could work for him. Or not. Two of Beth's phone pet peeves, he remembered, were numbers marked "unavailable"—she lumped numbers she didn't know in that category, too—and folks who didn't leave messages.

Making the call, even while drunk, was harder than Theo imagined. It was even harder than what he usually found himself doing at the beginning of every October since their divorce, which was mailing a Hallmark Mahogany card from the Schnucks store near his apartment to Beth a few days before the birthday of their would-be child.

Every year, Theo hoped the gesture would mend things between him and his ex-wife. And, every year, the card would come back marked "return to sender."

After the unanswered call to Beth, Theo spent most of the night at a pool hall in a bland drive-over town on the outskirts of downtown St. Louis. There, he was sure no one knew him. When he had his fill of cheap, warm beer and redundant sports conversation, he drove and parked near the Old Chain of Rocks Bridge at the mouth of the Riverfront Trail.

Theo liked this place at this time of year, when everything felt slower, controlled. He enjoyed the way summer's determined humidity still lingered under the crisp breath of autumn. The city's quietude under the ashen sky.

There was a gothic beauty to the factories of the industrial riverfront, now defunct for centuries, that mingled with the skyline at the trail's end. The rows of empty dark buildings with no windows were lifeless, dilapidated relics, opposite the lit brownstones across Interstate 70. But still precious because they represented the prime of St. Louis's manufacturing stamina.

In those buildings, Theo imagined brawny men with the built-up grime from assembly lines under their fingernails, in their pores. Men with families. Men with hobbies and dreams. Men with memories. Men who loved women. And, men who loved men.

It never occurred to Theo that the decrepit structures on the city's edge would one day remind him of the history classes he sat through during his community college days. Rote textbook lessons on the unexpected prowess of men who were part of the 1877 St. Louis general strike, a takeover born out of a national railroad strike that happened the same year. How none of it was ever linked to the beginnings of this whole Veiled Prophet ordeal that shadowed the city and, as he recently discovered, his own mother.

After seeing Raynah's photo of Justine as an undercover seamstress during the unmasking of the Veiled Prophet, Theo began wanting to learn his mother all over again, although from a safe distance. He wanted to dissect her. Undo the neatly arranged ideas he always had of her.

He accepted there were things he'd never understand. Even the fact that Justine had gone missing with a man she liked, and dated, was unfathomable to him. Something deep down didn't want Theo to believe that his mother—the homebody, Sir's lifelong devotee, smothering parent, former activist—now had a lover.

But, acknowledging that these parts of Justine existed somehow made her real to him. More human. For Theo, she became the lost link to seeing his place in the world with new eyes, not as a son, or ex-husband, or politician, but as a conflicted man.

Tangela's handwritten note came into Theo's thoughts. Of all his exes, she as the bona fide churchgoer had the least potential of being a public headache, but was still privately dangerous. His mind traced the words on the memo left jammed in his front door on what would've been the first anniversary of their relationship. Small but loose cursive letters tucked inside the lines on the paper that read:

You're a waste of a beautiful Black man. God bless you.

He resented being called a waste. He'd never told anyone, but he'd once seen Beans wasted and broken. Still married to Beth and working in construction at the time, Theo had spotted Sir's best friend in broad daylight as he veered off a walking path after lunch with his work crew, near the downtown riverfront's graffiti wall. He ran into the man who was once Bev's husband and the father of her kids.

Beans was one of several folks in a homeless encampment underneath a viaduct, across from steamboats on the water. He was an emaciated version of himself, and his almond-colored face was covered in sores. Theo watched him smash soda cans between his dirty hands, and before Beans could see him, he turned around and let the midafternoon breeze push back his tears.

In the car, Theo took another swig from the bottle. He saw Tangela's stinging letter again. Maybe he was a waste, in some ways. That's why he was leaving. Politics and St. Louis. At least for now. He'd fallen short of his commitments in both his private relationships and in the public eye. He could own that. He'd have to, if he wanted to get past it and start fresh, whatever that looked like.

"Son, this property's off-limits after hours."

Theo dropped the open bottle of rum underneath his passenger seat. He tried to study the cop, but all he saw was the stiff rim of the police cap outside the driver-side window. The shine of the officer's flashlight nearly blinded him.

"I understand, officer." He spoke slowly, as if rushed speech was an extension of rushed movement, which he knew could lead to a rush of terrible consequences. He wanted to move, to turn on the car engine, but he froze, remembering the last time he saw Pete alive. Both of them, shielding their eyes and their erections with trembling hands in the backseat of Pete's Chevy. The sound of gags and teeth being broken after officers forced Pete on the ground, on his knees, to suck the end of a billy club. Theo, obeying the cops' demand to walk home alone, without his partner.

"Understood, officer," he repeated. That no cop harmed, or even recognized, him since his night in jail after the run-in with vagrants back in June, was a relief. He hated complying, but he had to play it safe if he wanted to leave this place.

The officer didn't move. Theo closed his eyes on the flashlight's burn and felt himself slipping into panic. A weird sound escaped his mouth. He clutched the bottom of his steering wheel with both hands and held his breath against the sharp sweetness of the spilled rum on the carpet beneath his feet.

"Leave now," the officer insisted. "Don't make me tell you twice."

The flashlight disappeared. Theo leaned his head against the back of his seat and listened to the officer's boots tromp along the gravel.

*

The sun was becoming a round red pepper in the chalky sky. Grand Avenue gasped with life as schoolkids, uniformed workers, and garbage trucks littered its street corners.

Head still spinning, Theo zipped his jacket and exchanged his cash for gold coins at the self-service car wash's change machine. Sunlight hit his car at a weird angle as he worked a creamy lather from the soap gun onto his windshield, over the doors, on the tires.

Car washes were an old childhood comfort. One of the only places Theo felt like he could relax. It was a sacred, rejuvenating experience to wash away dirt and usher in all things clean and fresh. He thought of Lois crying when they were kids, scared of the massive conveyor belts that whapped Sir's Oldsmobile as they went through the tunnel wash. He'd been proud of his responsibility to put a protective arm around his sister, or cover her eyes until they exited the tunnel, and unwrap for Lois the Tootsie Rolls that Justine slipped to them in the backseat.

Theo chuckled. He was going to be an uncle again! Lois had given him the only positive, and very surprising, news this year. She was the only one aware of his leaving, and he made her swear it would stay that way until he was officially gone.

Unloading the machine's rinse tube on his car, Theo tried to conjure up more ways he could shield his sister and her unborn child from everything potentially destructive while he was away. No one really knew what Lois and Ahmad were doing, in terms of romance. He trusted Ahmad despite their irreparable friendship, but he made no assumptions and took it upon himself to do whatever he could, regardless of where he landed.

Where he was going, and for how long, was still a mystery. Somewhere in the East or South sounded most fitting. Someplace where he didn't have to hide, but wouldn't feel policed. Anyplace that still had a decent Black population and four distinctive seasons.

Chicago, Theo knew, was too close. Everyone would expect him to be there, if not somewhere in Springfield or Memphis, and he'd eventually wind up with more calls and visitors than the noiseless world he wanted. Maybe Charlotte, or Savannah. Even Baltimore. Possibly, he was a Philly guy. He'd heard D.C. was epic, but being the hawk-eyed political mecca that it was, he kept it off his radar.

The beeping change machine called for more coins. Theo fed it and sprayed the car with wax. At the carpet shampoo station, he pulled out all of his mats, including the rum-stained one under the passenger seat.

He sat on the block of concrete between the shampoo gun and vacuums, rubbing the last coins between his fingers. He spread out each coin on the concrete's smooth surface, only peeling his eyes away from them to redial Beth's number.

When she answered, Theo's stomach turned over on itself. He took in the sound of her voice—still kind, but wary.

High, but not whiny. The scratchiness in it that he favored when she just woke up.

She said "Hello" into the phone two more times. Each time, he silently mouthed the word back to her.

For a while, they both were just there. Just breathing. Theo looked up at the sun, closed his eyes and squeezed them together until he saw dancing white spots. Then, he saw the silk flowery scarf on Beth's kinky crop, matted from the pillow's strength. He smelled her tart morning breath and heard her right ankle popping as she turned it in circles on the bed. All the memories he silently summoned, until there was the soft click of her releasing the call.

Part IV

Justine

The sky's clouds looked so large and heavy, Justine could almost feel them preparing to crash down on her. She clucked her tongue, inhaling the damp, threatening smell of rain, and repositioned the pot of bone broth in her arms as one of Raynah's interns pulled out of her daughter's driveway.

The house seemed farther away from Justine, now that it wasn't Wesley's. The sidewalk was endless and so were the shrubs between their two yards. Justine glanced over at Myrtle's house across the street. The new bushes Ahmad had planted, in place of what was once her neighbor's robust lawn, looked fake and awful.

Still, as much as Justine hated to admit it, Ahmad had become quite the gentleman. Even Wesley would be surprised at the way he turned out. During the past few months, Justine had witnessed Ahmad go from being a fickle reverse transplant with nothing going for him but the obvious feelings he still had for Lois, to a stable and caring grandson for Myrtle. He spent a few nights with Myrtle each week, even when the new in-home care assistant was hired. He went with Lois to all of her doctor's appointments, and from her daughter, Justine learned he'd just accepted a new job as a staff writer for a local newspaper, making steady income with good benefits. So she couldn't expect everything Ahmad did to be 100 percent right, but he was proving to be there, nonetheless. She just hoped he'd do the same as a father this time. Lois couldn't afford to be a fool again, and Justine was done helping raise anyone's babies.

She stopped walking at the bottom of Raynah's porch stairs to catch her breath. Drizzle landed on her shoulders and arms. She could feel the water was strangely warm, like all of November so far.

She was tempted to turn back, but with the way things were moving so fast, Justine didn't know when she'd get another chance to do this. Rich was coming over later, and depending on how everything went this afternoon, Justine knew she might end up needing him the whole night.

Although Rich was readily at her side whether she asked him to or not, she tried not to be too needy by rationing the nights she spent with him.

It wasn't about Justine guarding her heart anymore; they were past that. It was more about helping Rich keep it together. He'd wept in front of her during their trip to Jefferson City in August to see his son in prison. The way he poured his feelings out was both terrifying and beautiful. Justine realized that, in over sixty years of her life, she had never seen a man cry before.

There were always the men in church who hollered, or in some pastors' cases, added theatrics to their sermons. But, to Justine, it wasn't the same as outright crying. She hadn't witnessed the men in her life show that type of vulnerability. Not her pops. Certainly not Wesley. Not Bev's beloved Beans, or even Theo, once he was past his minor years. It seemed that they were all too busy working, hardening, surviving.

That day, Rich's weeping changed Justine. His tears reworked something in her and inspired a gentle reclaiming of self. She quietly sat next to him in his Lincoln Town Car after he returned from visitation with his son inside the correctional center. There, she witnessed him own his tears, his mistakes, his uncertainties, and his struggles. Seeing him that way made Justine no longer care how worried Bev or her kids would be about her disappearing act. She wasn't concerned about the way Wesley would react if he were alive and saw her with Rich, because he wasn't and he couldn't. She didn't dwell on her regrets—what was or wasn't in her history—and wear them like invisible weights around her neck.

When Rich was done, he sniffled and looked at Justine with red-rimmed eyes that were apologetic.

"Here," was all she said, and passed him a handful of napkins that she'd taken from a gas station earlier that morning.

Thinking back, Justine knew she made the right decision to place a limit on the nights Rich stayed over at her house. But, when she allowed herself to indulge, she savored each moment with him, and drew strength that kept her from repeatedly doing stupid things, like intruding on any more funerals or wakes.

The only thing standing in the way for Justine now was the devil she called a daughter living next door. She tried not to think about what she was doing as she was doing it, or else she wouldn't be able to bring herself to go inside Wesley's old house at all. So much had happened there, in so little time. It would be impossible to follow through with anything if she let her mind wander. She was determined to give Raynah the leftover bone broth as a peace offering. And, if that didn't work, she needed to teach her daughter. Let her know she meant business.

Justine climbed up the stairs and rang the bell. She marveled at the surprise on Raynah's face when she opened the door. This so-called warrior woman with acid for blood and a laugh made from thunder.

"Can I help you?" Raynah asked. She folded her arms over her chest.

Justine forced a smile and held out the pot. "Made too much broth. Didn't want to let it go to waste."

Raynah stared suspiciously at Justine and then, at the pot of broth. She shifted her weight from one leg to the other.

"I know you're not going to let your mama stand out here and get wet over a pot of leftovers," said Justine. A roll of thunder rumbled in the distance. The light drizzle turned into a steady rain splattering the porch stairs behind them.

"I'm not hungry." Raynah didn't budge.

"Look, we need to talk. Just let me in, will you?" Justine pleaded. She felt fury beating into her temples. Raising her blood pressure. "I can warm this up on the stove and we can do some catching up over a bite."

"I said I'm not hungry. Another time. I have to go."

Before Raynah could close the door, Justine hurled the pot of broth inside the house. Raynah crouched and jerked to the left as the glass bowl shattered behind her. Brown juice and chunks of green, orange, and beige trickled down the wall in the small entrance. There was still the smoky, sweet smell of sassafras root under the earthiness of boiled vegetables. Justine entered the house and touched a piece of carrot stuck to the hallway's closet door.

"You're cleaning that up," Raynah said, her eyes fixed on the dripping broth.

"After you tell me why you're phoning Bev about Beans and his days as some militant cowboy."

"She wasn't supposed to tell you."

"What did you expect?" Justine asked her. "She's my best friend, not yours!"

The shock on Raynah's face turned to disgust and anger.

"Sit down," Justine said, closing the front door.

"Go home."

"I said, sit down."

Justine dragged a chair from the kitchen into what was left of the living room. Save for the exhibit knick-knacks surrounding them, Wesley's house felt less congested than what Justine remembered. Raynah had removed the carpet and somehow, the old smell of Wesley's vomit—but Justine hated the cigarette smoke taking its place. She leaned forward, elbows against her knees, and rubbed the knotted salt-and-pepper tufts of hair growing back on her head.

"The problem with folks like you is you get so smart, you turn out stupid."

"Mama, I won't have the insults," said Raynah. "You want to talk, that's fine, but—"

"Will you shut up for a minute? You're the one who wanted to go on this obsessive goose hunt. You wanted to expose your mama, right? The real Justine? Here I am, you got me."

"I thought you came over here about Beans," Raynah said.

"No, I came here to tell you to leave Beans out of this. Do what you want with that damn photo you claim you found. Use it in one of your crazy exhibits, I don't care. But stop it with the who-done-it-and-what-for. You leave Beans alone."

"Why?"

"What do you mean, why?" asked Justine. "Because he's not here to speak for himself."

Raynah rose and left Justine in the room alone. She heard her daughter rummaging through papers, books, and shelves. When she returned, she was holding a yellowed clipping with curled corners. Justine caught a glimpse of "Veiled Prophet" in the faded headline and herself as a young woman in a Sears uniform, kneeling before a white girl in a sparkling debutante's dress. She inhaled fast, but it felt like all the air had been sucked away. She coughed violently, hoping Raynah would be distracted long enough to fetch her a glass of water.

"You can speak for him, though," said Raynah, ignoring her act. She shoved the picture into Justine's hands. "Tell me, since you've decided to be so forthcoming today. Where was Beans in all of this?"

Justine placed the clipping in her lap and without looking at it, ran her fingers over the worn paper.

"Say something," Raynah insisted. "Did you two work
together on conspiring against those fools in the white
hoods? Was he the one who got you initiated into the
movement? Were you two lovers?"

"Lovers?" Justine looked at her daughter sideways.

"I don't know, I'm just trying to understand."

"You can't understand if you're talking like you don't
have sense."

Raynah chewed her bottom lip, like she was having a
hard time containing herself.

"Back then, it was easy to be part of the resistance," Justine explained. "We didn't have cell phones, or email, or
social media. That meant you didn't just show up at a location at such-and-such-time because you saw it somewhere
online. Organizers couldn't send mass invites about a
demonstration going down and expect folks to show up.
Not unless it was through the mail, and that was risky.

"But we were way more strategic, working with what little we had. Word usually got around through a paper flyer,
or people you knew, when and if you were looking to find
the word. You were bound to hear things, catch information, in the street, if you were paying attention. And if
you didn't want to know, it just wasn't there."

Outside, the wind howled and beat against the windows.

Justine shivered and rubbed the sleeves of her jacket.

"I can't remember exactly how I got the word," she continued. "I think it was through a friend of a friend, or old
neighbor from Pruitt-Igoe that I'd run into, here and there.
After the mess with that televised explosion, it could've

been anybody to put a word in my ear about getting back at the system, and I would've took them up on it. I was just that mad.

"So, anyway, I started going to a few backdoor meetings. The kind hidden in plain sight at a boarded-up headquarters, where you have to know the secret door knock to get in. At the time, there were mostly only Black men from my old 'hood and these well-to-do white girls who looked grittier than they actually were, in greasy hair buns and thrift-store overalls. Not many Black girls. And those who were there never stayed for long. Most of them ended up having to go find work when their own men couldn't."

"What?" she asked Raynah. "Don't look at me like that. Your father wasn't the cause of me leaving. Not to work, anyway. He wanted me at home, with you, where it turns out I should've been."

Justine held up the clipping with her fingertips.

"You've seen the picture. While you were busy snooping around on my dealings, I hope you also took the time to read about what happened to the activists on the frontline, especially the girl who slid down that cable to unmask the Prophet. Nearly cracked her rib. Car was bombed right in front of her place. House, ransacked several times."

Raynah pointed to a small shrine in one of the corners of her museum space. In a glass encasement, a host of newspaper clippings and photos surrounded a title in black, bold font: "The Veiled Prophet: Its Origins and a Scandal."

"Right," said Justine. "So, you can sit there, with that long, disapproving face of yours all you want. The truth is, I did what I did and got out while I could, long before folks could fix their mouths to make something out of nothing. A twentysomething Black girl from the projects in 1970s St. Louis couldn't stand a chance against the powers that be."

"That's great," Raynah said, "but it still doesn't answer my question. Where does Beans fit into all this?"

Justine slumped in her chair, disappointment running through her.

"All that I just told you, and you're still asking me about Beans. What gave you the idea he fit into this at all?"

"Why else would Pinch tell me something had her dad back in the '70s? She said whatever it was took him away from them later."

"Pinch?" repeated Justine. "You listen to Pinch? That heifer's been smoking wet since she came out of Bev's womb."

"Is that your excuse why I shouldn't take what she said to heart?"

"Yes."

"Fine, Mama," Raynah said, kicking the air with one of her socked feet. "There's something you're not telling me. You can say you don't want to talk about it, but don't act like nothing's there."

Justine stared at the cooked mess splattered on the wall. It was starting to look like a tree: trunk, branches, and leaves. She sighed, frustrated. There really wasn't anything there. Not with Beans. Sometimes, she wished, for everyone's sake and her conscience, that there was.

"Beans didn't start cracking up over some stunt with the Veiled Prophet," she said to Raynah. "He was very much like your father when it came to the movement and thought it was a waste of time. But he did have a gambling problem that got out of hand. Almost cost Bev her marriage and her kids. And it nearly cost Beans his life, when he couldn't pay a bookie on time. So, there."

Raynah looked straight ahead, running her tongue over her teeth. Justine knew the words preparing to come out her daughter's mouth before she could say them.

"And that caused him to run away nearly fifteen years later?" Raynah asked.

Justine closed her eyes, desperately hoping she could stop seeing Beans' face, or how she imagined Beans' face to look on the day Wesley told her what happened. But she still heard the sickening *whack*, as if she'd been right there at the scene. A quick, squishy thud. The sound of skull crunching under skin as the whacking continued. Bone mixed with blood and brains on the train track's hard, smooth steel shining blue under the moonlight.

"It was only supposed to be one good whack, to make him leave my boy alone. To teach him. The boy was already as good as dead out there when we found him laid out on those tracks, barely breathing and shitting his pants. What was I supposed to do? Carry him home to Myrtle that way?"

Justine had managed to block out the appearance of Wesley during his rambling, but she could still smell him, rotting. His sweat gave off an odor that was pisslike and vinegary. She couldn't remember how she and Wesley got on the subject of Theo, or Pete, or if they were even having a conversation at all. They didn't do a lot of talking during his last days; she just nursed him and he let her.

Things were breaking down in the strong man she once married, and nothing could be done anymore to stop Wesley from dying. He crouched, rather than sat, in the recliner in his living room, identical to the one he'd left behind at

Justine's house next door. His body looked like a robed, shriveled prune with a breathing tube.

It was still a wonder how he got that way, and so fast. In the end, Justine guessed his body started suffering from what his conscience and his heart could no longer handle.

Watching him confess, Justine just kept thinking what she could do for Myrtle. How she could fix the woman's brain, if it were still possible, by running over to her house and telling her the case was closed; she'd never ever have to hurt her mind, wondering how her grandson left this world again.

She remembered Wesley breaking her concentration and looking into her as the anger shadowed him.

"I just got so mad. I got so mad, I couldn't stop the whacking, and ... Beans, that son of a bitch could've got me off him if he hadn't been such a Goddamn chump. Nigger ran and left me on those tracks. You believe that, J? The nigger ran."

And she remembered him asking, begging, her not to spare any sassafras roots in his next meal of broth. He knew what would happen—all the stories about being poisoned—and he still wanted all of them. Every bit of the ones she'd plucked from Myrtle's tree and had planned to ration out over the month.

"Just leave them here and go away, J. If that makes it easier. I've seen you cook it enough to know the recipe by heart. I'll do it myself. Don't come back until morning." So, she did.

"Yes, that's what caused Beans to leave," Justine said to Raynah, unable to meet her daughter's eyes. She felt the rage rising inside her. "What, you don't believe me? Guess that's who I raised, huh? A brainy girl who's so tough, she's gullible enough to listen to a drug addict."

Justine balled up the newspaper clipping and hurled it at Raynah. She cried and cursed and hollered, until Raynah cried and cursed and hollered. Somehow, they both landed upstairs. Justine, in the bathroom, splashing faucet water over her swollen face. Raynah, in her room, smoking a cigarette.

Justine stopped in the doorway of Raynah's bedroom and held a washcloth over her nose to keep from inhaling smoke. Her daughter sniffled and pointed the lit tip of her cigarette at her.

"Sir might not have been the best person," she said to Justine, "but at least he didn't hide. My father taught me never to hide. He didn't lie to me, or to you, or to anyone, about who he was. He was truthful about everything that made him, him. That's more than I can ever say about you."

Justine looked at Raynah with terrible pity. She had never wanted to hold her daughter so much, so tightly. The idea of holding her hurt more than the idea of protecting Wesley, even in his death.

She saw Raynah, a thorny, laughing toddler, twisting her pudgy body in her grip. Spittle filming her little mouth as Justine blew into her navel. Their cheeks matching, dark brown and velvety, when Justine rubbed her face against Raynah's in her vanity mirror. The girl squirming out of her arms when they heard Wesley slam the front door. Falling flat on her stomach on the way to greet her father. Slipping on a flap of loose carpet that Justine had begged her husband to fix before the girl learned to walk.

Wesley, getting to Raynah before Justine could, and scooping her up in his arms. Glaring at Justine while he let the blood on her daughter's knee run down his cream-colored slacks. Her, telling Wesley to put the girl down. That she needed water, ice, a bandage. Him, shushing Raynah and telling her she was okay as she wailed into his shoulder. Rocking their daughter and still glaring at Justine, like she was the one who neglected the loosened carpet. Still telling Raynah she was okay until their daughter repeated it through her sobs, her face still buried in his shoulder.

"I otay, I otay."

"Yeah," is all Justine said to Raynah. She put the washcloth in the laundry chute and plopped down on the bed beside her daughter. Together, they stared at the television on top of the dresser, not watching.

"I didn't come here to fight with you," Justine finally said to her daughter when she got sick of hearing her own breathing.

"It's a little too late for that." The cigarette in Raynah's hand trembled as she brought it back to her mouth and inhaled. Justine let the words "too late" hang in the air between them. It seemed she was never on time when it came to doing the right things. She could only wonder what it would've been like if she had been forward with her kids about the life she had before she devoted herself to them. The heaviness of it all weighed on her, and she wished she'd waited to come see her daughter under different circumstances. But here she was, making due with a sour situation. No turning back.

Raynah busted out laughing, and Justine saw the child in her again. Her little willful toddler.

"What's so funny?"

"My mama, the revolutionary," Raynah said. "You look silly."

She tossed her cigarette in an ashtray on the nightstand and motioned for Justine to lay her head in her lap. Justine did, and she relaxed as her daughter kneaded her scalp. To keep from falling asleep, she focused on the television screen's footage of the recent Mizzou protests in Columbia. College students marching and shouting and holding up signs, their brazen faces scowling into the cameras.

Raynah pointed at the screen. "Damn, look at Claire!"

"Who?"

"My old intern."

Justine sat up and studied the albino girl with beige French braids. The sleeves of her oversized MU sweatshirt flapped the air as she toted a sign above her head. Her violet eyes, igniting with a persistence that Justine knew and understood. The idea of Raynah being an elder-to-be—a mentor—to this determined young woman on screen, thrilled Justine and made her hopeful. And envious! How she wished she could've been in a position when she was Raynah's age, to pass her willpower and activist energies on to the next generation instead of burying them deep inside her.

As the girl marched, Justine noticed she didn't look away from the camera, even as raindrops fell on the lens and lightning broke the sky above them in the background. The joy brewing inside Justine was overwhelming and caused her eyes to water. She promised herself she wouldn't cry.

Not now.

"How long do those kids plan on being out there?" she asked, settling back into her daughter's lap. "Storm's coming."

Raynah didn't respond. She wiped Justine's damp cheek with her shirt sleeve and continued massaging her scalp until Justine could no longer keep her eyes open.

Acknowledgements

The family in *Bone Broth* has lived with me for a long time. Sitting with their voices, their stories, and their resilience wouldn't have been possible if it weren't for a wealth of support.

I am immensely thankful for my friends and peers who graduated with me from the MFA in Writing program at California College of the Arts in San Francisco. We endured several workshops together, and I appreciate all the constructive feedback given to me when *Bone Broth* was just an infant. Dr. Opal Palmer Adisa – thank you for your generosity and your mentorship and for teaching us all how to honor the page and our duty as writers.

Heartfelt thanks goes to the wonderful sistas of We Tell Our Stories Film & Arts Collective: Cassandra "Mama Cassie" Lopez, Stephanie Duncan, Ann Penny Baten, Michelle Kern, Anita Martinez, and Natasha Corbin. And to the lively black women involved in the Cocoa Fly "Let Her Tell It!" reading series: Jenee Darden, Kelechi Ubozoh, Natalie Devora, and Yodassa Williams. To the AfroSurreal Writers—

Rochelle Spencer, Dera Williams, and Audrey Williams—thank you for your comradery and encouragement. I appreciate Dr. Adrienne Oliver and Tracy Baxter for being willing beta readers of *Bone Broth's* first draft. And, the kind souls in the Write Now! Workshop and Reverie Writers, led by Shizue Seigel, and Leporines—Alia Volz, Olga Zilberbourg, Jacquelyn Doyle, Frances Lefkowitz, Katie MacBride, JiaJing Liu, and Caryn Cardello—for helping me polish many drafts of this book. Much respect to the Hurston Wright Foundation, VONA/Voices, and Community of Writers at Squaw Valley for providing guidance and a nurturing environment. I am eternally indebted to the San Francisco Foundation and Barbara Deming Memorial Fund for believing in *Bone Broth* enough to aid in its development. Vermont Studio Center, Wellstone Center in the Redwoods, and Paul Artspace, thank you for your hospitality – you housed me so these ideas could one day flourish.

Warm thanks to elder activists Percy Green and William Lacy Clay, Sr. for allowing me to interview them in the early days of this novel, when there wasn't yet a clear direction.

Special shout-out to my Kimbilio family. Without your kindred spirits, I wouldn't have had the strength to revise and breathe new life into this novel.

Christi Craig of Hidden Timber Books, there are no words that explain how honored I feel that you took a chance on me and gave *Bone Broth* the home that it deserves. I'm so glad to have you as my publisher.

Tons of hugs to friends and supporters in the Bay Area – thank you for showing me what courage looks like. Much love to my family, teachers, friends, mentors and supporters in St. Louis and beyond, who've been behind me since day one – you are the reason I'm here.

Lastly, and mostly, to my best friends, Mommy and Daddy. I thank God for you daily.

ABOUT THE AUTHOR

Lyndsey Ellis is a St. Louis-born fiction writer, essayist, and cultural worker. She's passionate about exploring intergenerational struggles and resiliency in the Midwest. She earned her BA in English from the University of Missouri–Columbia and MFA in Writing from California College of the Arts in San Francisco. She was a recipient of the San Francisco Foundation's 2016 Joseph Henry Jackson Literary Award. In 2018, she received a grant from the Barbara Deming Memorial Fund for her fiction.

A VONA Voices and Squaw Valley Writers alumna, Ellis has had residencies at Vermont Studio Center, Wellstone Center in the Redwoods, and Paul Artspace. Her writing appears in several publications and anthologies, including *Joyland, Entropy*, Shondaland, *St. Louis Anthology, Catapult, Electric Literature, Black in the Middle: An Anthology of the Black Midwest*, and *midnight & indigo*. BONE BROTH is her first novel.

CPSIA information can be obtained
at www.ICGtesting.com
Printed in the USA
LVHW081448080621
689698LV00020B/619